Praise for Kendel Lynn's

BOARD STIFF

"A solid and satisfying mystery, yes indeed, and the fabulous and funny Elliott Lisbon is a true gem! Engaging, clever and genuinely delightful."

– Hank Phillippi Ryan,
Agatha, Anthony and Macavity Award-Winning Author

"Kendel Lynn captures the flavor of the South, right down to the delightfully quirky characters in this clever new mystery series. Elli Lisbon is the Stephanie Plum of the South!"

– Krista Davis,
New York Times Bestselling Author of the Domestic Diva Mysteries

"A sparkling new voice in traditional mystery."

– CJ Lyons,
New York Times Bestselling Author

"A cross between an educated, upper class Stephanie Plum and a less neurotic Monk. Put this on your list for a great vacation read."

– Lynn Farris,
National Mystery Review Examiner at Examiner.com

"Elliott is smart and sassy, takes no guff and pulls no punches. Packed with humor, romance, danger and adventure, this is a good mystery full of plot twists and turns, with red herrings a plenty and an ending that I found both surprising and satisfying."

– Cozy Mystery Book Reviews

OTHER PEOPLE'S BAGGAGE

"Lost luggage has never been this fun! With well-drawn characters, *Other People's Baggage* is your first class ticket to three fast-paced adventures full of mystery, murder, and magic."

— Elizabeth Craig,
Author of the Southern Quilting Series

"Kendel Lynn's *Switch Back* [in *Other People's Baggage*] is a clever, entertaining mystery with small town flavor and Texas flair!"

— Debra Webb,
USA Today Bestselling Author

"A cozy triple-scoop that tastes divine...the pleasantly contrasting novellas make it easy to finish off a story in one sitting."

— *Library Journal*

"Although mixed up luggage is the thread that connects this trio of globetrotting novellas, it's snappy dialogue, clever storytelling, and charming characters that are the real common denominators...I'm already hooked on their three new mystery series, and I've only read the prequels!"

— Maddy Hunter,
Bestselling Author of the Passport to Peril Mystery series

"Those who enjoy travel and mysteries like myself will definitely enjoy reading *Other People's Baggage*...The mix-ups are a creative theme for tying the stories together, and I loved seeing how each sleuth dealt with the problem. A very fun collection!"

— Beth Groundwater,
Author of the Claire Hanover Gift Basket Designer and
RM Outdoor Adventures Mystery Series

The Elliott Lisbon Mystery Series
by Kendel Lynn

<u>Novels</u>

BOARD STIFF

WHACK JOB
(*coming January 2014*)

<u>Novellas</u>

SWITCH BACK
(in OTHER PEOPLE'S BAGGAGE)

AN ELLIOTT LISBON MYSTERY

BOARD STIFF

Kendel Lynn

HENERY PRESS

BOARD STIFF
An Elliott Lisbon Mystery
Part of the Henery Press Mystery Collection

First Edition
Trade paperback edition | April 2013

Henery Press
www.henerypress.com

ISBN-13: 978-1-938383-32-8

Printed in the United States of America

For Babka

ACKNOWLEDGMENTS

I've been blessed and loved and encouraged to get to this point in my life, and I'm grateful.

Thank you to Hank Phillippi Ryan, CJ Lyons, Krista Davis, Gigi Pandian, Nancy Shields, Chris Cook, Lorin Oberweger, and extra love to my mom, Suzanne Atkins.

Thank you to my Sisters in Crime Guppies, the Beaufort County Sheriff's Office on Hilton Head Island, and all the little chickens in the Hen House. A special thank you to Diane Vallere, who always has my back.

ONE

I'm embarrassed to admit my most vivid memory of that night is of
ten minutes in the library with Nick Ransom. In my defense, three
of those minutes were damn good minutes, and I had no idea the
murder of a colleague was only a few hours away.

I was seeking refuge from the well-dressed and well-heeled at
a party for the Ballantyne Foundation when Ransom walked back
into my life. I stiffened at the sight. His smooth skin and sharp features made my breath catch, just as they had twenty years before.
He looked like Batman. Christian Bale Batman, not the other one in
the gray leotard and blue underpants.

"Elli Lisbon." He leaned in and kissed my cheek. "I'd heard
you were Director of the Ballantyne Foundation."

"Well, Nick Ransom. How disappointing. I thought you were
dead."

He rocked back on his heels and smiled. "No, not dead yet.
Though a sniper in Rio came close."

Nick Ransom, my college major. I loved him from afar until
he asked me out during our first class together. We rounded three
bases over five dates and would've slid home on the sixth had he
not left me waiting in the rain a week before Christmas. Two days
later he left a seven-word message on my answering machine: "Not
our time, Red. You take care." I never saw him again.

Until tonight. I'd heard Ransom had moved back to the island, so I knew I'd see him sooner or later. I'd just been counting on later. And certainly not at a private fundraiser I organized myself, including a specific list of attendees that did not include his name.

He ran his finger along the spines of the leather-bound books, as if browsing the Ballantyne's stunning collection of classics and first editions. They were stacked floorboard to ceiling on wide mahogany bookshelves with an elegant brick fireplace in between.

The warm smell of burning wood mixed with the tangy scent of aged paper and Ransom's intoxicating cologne. Sandalwood and ginger. The fire snapped, and I ducked around a rolling ladder to the other side of the fireplace.

"You look the same, Red," he said.

"I'm surprised you remember me."

"You wouldn't believe the things I remember about you."

I sucked in my stomach. Thank God I had the good sense to splurge on a new pleated floral dress and the cutest pair of buckle pumps. Yes, I needed to lose ten pounds. Okay, fifteen. But the thought of him seeing me naked? I vowed right then to stop eating cupcakes and get my butt back on the bike first thing the next morning.

Funny how I jumped to naked.

"So, Ransom, what brings you to the Big House? I didn't see your name on the guest list."

"Were you looking?"

I started to shake my head, a denial fresh on my lips when he stepped closer. His gaze held mine for so long, I forgot my own name. He took my face in his hands and kissed me as if the ship was sinking and the lifeboats were full. Thirty seconds later, his hands slipped from my neck to my waist, slowly gathering my skirt up by the hem.

Oh boy. I slapped my palm on the bookshelf, using it as leverage in case I accidentally slid to the floor. I drank in his taste. The feel of his chest beneath my hands. The feel of his hands beneath my skirt. It felt so good, so delicious. So familiar.

I pulled back. The years between us dissipated like sand slipping through an hourglass. The lines around his eyes faded and he looked at me with his same boyish grin. His eyes were dark, full of mischief.

He was a scoundrel and a shit. And he was standing in my sanctuary. Invading my Ballantyne. Uninvited.

I tilted my head up at him. "Well, that wasn't worth waiting for. Still all fumbly hands and sloppy kisses. You really should be better at this by now."

The mischief in his eyes dimmed and I patted him on the cheek. "Maybe it's not our time. You take care."

My heels sank into the deep wool rug as I crossed the library. They were higher than I was used to and I prayed I wouldn't trip on the way out. "See you in another twenty years," I said and closed the door.

Holy shit, I thought. Did I really just walk out on Nick Ransom? I couldn't have planned a better exit if I'd been given two weeks' notice and a script. I did a little dance across the foyer of the Big House just as Tod Hayes, Ballantyne Administrator, hit the bottom step of the center staircase. His normally neat brown hair had a decidedly disheveled look.

"Finally, Elliott. I've been all over this place looking for you."

"Here I am." I glanced over my shoulder, but the doors to the library remained closed. "Shall we go up to the party?"

Grabbing his sleeve, I practically dragged him up the wide steps toward the ballroom where one hundred and fifty guests drank and danced at the Foundation's May Bash fundraiser at the Big House on Sea Pine Island, South Carolina.

The Ballantyne manse earned its nickname for the obvious: it had the grandeur of a city mansion and the grace of a country estate. The house sat up high amidst acres of magnolia trees and live oaks, sharing its majesty with the whole plantation. Figuratively, of course. The Big House offered no tours, visiting hours, or party rentals. Receiving a Ballantyne invitation in your mailbox was akin to finding a golden ticket in a chocolate bar.

Tod was helping me man the Bash in the absence of the Ballantynes, who were on safari in India. Or maybe it was mountain climbing in Pakistan. They entrusted me with their life's work while away doing more life's work. Tonight that included acting as one part host and one part referee.

"So what's up? Is Mr. Abercorn dancing naked on the tables again?"

"Not quite," Tod said. "You have three fires to put out, though Jane is more of a firestorm of seething lava and flaming fireballs."

"Don't be so melodramatic." I glanced at my watch. It was already past eleven, dreadfully late for a party that started at five. How did I miss seeing Nick Ransom for the last six hours? My lips tingled at the thought of him being so close. Traitors.

Tod snapped his fingers. "Hello, Elliott?"

"Right, melodramatic. Things can't be that terrible, can they?"

"Jane is beheading board members, Mr. Colbert is serving guests from the canapés stuffed in his pockets, and Mrs. Kramer is singing with the band."

"That doesn't sound so bad."

"They're in the men's room."

"Naturally. Well, then, you take Jane, I'll take the other two." I stepped toward the gallery, where the men's lounge was located, but Tod stopped me before I lifted my left foot.

"Sorry, Elliott, I'll be taking the easy ones this time. You already got lucky once tonight."

At my quizzical glance, he said, "You have lipstick on your chin and your skirt is twisted."

I felt my cheeks go pink as I straightened my skirt. I hoped no one outside the ballroom noticed or told the Ballantynes about my inability to reign in the cuckoos. Or my inability to maintain my dignity in the face of a twenty-year-old broken heart. "This party is killing me. Literally killing me."

"Not literally."

"Yes, literally. Emotionally killing me on the inside, Tod. On the inside."

He rolled his eyes. "Good luck with Jane. Last I heard, she was on the terrace telling Leo Hirschorn to shove his humanitarian trophy up his ass." He waved and turned toward the gallery, leaving me to deal with firestorm number one.

Jane Walcott Hatting had been the chair of the Ballantyne board for the last eleven years. She owned an esteemed auction house in nearby Savannah, served as president of the local historical preservation society, and was the most unpleasant person on planet Earth. To find her, I merely had to follow the bursts of indignation through the crowd, like following a trail of burning buildings to locate Godzilla.

After a small detour to get my makeup redistributed to all the right facial features, I found Jane at the bar near the dessert table. She wore a tailored black dress and her expensive salon-cut hair framed her oval face and wickedly sharp eyes.

"Hey, Skippy," Jane said to the young bartender as she slid a martini glass across the bar top. "Do I look like James Bond? A martini should be gently stirred. It's a cocktail, not a can of spray paint. Try again, and this time haul out the good stuff. I'm not here for the company."

Ah, Jane. Such a people person.

"Good evening, Jane. Enjoying yourself, as always?"

She eyeballed me. "What the hell do you want?"

"Please stop harassing Leo Hirschorn. He's a respected member of the board."

"He's an embarrassment to the Foundation. A scheming buffoon with a loud mouth and a crass manner. He's done."

I smiled as a wealthy donor walked by. As soon as she was out of earshot, I said, "Keep your voice down, Jane. A Foundation project idea is not a scheme."

She gave me a look as flat as her tone. "You're so naïve, it's almost endearing."

"I'm not going to fight with you about Leo."

"This isn't a fight, Elliott. It's barely a conversation. As for Leo, he's off the board."

"That's not your decision."

The young bartender gently set Jane's fresh drink on a tiny napkin square. She belted it back, then slammed the glass down. The little olive on a stick flipped out and rolled onto the floor. "I don't care what I have to do, but we'll be sitting a new board at Monday's meeting." She snatched her beaded bag from the bar and stalked away.

This isn't going to end well, I thought.

I followed her through the ornate archway, but then she marched down the staircase and out the front door. I sighed. It's always a relief when the party's worst guest bids adieu without actually setting the place on fire.

Not two seconds later, Ransom appeared in the foyer with his arm around an exotic woman. She had dark hair to her waist and legs to her elbows and wore a clingy short dress that said Hot Damn! He tipped his head toward me, then followed Jane outside.

I snuck down to the library on wobbly legs. Ransom's cologne lingered in the air, along with a faint musky aroma of Cuban tobacco. I slipped into a tall leather wingback near the window and watched as a crew of valets in short red jackets sprinted to and fro, quickly fetching cars hidden behind the palm trees in the side lot.

A sleek silver sports car slid up to the walk. The valet hopped out as Ransom escorted his date down the path. He slowly kissed her neck, his hand low on her hip, and then poured her into the leather seat.

"Well, that was unnecessary," I whispered.

He turned his head toward the library as if he'd heard me. I don't think he saw me behind the glass, but I slouched down anyway. He walked around the car, slammed into the driver's seat, and sped away. I watched his taillights fade into the darkness, until they were gone.

So long, Batman.

I sighed and stood and went up to the ballroom. It took another two hours for Tod and me to shuffle the rest of the guests out the door. Funny how people are never mindful of the time when lounging around with someone else's booze. I finally approached the last three couples with a gift of fine wine from the cellar to enjoy once they made it home.

It was close to two a.m. when I climbed into my white Mini Cooper convertible and drove the short two miles from the Big House to my cottage on the beach, a mere fifty yards from the Atlantic. Exhaustion weighed down my limbs as if my bones were made of metal and the road was a magnet. I kept the top down to stay awake. I pictured myself in my striped pajamas, head resting on a fluffy down pillow. It was Sunday; I had a busy morning, but the rest of the day free. No Foundation, no meetings, no Jane. Nothing to do but nap. Maybe I'd even sleep through dinner.

Of course, I wasn't that lucky.

TWO

I was so tired, it hurt to wake up. I cracked open one eye and focused on the clock: 5:27. I opened the other eye. Dim stars glittered in the dark skylight in the ceiling above my bed. Morning had yet to break.

On paper, my Foundation director duties seemed prestigious. Organize fundraisers, research grant recipients, liaise between the board members and the Ballantyne family. But in reality, I felt less like a charity director and more like a camp counselor, herding misbehaving campers. Cleaning up their messes and breaking up their fights. And today was the worst: early morning mess hall duty for two different board members. First a quick run to Leo Hirschorn's to set up a breakfast meeting, then back to the Big House to set up the Coastal Conservation brunch.

But if I rushed, I could be back, snuggled under my quilt, before nine.

I threw on sweats, a clean t-shirt, and an old canvas beach hat to hide my snarled hair. It's red and wavy and hard to tame fresh out of bed. But it's not as if I have much of a beauty regime anyway. I don't color my gray (I only have like five strands) and I rarely wear make-up.

After a quick face scrub and swipe of a toothbrush, I gulped down a Pepsi. Even though I like my caffeine cold, let me tell you, gulping down an ice-cold carbonated drink at half-past five in the morning is not all it's cracked up to be.

In fifteen minutes flat—from alarm to driveway—I was on the road. The sun had begun to peek over the Atlantic as I streaked out the gate and onto the main highway.

Sea Pine Island is shaped like a shoe—a Converse sneaker, to be more accurate. The bridge to mainland South Carolina is at the high-top part and the lighthouse is at the toe. But rather than canvas—to carry this analogy to its most unbearable conclusion—the island is made up of thick oaks, pines, palms, an occasional shopping alcove, and a dozen or so plantations: housing communities fronted by large iron gates and armed guards.

I sped down Cabana Boulevard to the largest plantation: Harborside. It housed a ninety-foot lighthouse and a marina with the nicest yachts in a five-hundred-mile radius. The kind with onboard helicopters and motorcycles, in case you needed a vacation from your vacation.

The large traffic circle was quiet, as was the guardhouse. Leo had called in a pass for me. Without a resident sticker and a pin number, one generally needed an act of Congress to gain entry. Or at the very least, needed to be the pizza delivery guy.

With the pass tucked securely into the dash, I wound around the drive to Sparrow Road, then turned left on Ravenwood Lane, a curvy street of large stucco homes with manicured lawns, matching mailboxes, and sweeping golf course views. After I parked at number fifty-two, I hauled out a heavy box of brochures, forms, and a detailed diorama. Supplies for Leo's breakfast meeting. Even though I hated waking before the chickens did, I wanted to be the one to display the diorama. I designed it myself.

I knocked on the door and it slowly swung open.

I stepped in, and something crunched beneath my feet.

"Leo?" I called and flipped on the light switch.

My breath caught in my throat. Broken glass and ripped furniture littered the front room, and a stench from the kitchen nearly knocked me flat. Glops of spilled food from smashed jars pooled on the countertops. Spicy red salsa and pungent vinegar melded together on the bright white tiles. In a word: disgusting. I didn't know which way to breathe: through my nose and smell it or through my mouth and taste it.

Knives were strewn haphazardly on the floor. A single butcher's blade had been slammed into the breakfast room table. I shuffled forward. A piece of glass snapped under my left foot. I kicked something else with my right. Something solid, but malleable. Weighty and dense. I did not want to look down.

I looked down.

My toes were touching a large dark leather sofa cushion, cut across the seam. I almost giggled with relief. I peered past a broken chair into an oak-paneled den with a large desk beneath a bay window. And Leo Hirschorn dead on the floor.

His head was smashed into the base of a grandfather clock, covered in at least a gallon of blood. His eyes were open and he was staring right at me.

In two seconds, I screamed blue murder, whirled around, cracked my elbow on the doorjamb, dropped the diorama on my left foot, and ran.

I didn't stop until my shaking hands gripped the car door. I dove inside. My thoughts registered like a flashing road sign: Lock the door, start the car, drive like a crazy woman. I scrambled for my keys, finding them deep inside my left front pocket.

My sense finally returned when the key hit the ignition. A wild-eyed maniac had not run out of the house after me. I looked around. The neighborhood was quiet, almost serene, with dewy lawns and potted flowers on porches.

But I'm no fool. I got the hell out of there. I dialed 911 with one hand and drove with the other, eventually coming back around to park across from Leo's house in view of both the street and the front door. It still stood open and I swore I could smell the slimy food mounds from the kitchen. I grabbed the hand-sani from my pocket and slathered it from my fingers up to my elbows.

Within ten minutes, two police cars arrived. Within twenty, three fire engines, an ambulance, the medical examiner's wagon, and a handful of civilian cars crowded the street.

I spoke with the arriving officers first, blurting out my discovery in stops and starts. Including how I secured the scene, as required by South Carolina law for a private investigator (even in training), though not including how I screamed like a girl and ran from said scene.

They told me to wait by my car for the detectives, then they went inside. A short while later, I saw a familiar face: Corporal Lillie Parker. She helped out whenever we needed security at Ballantyne functions. She looked more like a cat burglar than a cop. Thin as a piece of string and graceful as a ballet dancer.

"Hey, Elliott," she said. "Crazy morning, huh?"

"What happened in there?"

"You tell me."

She took notes while I relayed the same story I told earlier. We walked away from the house while we talked. It helped me pull myself together.

"The Lieutenant will be here soon," she said. "He'll want to talk to you."

Lieutenant Sullivan had joined the Sea Pine Island police department when they still rode horses for patrol, or so it seemed. He advised me when I performed discreet inquiries for Foundation donors. Ones in which they didn't want to involve the police—or the press. Usually something simple like the maid lifted the silver or a relative got caught joyriding in a golf cart. With an advisor on the local police force, my minor investigations for the Ballantyne Foundation counted toward my required hours to obtain my official PI license. I had no plans to leave my job at the Foundation, but the license held a certain credibility for even the tiniest of troubles I tried to tame.

Parker and I reached my Mini, still parked out front. The street was chaotic, filled with cars, neighbors, and a crowd of specialists here to pick through every detail of Leo's life. Including the medical examiner, Harry Fleet. A burly black man who looked as though he purchased his antacid tablets in bulk. Rumpled shirt, baggy eyes, permanent scowl.

Harry and I didn't exactly have a pleasant working relationship. I once needed his assistance on a small matter where a generous Foundation donor kicked the bucket while in flagrante delicto—and not with her husband. Harry didn't appreciate my efforts to keep the matter quiet. He used phrases like "pain in my ass" and "get out of my office."

Parker noticed my glance. "Do you want to wait in back? It's quieter."

I nodded and walked through the backyard to a cheap patio set looking lonely with neglect. Dust and dried pollen covered the vinyl cushions and metal tabletop. It overlooked a pristine fairway. A foggy mist covered the greens, dissipating slowly as the sun broke over the horizon and began its day-long journey to the other side.

Two technicians with heavy equipment cases scurried out the back door toward a van in the driveway.

I quietly stood and inched closer, studying the activity from the comfort of the brick patio, away from the stenchy mess inside. Another tech carried out several clear evidence bags. A wine bottle with a short burgundy label. A fat wine glass. Maybe a long silver letter opener or an ice pick.

I'd always dreamt of being a hotshot investigator, but it didn't quite work out. I'd taken two years of criminology classes in college before I realized I'd never make it to graduation. I fainted twice in one forensics class and had to close my eyes during most of another. The smell of blood, death, and loose body parts would either gross me out or freak me out. Neither reaction impressed the professors.

I graduated with a Bachelor's in Criminal Justice, then started working at the Ballantyne. A few years later, as my discreet inquiries became more frequent, I decided to make my standing more official with a license to investigate from the State. They required six thousand hours of on the job training. I'd managed to accumulate just over four hundred. Apparently I'm more of a tortoise than a hare.

I sighed and glanced back inside. Then I choked.

Nick Ransom stood in the dining room. And he looked as tempting as he had the night before. Tailored dress slacks, a sport jacket, and a snug black polo.

Oh shit. I'm wearing sweatpants.

I turned around, dashed down the patio steps, and ran straight into Parker.

"What is he doing here?" I whispered and nonchalantly tilted my head toward Ransom and the back door.

"Lieutenant Ransom? It's his case," she said. "Lieutenant Sullivan retired to Florida last week."

"Him? He's a lieutenant with *our* Island Police department?"

"He's a looker, all right. But a pill. He asked for you first thing," Parker said and left me standing in the grass. She walked up the patio steps, opened the glass door, and called to Ransom.

I sank into one of the grungy patio chairs and tried to remember if I'd brushed my teeth. What is wrong with me? First my pants, now my teeth. Leo's dead, for shit's sake.

Ransom joined me a few minutes later. Relaxed, but guarded. "Didn't expect to see you so soon. Island's smaller than I remember."

"Like a Southern Cabot Cove."

He pulled out a slim notebook and silver pen. "Tell me about this morning."

I followed his lead and kept things professional, recounting my story for a third time, trying not to cringe as I remembered Leo's puffy face and the blood glops in his hair. I told Ransom the house looked a wreck and no one else was home. Which brought up an interesting question.

"Where's Leo's wife?" I asked. I hadn't seen Bebe here or at the party last night.

He ignored me. He scratched down a few words in his black book. His letters were dark and bold and impossible to read. Especially upside-down. "What can you tell me about Leo Hirschorn?"

I crossed my legs and leaned back in my chair, considering how much I could politely share. I didn't wish to speak ill of the dead, but Leo was not what you would call well-liked. Or even liked. He was loud, pushy, and a brash on his best day. But still a member of the Ballantyne board, and an underappreciated one at that.

"Leo owned Buffalo Bill's, a chain of discount appliance stores," I said. "The one with the brightly colored super sale stickers in the shape of sheriff stars. He relocated the main office from New Jersey to Summerton about five years ago. Active in the community. He accepted a seat on the Ballantyne board two years ago."

"Anything else?"

"He wears a ten-gallon hat." I winced. "Wore."

A golf cart zipped by on the small path at the edge of the lawn and parked.

"Did Mr. Hirschorn have any trouble at the party last night?"

I thought about the party. Ransom's hands under my dress. Mrs. Kramer in the men's room. Jane telling Leo to shove a trophy up his ass. "No, not really."

I looked away, torn between helping Ransom's investigation and protecting the Ballantyne's reputation. A tiny thwock echoed as the golfer took his swing. Within minutes, he was back in his cart, zooming out of sight.

The golf course grounds were immaculate, but the same could not be said of Leo's. His had an air of casual decline. All the trappings of wealth without the grace to care for it. Clusters of weeds gave the flowerbeds a trashy look, and small yellow circles of dead grass dotted the lawn like a game of single-color Twister.

I leaned forward. "What happened to Leo?"

"He's dead." Mr. Information.

"I noticed. And the mess in the house?"

He tapped his notebook against his knee, then looked at me for a full ten seconds. I thought he might actually answer my question. He didn't.

"Why are you here, Ransom?"

"Sea Pine Island needed an experienced, high-ranking investigator and I'm an experienced, high-ranking investigator. Seemed like a perfect fit."

I stared at him. He stared back.

He glanced at his notes. "What's the Shelter Initiative?"

"It's confidential."

A tech headed down the driveway pushing an ambulance gurney with a black zippered body bag belted on top.

"I don't think confidentiality matters anymore," Ransom said.

How sad for Leo. His dreams, his ambitions, his secrets, all zipped up and rolled away by a stranger. "The Shelter Initiative was Leo's project. He was forming a committee to build a new homeless shelter program for the county."

"And that's why you're here?"

"Yes. He was hosting a breakfast to garner support, but only for select members of the board. Very hush-hush."

"Why would a homeless shelter be top secret?"

"Not top secret, exactly. Think of the Ballantyne board as kids on a playground, and no one chose Leo for their team. Committees would form and he wouldn't get asked to join them. It's not that he wasn't good, but that his personality sometimes got in his way."

"So the Shelter Initiative was going to change that?"

"Definitely. He came to me with the idea. It was excellent. Thoughtful, compassionate, fiscally sound. Do you have any idea how many families on this island are homeless? They lose a single paycheck, and they're in serious trouble. Lose two in a row, and suddenly they have no place to live, no place to go, even for a night, shuffling from church to church, relying on the kindness of strangers. This Initiative would save more than their lives, it would save their hope."

"And this morning's meeting?"

"Leo didn't want anyone to find out about his idea and take it away from him. He needed allies on the board to support him. With their backing, he'd announce the Initiative at the board meeting tomorrow."

"I see. Do you know who was supposed to be here?"

I shook my head. Leo didn't tell me, and I didn't ask. I hadn't planned to be there when the guests arrived. Just get the diorama displayed and then zip over to the Big House.

Ransom pulled a clear evidence sleeve from his jacket and set it on the dusty patio table. A torn sheet of paper lay encased inside, ripped into ragged pieces. Several splotched in blood, including the one with my signature clearly legible beneath Leo's.

"That's the committee form," I said.

"I found it under Leo's body."

Based on the rips and bloodstains, someone wasn't happy about the form. Someone on the board? Someone who killed Leo? Ransom watched me while I fingered the plastic sleeve. My nerves started to itch. His demeanor had been slowly devolving from warm to cool and I was beginning to understand why. I think he was interrogating me.

Ransom resumed his notebook knee tapping. "I understand you worked closely with Lieutenant Sullivan. Some sort of unlicensed private investigative work."

"You make it sound illegal and insignificant. Besides, one does not have to be licensed to gossip. You'd have to arrest the whole island."

More silence.

"I make discreet inquiries," I said. "Perfectly legal ones designed to keep minor misdeeds from clogging up the police files."

Ransom raised an eyebrow.

"Look, I don't need your approval." My heart skipped two beats. With Lieutenant Sullivan gone, maybe I did need his approval. I needed some kind of advisor to sign off on my work.

I sat up straight, confident. "I'm good at what I do, and I'm quite professional."

He glanced at my hat. "Do you always get this dressed up for a breakfast meeting?"

"I was here to set up the meeting, not attend it."

He nodded and sat back against the cushion. Which was coating his expensive suit with garden grit, I hoped. "Maybe you weren't the first to find Hirschorn dead. Maybe you were the last to see him alive."

Heat rushed up my neck straight to my face so fast, it felt like a hot flash. "Me? That's crazy. I did not kill Leo Hirschorn and rage through his house. Some hotshot investigator you are. Do I look like a lunatic?"

He glanced at my hat again.

I flipped up the brim on my fisherman's hat with a flourish. "It's an island." To think I once let him get to third base. "Are we finished? Leo was a colleague and I certainly can't just chat away while he's dead in the driveway."

I stood. He nodded. I left.

"Don't get involved, Lisbon," he called out when I reached the walk. "This isn't one of your *discreet inquiries*."

I lifted my hand up without turning around. I had no desire to play Catwoman to his Batman. But I did wish I'd taken a shower and worn a pair of pants without an elastic waistband.

I stalked down the driveway and saw Corporal Parker and a technician standing by the Mini, clearly waiting for me.

"The Lieutenant asked me to search your car," Parker said. She had the good grace to look embarrassed as my jaw unhinged.

"Search my car? You want to search my car? Do you have a warrant?"

"Do I need one?" Ransom asked from behind me.

I whirled around and faced him with both hands on my hips. "I'm just wondering how serious a suspect you think I am. Did you get a judge involved in this ridiculous notion?"

He stared at me and I stared back.

"No warrant," Ransom finally said.

I turned to Parker. "Have at it. Then I'd like to leave."

I felt Ransom move behind me; his arm brushed against mine.

He leaned in close and whispered, "As long as you don't leave the island without telling me. First."

THREE

Monday morning bloomed sunny and clear, the perfect day to launch my two-pronged plan: forget Nick Ransom by ignoring him, and remember Leo Hirschorn by having another member lead the Shelter Initiative in his honor.

Normally I'd ride my bike over to the Big House, but today was the first board meeting of the new season and I was wearing my good clothes: a dobby voile blouse with three-quarter ruffle sleeves and blue cuffed capris. I didn't want to risk a wipeout and show up with ripped pants and bloody palms. Of course, my bike is a three-wheeler, but it wouldn't be the first time I tipped over.

The side lot was jammed full, so I parked near the front walk. Probably the largest turnout for a board meeting since we stopped serving liquor three years ago. Officially, there are seventeen seats on the board; unofficially, the Foundation needs only seven members for a quorum. However, with the news of Leo's murder spreading faster than warm honey on a hot biscuit, you can bet every seat would be filled.

I waved to Zibby Archibald, the oldest member of the board at eighty-seven. She wore a lovely wide-brimmed hat with flowers around the rim. I'm pretty sure it was on backward. The bow faced front with the ribbon tails hanging down, one over each eyeball.

I opened the heavy door and headed to my office at the back of the house. Mr. Ballantyne converted the music room when he officially gave me the directorship eight years ago. I loved the high ceiling and tall windows with white plantation shutters. A vase of pink hydrangeas and soft yellow roses as big as softballs sat center on my desk. The gardener delivered fresh flowers to my office every Monday morning.

I sank into my chair just as Carla Otto, Ballantyne head chef and resident mother hen, walked in carrying a platter of fluffy croissants with blackberry jam, sweet butter, and a large sprig of plump red grapes. She believed in infusing her food with both love and soul. I've eaten her pastries and I can say it works.

She handed me a plate and a tall glass of Pepsi. "Good Lord, woman, did you see the parlor?" Carla asked.

"I know! I'm expecting bedlam." I took a bite of croissant. Soft flakes rained down on a small stack of messages piled on my desk. I brushed them off and took a quick peek. Mostly calls regarding Leo Hirschorn—his murder and the seat he left vacant on the board. Including one from a reporter at the *Islander Post*. Probably needed a quote from Mr. Ballantyne. Nothing that couldn't wait. "What have you heard so far?"

"Wait for me," Tod said as he crossed from the doorway to my desk. He slathered a croissant with butter and jam, then settled into the chair across from me. "Okay, go."

"You first, Elli, you were there," Carla said.

I told them a quick version of the events from Leo's house: the mess, the murder, and the missing Bebe.

"I hadn't heard that yet. Where exactly was she, if she wasn't home with her husband?" Carla said.

"With somebody else's husband?" Tod asked. "Kidnapped for ransom? Hiding in Switzerland? Buried in the backyard?"

"Easy, Clouseau. I sat in that backyard," I said and shuddered. "I can't believe I found Leo."

"Well, you almost didn't," Carla said. "Joey dropped off the fruit from Fresh Market this morning, said he saw Tim Hanson at the Gullah Café for Sunday brunch. Tim works for Palmetto Propane and was supposed to drop off a tank for Leo at six, but was running late. Could've been him to find Leo dead in the den."

For most, living on an island means natural gas is a luxury. For Sea Pine Island, it's non-existent. If you want to cook on a gas stove, you need propane.

"Why was Tim there so early in the morning?" I asked.

"I have no idea," Carla said.

Tod glanced at his watch. "Elli, we'd better get to the meeting. Jane's liable to lock us out."

"Not today," I said. Leo worked his butt off for the Shelter Initiative and I was getting it on the agenda.

Carla went to the kitchen and I followed Tod into the parlor, the formal boardroom in the Big House. Sixteen men and women mingled near a dark oval table in the center. Its polished wood surface gleamed smooth as glass. It had intricately carved feet and matching high-backed chairs with silk cushions. The last few members quickly took their seats.

Jeremy Turco sat midway down the table. The youngest member of the board, but with the oldest money. Like before they printed it on paper.

Chas Obermeyer sat at the far end of the table. He worked at Charter Bank, Vice President of something. He was good-looking in an aging ex-Prom King sort of way. Wavy blond hair, but thinning on top; wide shoulders, but a doughy middle.

Deidre Burch chose a chair on the right side of the table. She had a bouncy gray bob and kept a pair of orange reading glasses on a beaded string around her neck.

And Jane Hatting, she of the flaming Godzilla firestorm, towered at the head of the long table wearing a tailored pantsuit in a striking shade of fuchsia. She wore a flower pin on her lapel and pearls around her neck.

Every seat was filled, save Leo Hirschorn's. I remembered Jane's threat of sitting a new board at this meeting and wondered if she knew something I didn't.

I sat in my usual armchair just behind Jane to the left; Tod sat in his on the right. We weren't actually on the board. We were more like observers. Or, as with our party hosting duties, referees. I took a deep swig of Pepsi and prepared for Jane's opening remarks. I wasn't sure if she would assume her usual acerbic attitude or opt for some measure of grief over Leo's death. However, I was so ill-prepared for the boundless joyful song that sprung from her lips, I snorted Pepsi up my nose in an attempt to avoid spitting it across her backside. Carbonation bubbles dribbled down my throat. I coughed and Tod thumped my back as if I was a child choking on a chicken bone.

All the while, Miss Sunshine pattered on, her voice so cheery, I expected blue birds to dance above her head. "—this glorious day. I'm excited to seat some fresh new blood. Shall we begin?"

Fifteen faces stared silently at this creature in a bright pink suit.

"What have you been drinking?" Jeremy Turco said.

"So, I'm in a good mood. It happens. No need for a roll call, I see we're all here," Jane said. She flipped open a wide leather portfolio. Humming.

"Oh no, dear, poor Leo isn't here," Zibby said and adjusted her backwards hat.

"Nope. I guess he won't be getting his seat renewed," Jane replied. "Now, any nominations? I have a short list prepared."

"Jesus, Jane. That's cold, even for you," Chas Obermeyer said.

"Maybe we should say something about Leo first," Zibby said.

"Like who killed the man," Deidre Burch chimed in, her readers now perched on her head. "Anyone know who did the deed? You're looking particularly chipper, Chas."

"Yeah, and you're a little green, Deidre," Chas replied, sounding even more like an old football star, biting back at the nerd in the class.

I put my hand up to stop the blithe banter, but Deidre interrupted me before I could speak. "Oh, don't look so shocked, sugar. We're all thinking somebody here is guilty."

I dropped my hand and thought she might be right. I studied the faces around the table. Who here knew about Leo's Shelter Initiative? Did they kill him to stop it? But why stop a homeless shelter?

"Could've been Leo's wife," Jeremy said. "He was swinging some major babe around the party. Red dress, serious arm candy, man. Definitely not Bebe Hirschorn."

"Do you think Bebe iced him?" Zibby asked.

Several board members leaned forward. Whitney Tattersall was so transfixed, she put her elbow in a pat of soft butter.

"Well, I didn't see Bebe at the party," Whitney said. "Do you think she left him?"

"If she saw Leo with a babe, she would've been pissed," Deidre said.

"Who wasn't pissed at Leo?" Jane said. "He was an ass and now he's dead. His loss, our gain. Now we can put someone more deserving on the board and I never have to see that ridiculous cowboy hat again."

"Well, gee, Jane, tell us how you really feel," Chas said.

"At least I'm honest."

"But Jane, dear, the hat was part of his business," Zibby said. "It made Buffalo Bill's famous."

"Oh, please. They don't have cowboys in Hoboken," she replied. She placed her hand on the table and cleared her throat. "Look, my concern isn't Leo Hirschorn. Not anymore. My concern is this Foundation. Keeping it strong, keeping it focused. We need to devote our time to the important things."

"Yes, I agree," said Preston Wilde, a semi-retired tax attorney. He looked down his nose in disapproval. "This gossiping is highly inappropriate. We should move on."

"Perfect," I said. "I have an important Leo item I'd like to present. One in his honor."

"Thank you, Preston," Jane said, ignoring me completely. She pulled a neatly-typed agenda from her portfolio. "Finally, on to board business."

The door swung open and Carla quietly stepped in with a wave to get my attention.

"Not now, Carla," Jane said. "We're in a closed-door meeting. In case you didn't notice, what with the door closed and all."

Carla ignored her. "I hate to interrupt, Elliott, but you've got visitors. The kind who carry guns."

She stepped aside as Nick Ransom and two uniformed officers entered the room. Ransom wore his badge on his belt, his gun under his arm, and his shirt clung to his chest for dear life. He looked at me for a full five seconds and my palms started to sweat. Then he slowly surveyed the rest of the room. The bountiful breakfast, the curious upturned faces around the table, and finally, his target.

He approached Jane while the two officers remained in front of the parlor doors. They looked like sentries guarding the palace entry. "Jane Hatting?"

"Yes, I'm Jane Walcott Hatting. What can I do for you?"

"Lieutenant Ransom." He unclipped the leather case from his belt and showed her the gold and silver shield. "I need to ask you about Leo Hirschorn. Down at the station."

Jane didn't so much as blink toward his badge. "As you can undoubtedly see, I am otherwise engaged. If you leave your card, I'll have my assistant set an appointment for later this week." She turned back to face the board.

"Ms. Hatting, I'm not asking."

No one said a word. Every face frozen in such rapt attention, I could've sold popcorn and chocolates.

"Am I under arrest?" Jane asked.

"Should you be?" Ransom said.

He reached out to take her arm, but Jane was having none of that. She whipped her arm out of his reach and her elbow smacked me right in the face.

My eyes pinched shut in pain. I saw stars. Tiny pinprick-sized glowing shooting stars.

Tod rushed over. "Elliott, are you okay?"

I nodded and held my hand over my mouth, hoping blood wasn't dribbling onto my blouse. It cost three hundred bucks.

"I'll get ice," Carla said and rushed to the buffet bar in the corner.

Preston Wilde marched over. "Answer the lady's question. Is she under arrest?"

Ransom looked down (a good foot and a half). "And you are?"

"I'm her attorney, Preston Wilde."

Ransom raised his eyebrow at Jane. "That was fast. She's a person of interest in the murder of Leo Hirschorn."

Ransom nodded to one of the officers, who then stepped forward and led Jane from the room.

She didn't say a word.

Carla handed me a napkin filled with ice cubes, which I gently placed on my face.

"Well, today sucks," I said.

Ransom leaned down and pulled back the ice pack. His finger softly touched my cheek. "It's only going to get worse."

FOUR

"Holy crap, Jane killed Leo."

"I knew she'd kill someone eventually."

"Surprised it took her this long."

I turned to Tod and opened my notebook with my left hand, the right still attached to the ice pack on my face. "We should adjourn. And quickly," I said, nodding toward the board members chatting around the room. "We'll pick a new date when Jane's free."

"Like in fifteen to life," Tod said and plopped into Jane's seat at the head of the table.

I moved the ice pack from my lip to my forehead and closed my eyes.

"I'm thinking it'll be the electric chair," Carla added. "The jury's gonna hate Jane. Probably hand down their verdict while the D.A.'s still delivering his closing argument."

"Stop," I said. "Let's just adjourn the meeting and get everyone out of here."

"Sorry, but that's just not going to happen," Tod said. "You can't buy gossip this good."

"I better get more croissants," Carla said and left the parlor carrying an empty silver platter.

I glanced across the room. Members bustled over to the buffet to refill their breakfast plates and coffee. Some took off their suit jackets and cardigan sweaters. One gal flipped off her shoes and tucked her legs up under her.

Tod was right. It would take something bigger than me to shut this sucker down.

"Fine, Tod. But not all day, okay? Try to wrap by lunch," I said and pushed my hair back. "How's my face?"

"Not horrible, and no blood. You've certainly looked worse."

Good enough for me. I grabbed my notebook, dropped my make-shift ice pack on the buffet, and left the parlor. I closed the doors behind me with a sigh.

In the foyer, Ransom stood talking to the two uniforms. His hands were in his pockets and he smiled at me. Mr. Casual. Mr. No Worries.

He worried me.

"So what's going on?" I asked when I reached him.

"How's your face?"

Preston Wilde stuck his head out from the library. "Lieutenant Ransom? My client and I need more time. We'll meet you at the station this afternoon."

"That's not the way it works," Ransom replied.

"We would appreciate the courtesy, Lieutenant," Preston said. His voice became friendly, a tax man used to dealing with the uncooperative nature of bureaucrats. One surly detective was probably no more than a 1040EZ form he could fill out with a crayon.

"Fine. One hour. But if she doesn't show, I will find her, handcuff her, and parade her down Main Street straight to a jail cell." Ransom nodded to the two uniforms, and they left through the front door.

Ransom put his hand on my arm. "May I have a minute?"

"Only if you plan on answering my questions this time."

He leaned in. "Only if you plan on making them personal."

His hand lingered on my arm as Carla walked up with the platter full of fresh croissants. The warm buttery aroma preceded her by a good ten feet. "Croissant, Lieutenant? Hot from the oven."

He smiled, but declined.

"Elli, I hate to interrupt, but Mr. Ballantyne is on line two." She looked up at Ransom. "Lieutenant, you don't need to rush off,

I'm sure she'll only be a minute. You wait right here and I'll bring out some fresh coffee." Carla walked away before he could answer.

"I need to take this," I said to Ransom. "And you do not need to wait."

He sat down in one of the wing back chairs and grinned. "I don't mind."

Of course not.

I passed the parlor on my way to my office. The members were still sequestered behind the double doors. Popping champagne bottles, no doubt, celebrating board life without Jane Hatting.

Sinking into my desk chair, I wondered how to break it to Mr. Ballantyne about Jane. He was going to be crushed. He personally chose Jane as chair; every year he renewed her seat. No votes, only his appointment.

I picked up the handset. "Mr. Ballantyne, how are you?"

"Elliott! Hello! Hello! How wonderful to hear your voice," Mr. Ballantyne shouted into the phone. He sounded as if he was using a battery-operated hand-crank telephone circa 1897. "We've just finished a late dinner. The food, Elli! So rich, you would adore it. And the tigers in Ranthambore. We took the train from Mumbai. It's magnificent here!"

Ah. Safari in India. I pictured the Ballantynes with matching leather rucksacks and pith helmets on their heads, trekking across the savannas, aiding small villages and tiny children. I missed the Ballantynes. They'd been gone nearly a month this time.

"About Jane," Mr. Ballantyne continued. "I'm going to need your help sorting things out with the police."

"How can you possibly know about Jane? I heard not ten minutes ago."

"The chief phoned me this morning, and I've just hung up with Jane. She assures me she has nothing to do with Leo's murder, nothing at all, Elli, and I believe her. I need you on this one; I'm counting on your expertise. You've helped many a donor out of a pickle before, you can do it again!"

"But Mr. Ballantyne, this is a murder. I'm afraid I don't have much expertise with those." As I protested, my mind raced. I grabbed my notebook and started listing questions from yesterday's excursion to Leo's house: Why the mess? Where was Bebe?

"You can do it, my girl! Clear your plate. This is your top priority, your top priority, Elli. We owe Leo and we owe our Jane. I know you won't disappoint me!"

I scribbled as we spoke: Police suspect Jane. Why? "I suppose I could poke around a bit. I don't have any other inquiries at the moment." How much harder could this be? A stolen golf cart, a missing brooch, a man shoved into a clock...My heart sank a bit as I thought of Leo. He definitely deserved better.

"Oh, yes, just one more inquiry. Zibby Archibald has a small peccadillo. It's a petite problem, really, but it's upsetting her deeply. She's Vivi's cousin, adores her like a baby with a kitten. After you patch up Zibby, keep your full attention on Jane. We're off to bed, my dear. Tomorrow the Keladevi Sanctuary."

"Goodnight, Mr. Ballantyne," I said, but he was already gone.

"I hope you weren't talking about poking around my investigation," Ransom said from the doorway.

I slapped my notebook closed. "What happened to waiting out front?"

"I'm not the type of man who waits." He slipped into the chair facing my desk. He crossed his legs, resting an ankle on his knee.

I tucked my notebook in a bottom drawer, then sat straight behind the roses on my desk. A lovely barrier between me and the pushy Nick Ransom. I squirted some hand-sanitizer into my palm and rubbed my hands together while I contemplated my options. Throw him out or hear him out? Or both? Hear him out, *and then* throw him out.

"That's quite an industrial-sized bottle you have there." He nodded at the big plastic pump filled with green gel. "Is that in case the plague descends?"

"You're a funny man, Lieutenant. But what can I do for you?"

He moved the flowers to the credenza in the corner. "First, you can stop calling me Lieutenant. It's Nick. I like it when you call me Nick."

"What's with the hot and cold? Saturday night you were all smiles,"–and hands, I thought to myself—"but Sunday you were downright dictatorial."

"Sunday you were a suspect."

"But not anymore?"

"Your alibi checks."

I felt my jaw start to clench. "I didn't give you one to check."

"Hotshot investigator, remember? I'm that good."

I played with the clicker on my pen, studying Ransom while he studied me. Click-click, click-click. He was strong and smart. But then, so was I. He probably had lots of experience investigating murders and shooting guns. I worked with charities and rode a three-wheel bike. Damn. I needed his cooperation more than he needed mine.

"So, Ransom, this is your meeting," I said. "What's on your mind?"

"Tell me about your Ballantyne Foundation."

"How about we talk outside?" I rose from my desk, carefully avoiding brushing against him as I walked past. "By the way, the flower vase you moved? The gardener delivered it this morning. He has a nasty cold. Going on two weeks. It's not the plague, of course, but no way I'd touch it."

I thought I heard the distinctive sound of a small pump behind me.

On the back terrace, a sparkling lap pool stretched twenty-five yards across a fieldstone patio. I walked down the steps to a large sitting area where a cluster of chairs faced the pool and the back lawn. "The Ballantynes have over seventy-five acres. There's croquet, tennis, a formal English garden, and the largest vegetable garden on the island. Carla grows the most flavorful bell peppers. So crunchy, you can eat them like apples."

"Where did all the money come from?"

"Mr. Edward Ballantyne, the first, earned his money the old-fashioned way. He inherited it. And he liked to spend it," I said as I offered Ransom a seat across from me.

The late spring temperature was already over eighty degrees and it wasn't quite noon. I cranked open a large market umbrella to shade us from the sun. "When Mr. Ballantyne died suddenly in 1959, his only heir, the Mr. Ballantyne of today, took the Foundation reins without restrictions. At twenty-two, just out of college and on the eve of the civil rights movement, the young Mr. Ballantyne made sweeping changes. Especially when he learned the depth of the family fortune. Billions."

"Did you say billions, with a B?"

"Yep. He married his sweetheart, Vivienne White, three years later. Together they directed the Foundation to reach out to numerous charitable organizations—educational, environmental, social—and have been giving away money ever since."

Ransom leaned forward. "And the board? How does that work?"

"Members arrange fundraisers and community outreach programs. They review grant packets, sometimes over a hundred applications at any given time. They nominate top picks at general meetings. The packets are handed off to Tod and me for processing."

"Was Hirschorn favoring a particular grant?"

"Not that I know of. This morning's meeting was the first of the season."

"Would someone kill for his vote?"

"Unlikely. A single vote won't do much good, and honestly, Leo didn't have much favor with the rest of the board. It's a very involved process. After Tod and I finish our research, we present the applications to Mr. Ballantyne's private committee, they make the final decision."

"And how do you jump from doling out funds to investigating murder?"

"I don't investigate murders. Just the occasional mishap."

I waved my arms toward the back lawn. The thick green grass hosted an orchard of crape myrtles, blooming magnolias, and massive oaks with Spanish moss hanging from them like tinsel on a Christmas tree.

"See that swing?" I said, pointing to an old wood-board swing tied to a thick branch swaying lazily in the breeze. "All my best childhood memories are from right there. Sometimes I think Mr. Ballantyne hung it just for me. I'd swing while my parents attended the Big House parties...the few times they brought me, anyway."

I glanced back at Ransom and caught him staring at me.

"It's peaceful," he said softly.

"Yes, well, island life is slow. Afternoons spent on the golf course or sipping lemonade by the pool. Our citizens stay out of trouble. For the most part. And when they don't, I step in and fix it."

He leaned back in his chair and laughed. "I see. So you're a fixer. Like the Wolf."

"Yes, that's exactly what I'm saying. Don't let my southern hospitality fool you. I'm a character right out of *Pulp Fiction*, the one you turn to when you need to clean up a dead body."

"Don't overreact. It's just that a mishap isn't the same as a murder. You simply can't handle something this big."

"You don't know what I can handle."

"I was in your evidence collection class. You grabbed my pants and slid to the floor in a dead faint during a crime scene slideshow. It's how we met, remember?"

My palms started to hurt. I'd squeezed my fist so tight, my fingernails nearly drew blood. I slowly released them. "Things have changed. I've changed."

"Elliott, you have a nine gallon barrel of hand-sanitizer on your desk. You aren't ready to get this dirty."

"I guess we'll see," I said and stood. "Now, if you've finished mocking me, I'd like to get back to work."

He slowly picked up his jacket. "I'm not mocking you, Elliott. I'm serious. This investigation doesn't concern you."

"Have you not been listening? Of course it concerns me. You are questioning one board member about the murder of another. This isn't a job, Ransom, it's my life. The Ballantynes treat me like a daughter; they're my only family. They were there for me when my parents died. You left. They were all I had. I won't let you shred their reputation while you witch hunt my board. Besides, your chief called my chief last night." I stabbed his chest with my finger. Twice. "I'm in this."

Ransom stepped forward, his jaw tight. "What did you say?"

"Mr. Ballantyne asked me to find out who killed Leo Hirschorn and I'm going to." So maybe not exactly what Mr. Ballantyne asked, I thought, but close enough. The extra investigation hours could go toward my PI license, and that also helped the Ballantyne. "I don't answer to you. We've always had the cooperation of the Sea Pine Police, and based on my phone call, this won't be any different."

"It will be on my terms," he said, an edge in his voice.

"If you'd like to think that, have at it. Now, when I said afternoons spent by the pool, I didn't mean me. I have a job." I walked along the path by the garden toward the front. "I really liked Lieutenant Sully," I muttered.

"Maybe you'll like me, too," he said over my shoulder. "Just stay out of my way and we'll be fine."

"You do the same, Lieutenant."

I left him in the parking lot and stalked up the front steps, irritated he called me out on my forensic fainting. I may be squeamish, but it's not as if I was performing Leo's autopsy. I just needed to find his killer before Ransom arrested Jane and ruined my life. I'm going to need real help, I thought as I marched back to my office. So I'm going to do what any self-respecting woman would do in this situation. I'm going to beg Sully to come back.

FIVE

It looked as though the board meeting finally adjourned; the parlor was empty and members gathered in the halls. I tracked down Zibby Archibald outside the ladies room on the first floor. I wanted to get her peccadillo settled and move on to the Hirschorn murder right away. Ransom's investigation was in the fast lane and mine was still in the parking lot.

Zibby accepted my invitation to lunch at Molly's in an hour. It gave her time to dash home and walk her Pomeranians, and me time to make four quick calls.

I flipped through the Rolodex on the corner of my desk. Tod tried to get me to computerize the index cards, but I had so many of them, the task seemed too monumental. I found the card I wanted and dialed the phone.

"Where the hell are you and when are you coming back?" I asked when Lieutenant Sullivan answered. "By the way, it's Elliott Lisbon from the Ballantyne Foundation."

"Didn't they tell you? I retired. I live in Key Biscayne now."

"How do you retire from an island? Aren't you already halfway there?"

He laughed the boisterous laugh of the unencumbered. "Me and Ginny were visiting her sister last month. She's got a stilt house right on the water. A twenty-two foot Wellcraft ten feet from the house. We had a great time. Fishing like I've never seen. Turns out the place next door was for sale."

"But Sully, why so fast? You may not know this, but we've got fishing right here. And boats, too." I fiddled with a paper clip while I spoke, unwinding it until it was straight.

"Yes, but Ginny's sister is alone and not doing so great, getting along in years. Likes to have us around." He cleared his throat. "Now what's this all about, Lisbon?"

"You're my go-to guy at the station. I need someone with official access. A silent partner to liaise between crime and the Ballantyne. You sign my papers, Sully. Who's going to advise me?"

"Well, I hear this new fella is smart as a fox."

"He's a fox, all right. And he doesn't like to play with others. Already giving me a hard time and I haven't even started." I tried to put the clip back to its original state and ended up snapping off the ends.

"He'll come around. Contact Lillie Parker. She's always liked you. By the book, but not afraid to get things done. Look, I gotta run. We're going out for conch salad. Best I've ever had. Call me if you're ever down this way."

"Sure, Sully, take care." I hung up and spent a good five minutes brooding. I'd forgotten to beg. And ole smart as a fox Ransom was flat out not going to share his spoils with me. At least not the ones pertaining to the murder of Leo Hirschorn. I needed to outwit the fox in his own henhouse and sniff out my own spoils.

I decided to make the next call an easy one. I dialed the number from memory: the *Islander Post*. Tate Keating answered on the first ring.

"Hey Tate, it's Elliott at the Ballantyne. Just returning your call. Mr. Ballantyne is in India, but he wanted me to tell you how much he admired Leo Hirschorn and his dedication to the community. He'll be remembered as a champion for the underserved, and the entire Foundation family will miss him."

"What's he say about his chairwoman being dragged out of the Big House by the cops for questioning? Why did she kill Leo? I heard it was brutal. Torrid affair, or to cover up a scandal at the Foundation?"

I gripped the phone. "That's ridiculous speculation and completely untrue. Jane was not dragged anywhere, and there's nothing to cover up. You know you can't print gossip." I started pacing. So much for my grand delusion of a puff piece on Leo's legacy at the Ballantyne.

Traffic sounds floated through the earpiece. It sounded like a party. Loud music and horn-honking. "I'm just getting a feel for the story. I'll fact check before we print. Can I quote you on any of that?"

"Just the statement from Mr. Ballantyne. No comment on the rest." I put a smile in my voice. "Come on, Tate. We've worked together for years. The Foundation does a lot of good for this community and doesn't deserve scandalous press."

He chuckled. "It's been only one year and the Foundation didn't do any good for Leo. Gotta run. If you change your mind on the quote, call me."

I sank into my chair, slightly numb. Jane's mortification would be legendary if the world thought she was boinking Leo. Mr. Ballantyne's embarrassment would be categorical if his life's work was reduced to a tacky tabloid scandal.

The implications of Leo's death and Jane's involvement were beginning to make my stomach sink. Maybe I shouldn't have antagonized Ransom; that second chest poke may have been unnecessary. I remembered something about catching more bees with honey rather than kicking a hornet's nest or some such bee wisdom. Either way, I had a feeling I'd end up stung.

I grabbed the phone and left a message with Jane's assistant. I needed to speak with Jane immediately and said so. While she probably wouldn't divulge her private attorney conversations, I needed to know what happened with Ransom. Why he singled out her for questioning. Other than everyone knew she hated Leo and half the party-goers heard her threaten him.

I flipped through the pages in my spiral notebook, stopping at what I'd written regarding Leo's ransacked house. I underlined the word "shambles" twice. The symphony of destruction in the kitchen was more than a ransack, it was pure rage. And where was Bebe? She makes plans for the night of the May Bash, a party specifically honoring the board members, and her husband also ends up murdered? Quite a night to be away. Why wasn't she being dragged to the police station?

I found Bebe's number in the Ballantyne directory and dialed; it rolled straight to voicemail. I silently debated whether or not to mention Leo. I wasn't sure she even knew he was dead. In the end, I simply asked her to call me.

My stomach gurgled and I realized it was time for my lunch with Zibby Archibald. I grabbed my hipster handbag and left the Big House.

Molly's by the Sea was tucked behind a row of sand dunes in Sugar Hill Plantation, a large rambling residential community with hotels, condos, restaurants, and two bike rental shops. I sped up to the guard house for a day pass. It's much easier to enter a plantation when they have a restaurant behind the gates. I drove down Sugar Hill Drive two miles to the sea, arriving at the three-story Victorian house-turned-restaurant only five minutes late.

The hostess escorted me to a table for two on the back porch with long views of the ocean. Zibby was waiting for me. She had placed her hat on the railing and tucked a pale pink napkin under her chin.

"Zibby, I'm so happy you were free," I said after I scooted in my chair.

"Always for you, dear. Lovely day to lunch by the ocean."

"I haven't been to Molly's in months. I've forgotten the selection." I scanned the three-page menu. Everything sounded delicious.

A waitress appeared with a bread basket, then rattled off the specials. I ordered a honey roasted turkey and brie on brioche with raspberry mayonnaise; Zibby tried the catch of the day: fresh fillet of flounder. Deep-fried.

"What an exciting meeting today! Can you imagine Jane being dragged in? Maybe they put her in handcuffs. Here we are dining by the beach, and she's probably being served bread and water," Zibby said. She grabbed two pumpernickel rolls from the basket. Buttered one, stuck the other in her purse.

"Jane wasn't arrested. They only needed to ask a few questions. With her being the board chair, it's probably routine," I said, trying to dampen the gossip the best I could. I also didn't point out that they stopped serving bread and water to inmates in the 1800s.

I steered the conversation to safer territory once the server delivered our lunch. Zibby was an old Southern luncher—gossip over lunch, business over dessert. I ate quickly.

"Were you friends with Leo?" I asked.

"Oh, not really. Nice young man, though. Promised me a good deal on a new refrigerator. I never did get over to Buffalo Bill's. And now I'm not sure I ever will," she said. She stirred her iced tea with a fork and ate her catfish with a spoon.

"Did you see him at the party Saturday night?"

"You know, I don't think so. Mr. and Mrs. Fetterbush kept us entertained with stories of the pirates off Sullivan's Island near Charleston Harbor. We hardly even left the table."

We settled into a comfortable conversation, chatting about the rise of piracy in the Atlantic and how the island needs more shopping trolleys and a better surf shop.

The waitress finally arrived to clear our plates and offered dessert. I wanted to pass—I did, really—but I needed to get on with Zibby's tiny transgression. I chose something light: lemon cookies with a thin layer of white icing. Barely any calories, I'm sure.

"Mr. Ballantyne tells me you need my assistance with a small matter," I said.

"Oh yes, dear. I'm so happy you brought that up." She leaned in conspiratorially and whispered loudly. "It's the Wharf. I've been banned! Escorted me right out the front."

It hurts to swallow a cookie whole. "Banned you? Whatever for?" Who bans an eighty-seven year old woman? She might be eccentric, but she had more money and manners than necessary, even for the South.

"It's a bunch of twaddle, Elli. One time I left without paying. One time!" She ripped open a sugar packet and sprinkled the crystals into her water glass, then stirred it with a knife. "I told the nice waiter to bring my check, but he never came back. I'd have missed Jeopardy if I waited any longer."

"It sounds pretty harsh for such a small incident, Zibby, especially the Wharf."

Nestled on the Intracoastal Waterway, Wharf patrons were treated to spectacular sunsets over the Palmetto Bridge while they dined on French-fusion cuisine. Certainly not the type of establishment to toss little old ladies out the front door.

"I know, dear. Called me a flibbertigibbet, of all things. I knew I had to pay, I just couldn't wait. It's my favorite restaurant. What ever shall I do if I can't go back?"

Tears spilled onto Zibby's cheeks and she sniffed back a sob. She dug into her enormous leather pocketbook, pulling out a pack of tissues. "It's George. We ate there every Thursday night for eight years. Every single Thursday, Elli." She dabbed her eyes and tucked the tissue up her sleeve. "It's been two years since my George passed, but I still go to the Wharf on Thursdays."

I patted her hand. "I'll talk to them." I'd met the head chef and owner, Paul Carmichael, years earlier at a cooking competition. This didn't sound like it would be too difficult to fix. Wouldn't take but an hour, then I could get back to Leo and Jane.

"Would you really? George and I never skipped an episode or a dinner at the Wharf. I already missed last week. Two in a row would be unbearable."

"Don't worry. I can fix this," I reassured her.

"You're a dear. If you ever need a favor from me, you just ask. I'm not one to take and not give."

"I do have one thing that would be a big help. Leo was forming a new committee for the board. It didn't make the agenda at the meeting and I need someone to take it over."

"How sweet of you to ask, but I'm afraid I gave up chairing committees for Lent this year." She tucked her pink napkin into her purse and smiled.

I nodded as if that made perfect sense.

After I paid the check, we walked to the parking lot and said our goodbyes. She climbed into a very large Cadillac sedan, one built for a family of ten and modified with a crank-down convertible top. With a wave and a honk, she zipped out of the lot.

I checked my voicemail. Nothing from Bebe or Jane. Jane might still be at the station. But if she was there much longer, I was going to start worrying about how much evidence Ransom actually had. I stuck a straw hat on my head to keep my hair from whipping into my eyes and drove down Cabana Boulevard with the mid-afternoon sun hot on my face.

The far north end of the island was as beautiful as the rest. Where most cities have main roads clogged with shopping centers and acres of asphalt parking lots, Sea Pine's are not. Every center, development, and drive was bermed by fields of trees, grass, flowers, and plantings to rival the Amazon. It can be frustrating at first—take you ten minutes before you realize you passed what you were looking for two miles back. But once you get used to it, it was a snap.

I turned onto Old Pickett Road, then drove the three miles along the sound to the Wharf. It was only two-thirty, but I figured the staff would be prepping for dinner, the only meal they offered during the week. I parked beneath a sprawling oak and hoped I wouldn't come back to a seat full of Spanish moss and squirrel poop.

The hostess station was vacant, so I wandered into the main dining area. One staffer was laying stiff white cloths across a series of four-top tables while another staffer folded tan napkins into pretty little fan designs. Their color reminded me of the caramels Carla makes every Christmas, the homemade kind cut from a pan and wrapped in wax paper. Maybe I should've had the caramel cake for dessert.

"Excuse me, is Chef Carmichael in?" I asked the busser with the napkins.

He nodded toward the kitchen.

I stepped through the swinging door and walked around the back side of a baker's rack. Pots and pans rattled as two sous chefs manned an enormous commercial stove. The room smelled of rosemary and zesty garlic sizzling in a pan.

I spotted Chef Carmichael in a dark blue chef's coat. A stocky man, built like a wrestler and bald as an egg. He was arranging bite-sized appetizers on a tray with a grace that belied his build.

"Excuse me, Chef Carmichael? I'm Elliott Lisbon with the Ballantyne Foundation. We met in New Orleans a few years back. Do you have a moment?"

"Ah, the lovely Ms. Lisbon. Come in. Here, you must try the amuse-bouche for this evening. Prosciutto, arugula, sweet melon, and aged balsamic."

He placed several on a plate in front of me before I came to a complete stop. I smiled and obliged, trying to gain favor where I could find it.

It was fantastic.

I savored every morsel of that little delicacy. Two more remained and I wondered if I should have another. Seemed rude not to. However, I did refrain from licking the plate.

"What can I do for you, Ms. Lisbon?" He set aside the small plate and selected a particularly large chef's knife from a rack. He sharpened the smooth blade, swiftly scraping it against a steel rod.

"It's about Zibby Archibald, Chef."

The smile left his eyes. "Not a chance. You're wasting your time and mine." He returned the metal rod to the rack, then chose a white onion from a large bowl at the end of the island.

"But Chef, surely one small indiscretion shouldn't result in a lifetime ban."

"One? Ms. Lisbon, that dotty old broad has skipped out five times. Five! This year." WHACK! He hacked the onion in two like a Samurai chef in a cooking competition.

"First, please call me Elliott." I smiled and folded my hands on the table. "Second, Mrs. Archibald may be senior, but she's a beloved relative of the Ballantynes."

"Of course, I didn't mean to be insulting. But that beloved relative will not be dining here. Ever. I've alerted the entire staff. The last time the hostess seated Mrs. Archibald, I was on vacation. It will not happen again." He selected one half of the split onion, then the other, slicing them at a speed that made my fingers itch and my eyes water.

"Chef, there must be something we can do. She isn't skipping out; she just wants to get home." I lowered my voice. "For Jeopardy. It's important to her."

He scraped the diced onions into a small bowl, then grabbed another onion.

WHACK!

I backed up and leaned against the sink. "How well do you know Zibby Archibald?"

"She dyes her hair to match her clothes. Her husband died and left her a little nest egg. And, oh yeah, she likes to dine and ditch."

"Chef, I hate to sound crass and discuss money, but Mrs. Archibald's little nest egg could keep a small country in cheeseburgers for several years. Steaks, even. The Wharf is absolutely Zibby's favorite restaurant. She dines here once a week."

"Not anymore."

"What I'm saying, Chef, is Zibby Archibald is the best advertising you have. She raves over your she-crab bisque to anyone who will listen. And she serves on a dozen boards."

"I do a brisk business. I've built the Wharf into the top-rated restaurant in this state. I don't need Zibby Archibald's influence." He waved his knife around. Sous chefs and prep cooks were chopping, slicing, dicing, peeling, shredding, whisking, and whipping as if the Queen were coming to dinner. "Besides, the Ballantyne isn't what it used to be."

"Excuse me?"

"One member is a thief, another's dead, and your ringleader is in jail. What's next? A counterfeit ring in the wine cellar?"

How did he hear about Jane? I mentally counted to three and forced a smile. "Jane is not in jail. And Zibby is not a thief. This is just a misunderstanding. Certainly we can find a compromise."

He swept the loose onion bits from the table. He wiped his knife with a white cloth, then returned it to the rack. Finally, he turned toward me. "I want the Palm & Fig Ball."

So much for distancing himself from the scandalous Ballantyne.

The Foundation hosted a lavish holiday gala each December. Renowned chefs throughout the South bid to co-cater the event and Chef Carmichael had never been selected. It was decided by committee, not me. But I suspected he knew this.

"I have no influence over the committee that chooses the chef for the Palm & Fig. Though we are hosting the Gatsby lawn party next week, benefitting the middle school. New sports equipment so everyone can play. It's short notice—"

"Perfect," he interrupted. "I'm honored you asked."

"And about Zibby, your most loyal customer?"

"I cannot let her dine for free. Surely, that's asking too much of me."

This from the man who just asked me to leapfrog a ten-member review board and hand him the ultimate catering prize. "Of course not. She'd be happy to leave a credit card on file, you can charge her monthly. Will that work for you?"

He unfolded his arms and smiled. "Anything for the Foundation. Mrs. Archibald is welcome anytime. Now about the Gatsby lawn party, I'm available Saturday for menu planning. It will be such a delight to work with Carla again!"

"I'm sure she'll feel the same," I said. "Thank you, Chef, I'll see myself out."

I think I gave in too soon. I certainly gave up too much. What Carla would feel was so far from delight, it would take a dictionary and a picture book for her to recognize it.

She and Chef Carmichael had a teensy tiny rivalry. It started in culinary school and escalated at a competition in New Orleans with Carla dumping a pot full of shrimp gumbo on Chef Carmichael's head. It was neither pretty nor pleasant and I had essentially offered to host a re-match.

The sun was starting to sink when I climbed into the Mini. Okay, maybe not sink since it was not yet four o'clock, but it had definitely moved lower and I was tired and wanted to go home. I called Zibby with the good news. She was ecstatic. Maybe things were looking up.

They weren't.

SIX

I zipped down Spy Hop Lane to my cottage. When I turned into my driveway, Ransom's prophecy that my day would only get worse rang in my ears.

"No, no, no, no, no. No," I said aloud.

Ransom stood in front of the house next door. He had two cardboard boxes at his feet and a moving van in the driveway.

"Maybe he's just helping Mr. Wallaby," I said frantically to my empty garage. "The police do that sometimes, right?" I hadn't actually seen my neighbor, Mr. Wallaby, in weeks. This can't be good, I thought.

I hopped out of my convertible and walked over to Ransom's—the same slick Mercedes from Saturday's party.

"Hey, Red," he said, leaning against the driver's side door, feet crossed at the ankles. A man without a care in the world.

"Those boxes wouldn't be for Mr. Wallaby, would they?"

Tiny lines broke out around his eyes as he smiled. "Nope. He went to live with his brother in Florida. I'm moving in."

What's with Florida snatching away my buffers? I'll need to start browsing brochures for condos in Boca just to get my life back.

"But why here?"

"Oyster Cove is the perfect plantation. Close to the station, the hospital, and the airport. And it's on the ocean."

"Uh-huh. One in five houses on this island is vacant, including in this plantation."

"I like having a friendly neighbor," he said.

"You knew it was right next door to me?"

"The icing on the cake, Red. I bought it on the spot."

"You *bought* this place?"

He raised an eyebrow. "You seemed to manage it."

I squinted at his car again. "Beachfront property, a hundred thousand dollar car. Seems kind of steep for a cop."

"Five hundred."

"What?"

"The car. It was five hundred thousand. It's a McLaren Roadster. It has a racing engine."

Are you shitting me? "What, no Lamborghini?"

"Too splashy."

I nodded. "Sure sure. Nothing says subdued like a Mercedes with a racing engine."

I knew Ransom came from money—his parents were a Charleston power couple who spent Saturday afternoons at the stables, Sunday mornings at church, and Monday evenings at the club—but they didn't rock this kind of cash. "Seriously, how can you manage this on a cop's salary?"

"That's rather personal, don't you think? We should have dinner first."

"We're definitely not having dinner." I watched as two large men in jeans continued to embed Nick's life next to mine, one end table at a time. "Why are you trying to get back in my life?"

"Maybe I regret the way things ended."

"Well, gee, Nick, do you always move this fast? It's only been twenty years."

"The message was the best I could do. We both knew the FBI could move me out any time. Just bad timing."

"Whatever, I'm not pining. I barely even remember you." Or the sound of your voice on the machine as I replayed those seven words over and over and over again.

A mover carrying a carved mahogany bedpost interrupted us. "Where does the bed go? That's a beautiful picture window in the master bedroom. You rather it behind you, or do you want to see the beach from bed?"

My thoughts jumped right back to naked.

Ransom grinned at me and I backed up. "I'm not that friend-ly."

"See you around the neighborhood," he said as I walked away.

I hurried back to my cottage. A half-million dollar car? He truly was Bruce Wayne. Son of a bitch. I really did have to give up cupcakes.

I kicked off my shoes and fell onto my couch. How could I live next door to Nick Ransom? I couldn't move; my cottage was perfect. Galley kitchen, living room, and half-bath downstairs; two bedrooms and a bathroom up. My parents left it to me twenty years ago, which is how *I* ended up living on the beach on an island on *my* salary.

We used to drive down from Michigan every summer. I hated the drive, but only because riding in a car for seventeen hours sucks. We stayed in Summerton, not Sea Pine, in a rental house on the May River. I would read by the riverbank while my parents championed the poor, supported the arts, and sailed the ocean blue.

My parents did their best to include me, but their complete absorption in one another before I arrived post-retirement didn't leave much room for a third wheel. They remained devoted as love birds until mom died when I was twenty. Dad passed six months later, leaving me orphaned, debt-free, and a cottage on Sea Pine Is-land I didn't even know they owned.

I stared at the shelf above the sofa. It held vintage games: wood dominoes, a Batman super-micro Bat radio, a Wonder Wom-an Bend 'n Flex, and a game of Clue in mint condition.

"Who - Where - How?" the Parker Brothers on the orange box asked. That's what I needed to figure out. Forget Nick Ransom, I thought. I needed to help Jane Walcott Hatting stay out of jail.

Now there's a sentence you don't hear too often.

I pulled out my notebook and created a separate page for each person involved in the case. So far I had Leo, Bebe, and Jane.

Jane was my biggest problem. She was wickedly unpleasant, but that wasn't the same as being uncontrollably violent. That required a passion I'm not sure she possessed. Mr. Ballantyne expected me to clear her, Ransom seemed determined to arrest her, and Jane could probably give a crap either way.

I spent some quality time with a bottle of Dos Equis Lager and a thin crust pizza. I checked my voicemail. Nothing from Bebe or Jane. Bebe I could understand, but not Jane. I needed to talk to her whether she wanted to or not, so I rang her again. Same result. I left a terse message and hung up the phone.

The next morning I fast-walked along the beach amidst the joggers and dog-walkers. I spent thirty minutes on the sand and returned to my cottage feeling frustrated instead of refreshed. It was already day two of my investigation and I had nothing to show for it but a string of unanswered messages and a front page headline that made me nauseous: Ballantyne Chair Questioned in Murder. Written in bold black letters with Tate Keating's name as the byline.

I read the article with trepidation, but it turned out the headline held all of bang. Other than saying Jane was being questioned, it talked about Leo's business, family, and work at the Foundation. I knew better than to relax. Tate's scent for the sensational made Geraldo look like an amateur.

And Jane wasn't helping. I decided if she ever did return my call, it would probably be from a pay phone at county lockup. Forget the phone; I needed to go to Savannah.

I sailed over the Palmetto Bridge from Sea Pine Island into Summerton at half-past ten. The tide was still high and the strong smell of the buried oyster beds blew over me as I drove, quickly evaporating as I wove through a mass of traffic, Savannah-bound sightseers off to visit the city's historic homes, art galleries, ghost tours, and all those gardens of good and evil.

Thirty minutes later I crossed the Talmadge Memorial, a cable bridge suspended almost two hundred feet over the Savannah River. The convention center sat across the bank overlooking the waterfront shops and restaurants. I turned right onto Whitaker and made my way into downtown where the streets were paved in brick and lined with live oaks dripping tendrils of Spanish moss.

I parked on Abercorn Street, a block from the Walcott Hatting Gallery, a fixture in the neighborhood since Jane's grandfather opened the doors in 1927. I stood outside the arched doorway, under a navy awning that faced Calhoun Square and a statue of General Oglethorpe, staring at my phone. Hoping it would ring. Parker calling to say they caught Leo's killer. A disgruntled employee, a jealous relative, a random serial killer. Somehow a serial killer was more appealing than poking into Jane's personal life. I was pretty sure Jane would agree.

I shoved my silent phone into my pocket and entered the main gallery room. Fifty feet long and thirty feet wide, it resembled a turn of the century sitting room. One in a really big house. Petite settees and wing chairs were grouped down the center of the room, facing walls decorated with heavy silk wallpaper. Paintings (of both the heirloom and local artist variety) covered nearly every inch of paper. Armoires, writing desks, and antique tables held valuable antiquities: jewel boxes, Fabergé eggs, first edition leather bound books, and porcelain plates.

No one greeted me, so I wandered through the auction area and eventually found Jane in a back workshop stuffed with old sewing machines. She wore paint-stained cargoes and a light denim smock. I couldn't have been more surprised if I found her naked. And she seemed pleased to see me, too.

"What the hell are you staring at?"

"I'm not staring, just admiring your outfit." Add some yellow rubber gloves and a bandana and she'd be perfect for a 1950's Pledge ad.

"I'm supposed to clean all this machinery in a silk suit?" She continued to scrub an old black Singer sewing machine. Its golden decals shone under her polishing. The bobbin looked brand new. At least I think it was a bobbin. It's the only technical sewing language I know.

"These seem a little street for your swanky shop."

She glanced at me. "I'm surprised you know the difference. They belonged to one of my father's first patrons. I'm doing a favor for the family, raising money for the ladies guild she founded. Coincidentally, these same ladies will be the ones purchasing." She went back to polishing. "Are you here to discuss my business or apologize for the headline in this morning's paper?"

"Neither. I didn't write the headline."

"I believe 'media' falls under your job as director. You're supposed to keep the reporters from slinging mud at the Ballantyne walls."

"I'm working on it. I have many duties as director. Like helping with Leo's murder. What happened at the police station?"

Jane barked out a laugh. "Jesus, Elliott, you can't be serious. Edward said something about getting you involved or some such nonsense."

"It's not nonsense. And yes, Mr. Ballantyne asked me to look into Leo's death."

"What does it matter? Whoever killed him did the Foundation a favor." She rubbed the same spot so hard, I thought she might sear through the enamel finish and crack into the cast iron.

"It matters because the police think you did it."

"Quit being such a drama queen. Questioning me was just for show. Drag in members of the Ballantyne, make a splash in the paper, let the public see those tax dollars at work. No stone unturned and all that crap."

"Not 'members of the Ballantyne,' Jane. Just you. Lieutenant Ransom considers you the prime suspect. And by prime, I mean only. They've got something and they're trying to make it stick."

She stopped scrubbing and looked me right in the face for the first time since I walked in. "Suspect? They actually think *I* killed that loudmouth weasel?"

"Yes. Despite your obvious grief over his passing." I leaned against a splintering wood worktable covered in old paint splatters, resting half a butt cheek on the sharp corner. I didn't want big fat tarnish stains on my rear end all day. "What happened at the police station?"

She walked over to a large hutch in the corner where she perused several stacks of tin cans, each with a different kind of polish or cleanser. Neatly lined up, labels facing out. "I can't tell you everything, I was with my attorney," she said with her back to me.

"Preston Wilde won't mind if you tell me."

"Yes, well, Preston might not, but Gregory Meade will."

"Gregory Meade, the *criminal* attorney?"

"Of course, the criminal attorney. I was at a police station, Elliott. I'm not an idiot." She eventually selected a fat black can from the shelf and carried it back to the table. She untwisted the wide lid before setting it aside.

"Jane, as much as I enjoy your company, can we please move this along?"

"You can leave any time. I didn't ask you here." She scooped out a dollop of white paste and began smoothing it on all the silver parts of the Singer.

"Did Lieutenant Ransom tell you why he brought you in?"

"Someone told him Leo and I argued at the party. I told him he heard wrong."

"You can't lie to the police. Half the guests heard you arguing with Leo on the terrace. How do you think I found you at the bar?"

"I assumed you used your stellar investigative skills. But I didn't lie. Leo and I weren't arguing. Just a normal conversation. He wanted a guaranteed renewal for his board seat and I told him over my dead body."

I mentally slapped my forehead. "Geez, Jane, what else did you discuss during this normal conversation?"

"I don't know exactly, I wasn't recording the damn thing. I may have said something about him running his fat mouth all the time. And something else about his stupid trophy."

"I heard you told him to shove it up his ass."

She shrugged. "It's possible. He didn't deserve to be Humanitarian of the Year."

"Did Leo mention his Shelter Initiative?"

"Was that his big committee proposal? He didn't say what it was, only that he was presenting something at the meeting. I told him I would kill whatever he proposed before the papers were signed."

"Why kill it if you didn't even know what it was?"

"Leo was conniving and self-serving. Whatever scheme he planned to disguise as a charitable project would only hurt the Foundation. I'd had enough. Someone needed to protect the Ballantyne from that snake."

I ran my hands through my hair. No wonder she was Ransom's prime suspect. Hell, after this conversation, she was *my* prime suspect. "Where did you go after the party?"

"None of your business." She smoothed on more paste. The silver was now so shiny, I was nearly blind. But she kept polishing. And polishing. The silence stretched from seconds to minutes. I got a bad feeling.

"Did you go to Leo's house after the party?"

"Nope."

"So, then, where were you after the party?"

"I said it's none of your damn business."

"Jesus Jane, I'm helping you here. Though you're making me not want to. Please tell me you told Ransom where you were."

"I told that asshole exactly what I told you."

"Not like that, I hope."

She threw down the tarnished rag. "Well, shit, am I supposed to change my personality to please one pushy detective? I don't care what he thinks. Now wrap it up and get out. I've got an auction in a week."

"Did Ransom tell you about any actual evidence they have?"

"Nope."

"Did you ask?"

"Gregory did, but they wouldn't say." She picked her rag back up and wiped away the excess paste from the edge of the machine.

Whatever else Jane knew, she wasn't sharing it with me. "I'll call you in a few days with the date of the new board meeting. If anything happens with the police, or you remember any more about Leo, call me." I opened the workshop door and was halfway through when she stopped me.

"There's one more grantee for the roster, a late addition for the meeting. We need to skip the preliminary board review. Make sure it's on the schedule."

"What grantee? No one told me," I said.

"Why would they? Just make the time so we can get it approved."

She turned back to her shiny old Singer and I left. I may have slammed the door with all my might.

SEVEN

I drove back to the island with the sun high in the sky; the temperature was over eighty-five. Some people don't like it hot. Me? I love it. I was raised in the freezing miserable bitter nasty snowy cold and was never as happy as the day I packed my bags and left.

I had planned on having lunch at Vic's on the River in Savannah, but I was too irritated to stop and didn't want to waste the view on a cranky attitude. Instead I spent the forty-five minutes in the car with a drive-thru cheeseburger (ketchup only) and fries while imagining what Jane would look like in a bright orange jail jumpsuit with her arms painted green with tattoos.

I arrived back at the Big House at ten past noon. I threw my handbag in the drawer, then crossed the hall to Tod's office tucked beneath the stairs, no bigger than a roomy broom closet. With over seven thousand square feet on the first floor alone, he could've chosen a different room, but he liked the tight space. He said the dark corners, crooked chandelier, and lack of windows creeped out the board members. His black suit and dead pan expression completed the effect. Like a young recluse undertaker in a Hitchcock film.

"When was Leo's fight with Jane?" I asked and plopped into a creaky chair opposite his desk. "How long before you found me in the foyer?"

"Maybe twenty minutes. You think she killed him?"

"Better odds than not after speaking with her this morning, but Mr. Ballantyne wants me to prove otherwise."

"You might as well try to prove the Earth is flat."

"Thanks for the encouragement."

"You want encouragement, go talk to Carla."

"I'm avoiding her," I said and picked imaginary lint from my shorty pants. "I sort of promised Chef Carmichael he could co-cater the Gatsby."

He raised his brow in question. "Sort of?"

"It was the only way he'd allow Zibby back into the Wharf."

"He kicked her out?"

"Long story. But I worked it out."

"If you think so," Tod said and went back to the paperwork on his desk. "Just make sure I'm not around when you tell Carla. I don't want her to think I had anything to do with this nut roll."

"It won't be today. I have to work up to it first."

I walked back to my office and checked my voicemail. One message. From Matty Gannon, close friend and headmaster of the private Seabrook Preparatory School. We met on a blind date eighteen months earlier, he was handsome and sweet and rugged, but somewhere between the filet mignon and the apple brown betty, his brother joined us. After that, the night slipped from friendly to friendship, and somehow it never flipped back.

Matty wasn't in his office, so I left him a message in return. Then I opened my notebook to a short list of questions I'd prepared and dialed Lillie Parker at the police station. I got lucky; she was at her desk.

"What's the deal with Ransom?" I asked after we said hello. "They must pay a lot more in Virginia."

She laughed and lowered her voice. "Retired FBI, but got his money from stocks, not salary. He invested in one of those search engine sites, then sold his shares before the market tanked."

I doodled on a fresh page. FBI in 3D. "Retired? From the way he acted yesterday, I'd say he's forgotten that part."

"Seriously. He knew a chief who knew a chief. With Sully's retirement, Captain Finnegan brought him on board. I guess the Lieutenant wanted a slower assignment."

"I wonder how that's working out. Listen, you know how I sometimes assist the community in resolving minor indiscretions?"

"Uh-huh."

"With Leo being a respected member of the board, the Ballantynes have asked me to step up and include this, um, situation."

Silence.

"I've already told Ransom. He didn't like it, but hey, he didn't like my hat either," I said with a chuckle.

More silence.

I started talking faster. "Look, Parker. I spoke with Sully and he thought you might be my sponsor. You know I'm working toward my PI license. Maybe you could even toss me a bone from time to time. Nothing major; just a few scraps to help a girl out. Of course you know I'll return the favor."

I held my breath. I added the name Parker to my doodle pad. Made a very sophisticated daisy out of the P. Added some lightning bolts to the FBI drawing.

"Fine, I'll talk to the Captain," she finally said. "But you cannot withhold evidence from me. You cannot get in the way, obstruct, hinder, or hamper."

"Never."

"I'll expect full disclosure on your end, Elliott."

"Absolutely. Always You bet," I agreed. "Now, I have just a couple of questions."

"Make it quick."

I flipped the page over and jotted notes as I spoke. "What evidence do you have against Jane?"

"No chance. Next."

"Where was Bebe Saturday night?"

"Out. Ask her yourself, she moved into the Tidewater Inn while her house is a crime scene. Princess Suite. Pretty nice digs for a grieving widow, you ask me. Next."

I quickly scanned my question list. "Time of death?"

"Between eleven-thirty p.m. Saturday and twelve-thirty a.m. Sunday."

That explained Ransom and my alibi; I didn't leave the Ballantyne until almost two. And why he considered Jane an option. She left around eleven.

"How was Leo killed?"

"It's complicated, and I can't share," Parker said. "But we're not the only department who knows the answer. We got our confirmation from somewhere, right? Now I really gotta go. Good luck," she said and hung up.

I knew just who she meant. Dr. Harry Fleet. He spends his mornings at the hospital and his afternoons in his office. I checked my watch: 2:05 p.m. If I timed it right, I could stop by in an hour and catch him well before dinner. If I delayed his usual mealtime, his normal grumpy mood could turn churlish. I could call, but he'd hang up on me. With Harry, if it's important, you show up in person.

Next I dialed the Tidewater Inn. Mrs. Bebe Hirschorn was indeed a guest, but her phone rolled to the hotel's voicemail. This time I said the Ballantyne wanted to honor Leo with a new fund. Then I called Ocean Blooms and sent her a big bouquet of roses and lilies with a personal note about sympathy and strength. See if that gets a response.

I leaned back in my chair, staring at the flower boxes outside the window. Trailing petunias, daisies, and clusters of magenta Sweet William attracted a pair of butterflies. Their lemon yellow wings flapped lazily around the planters.

Parker didn't give me much; Sully had been way more generous with his scraps. Difference in their personalities or the type of case? I admit murder wasn't my usual type of case, though some incidents escalate rather quickly.

Last year a former board member asked me to investigate her shoe closet. It rivaled the Nordstrom shoe department. I'd never seen so many pairs in one single place. Well, every day for four weeks, a different pair went missing. Hardly even noticeable, the closet was so vast. Turned out the nanny was selling them on eBay to supplement her salary. After I exposed the nanny as the thief, she stole another fifty pairs and set them on fire on the Big House lawn.

It seemed the more complicated the case, the less cooperation I was going to get. I wasn't looking forward to questioning Harry. Easier to pull weeds with my teeth than to get information out of Harry Fleet. Then there was Bebe Hirschorn. I needed her to provide the missing details about Saturday night. Like why she skipped the party and why she didn't notice her husband dead in the den.

Which reminded me of Tim Hanson, the propane delivery man who might have discovered Leo's body if he wasn't running late. Time to throw out a line and see what I could catch.

I reached for my Rolodex, found Palmetto Propane, and dialed the main office. Five minutes later, the receptionist connected me with Tim.

"Hi, Tim, I'm Elli with the Ballantyne Foundation, and I'm on the committee for the meeting Leo was hosting the other morning. Actually, I think you and I almost ran into each other out front. But you know, I can't find a single order for propane, especially for a Sunday delivery. This paperwork's a mess."

"Yeah, last minute rush. Hirschorn wanted a new set of larger tanks, had to have them that morning. Some special breakfast or something. I wouldn't have even gone out there if he hadn't promised he'd pay in cash, plus a bonus."

"Cash?"

"His last two checks bounced and Sally in accounting said it was cash or go without. Guess he found the cash."

"Thanks much, Tim. I'll make a note for the file. You have a great day now," I said and hung up.

Interesting. But what was more significant? The fact that Leo couldn't cover his checks or that he was suddenly flush the day he died? What was special about the day he died?

I rifled through one of my desk drawers until I found the folder for the May Bash. Since it was a formal dinner, I had created a seating chart for the guests. I skimmed the names of Leo's tablemates trying to find someone to question. The key to a discreet inquiry lies in the whole discreet part. I couldn't grill every guest from the party, that was a luxury for the police. I had to be more selective.

Leo wasn't the only board member at his table, Whitney Tattersall was, too. Another interesting tidbit. She didn't mention it at the board meeting. At least while I was there. I added her to my call list just as my phone rang.

"Elliott Lisbon," I said.

"Elli! My dear, how wonderful to hear your voice," Mr. Ballantyne shouted into my ear.

"Mr. Ballantyne, how are you? How is India, sir?"

"Fantastic, Elli. We've met a dashing young couple. Australians! We're bringing them home for the Gatsby next week." The line crackled with light static. "Are you there, Elli? Can you hear me?"

"Yes, I'm here. We're preparing for the party now. Tod mailed the invitations three weeks ago. He told me all the grantees have RSVP'd."

"Speaking of, my dear girl. I've moved one up the list: Mumbai Humanitarian. I don't want Mumbai to wait another day! Very close to my heart, very close."

Mr. Ballantyne likes to choose causes that mean something personally. He went on to tell me about the poverty-stricken areas in Mumbai. Of fifty-foot trash heaps and contaminated watering holes. They sounded dreadful. "But you call Reena Patel; her office is on the island. She'll fill you in on this tragic state. Tod has an extra packet for you. This should be on the books for approval at our next meeting, Elli."

I wrote down the organizer's name and a note to make an appointment. "I'll take care of it, sir!" I found myself shouting back, even though I'm pretty sure he could hear me just fine. "But on this other matter of Leo Hirschorn, can you use some of your connections to find out some things for me? I'd like information on his financial situation, business and personal. His debts, life insurance, who inherits his estate. It would be a big help."

"I understand, my girl, I understand. I'm on the case! I must ring off now, time for bed. I stayed up late to make this call. Tally-ho, Elli!"

"Tally-ho, sir."

I made a note to add two more guests for the party, the Ballantyne's Australian friends. Carla generally cooks up plenty of extra food—no one passes up an invitation to Big House, especially the Gatsby lawn party—but I wasn't sure about Chef Carmichael.

The annual Gatsby at the Big House was a throwback to lazy summer days of the roaring twenties when the wealthy gathered for simple games and fancy libations. Ladies wear cloche hats, low-waisted dresses, and buckle shoes. The men don knickers, soft caps, and dress shirts with rolled-up sleeves. I, myself, had a darling dress I couldn't wait to wear. But that was next week. I first had to get through this one.

I popped over to Tod's office for the Mumbai file.

"Top priority, Elliott, top priority," he sang.

"I know, thank you. All my assignments are top priority. I have no bottoms."

I shuffled back to my office and called the number for Mumbai Humanitarian listed on the application. The young receptionist informed me that Ms. Patel was unavailable to speak with me, but I could leave a message. I booked an appointment for nine o'clock the next morning instead. A top priority couldn't wait for a return call.

And neither could Harry.

I shoved my notebook in my hipster, grabbed my keys, and hollered goodnight on my way out the door.

The medical examiner's office was attached to the back of Island Memorial Hospital in a building that resembled a pretty brick colonial house with shutters on the windows, white raised-panel doors, and black embossed address plates. Most folks didn't realize the unmarked door at the end of the walk held all the dead people. Sea

Pine Island had a full-time medical examiner. Even though we're a small island of thirty-thousand residents, Harry served the entire county, which added another ninety-thousand people.

I entered the closet-sized lobby and signed my name on the clipboard nailed to the wall, then pushed the button near a plain side door. It had a combination pad and deadbolt lock.

A faint buzzer sounded on the other side. A minute later, an intern in pale blue scrubs poked his head out. "Can I help you?"

I showed him my driver's license. "Elliott Lisbon to see Dr. Fleet."

"Is he expecting you?"

"No, but I'm sure he won't mind."

He looked at me skeptically, but opened the door wide enough for me to sneak through. I followed him down a narrow corridor with vinyl speckle floors and dull beige walls. It smelled medicinal, stringently clinical. Like bleach and ammonia and other chemicals I didn't want to think about. The intern pointed me to a door on the left and kept walking.

Harry stood facing a barrage of books opposite the door. The shelf spanned the entire wall straight to the ceiling. Hundreds of books, some over four inches thick, were crammed haphazardly, tottering sidewise as if angling for better position on the shelf.

I knocked on the doorjamb. "Hi, Harry."

"What the hell are you doing in my office, Lisbon? You're not allowed back here," he said without turning around.

"I'm helping with the Hirschorn murder." I scooped up a stack of files from one of the visitor's chairs and looked for a place to set them. Files, books, and papers covered every surface: desk, chairs, floor, shelves. I kept the stack in my arms and sat.

Harry selected a book and thumped into his chair. "Helping, my ass. Does the Lieutenant know you're down here sniffing around?"

"Of course. I spoke with Corporal Parker this afternoon." Not really a lie. For all I knew, she told Ransom. "I just need a minute, Harry."

"Do I look like I have a minute?" He gathered some papers and shoved them in a file, then started a fresh sheet. He worked as if I wasn't there.

I took that as a good sign. "Just tell me about the murder weapon and I'll get out of your hair."

"Seems to me the police you're helping would've already offered that up."

I shifted the files on my lap and leaned forward. "Parker specifically suggested I meet with you, get your perspective on the murder, Harry. From the horse's mouth, so to speak."

He raised his head and stared at me.

I smiled to add a little sugar on top.

"Blunt force trauma to the back of his head. Bruising, indentations match a trophy found near the body."

Shut. Up. Did he say trophy?

"Also found GHB in his system—"

"The date rape drug? On Leo?"

"—mixed with diazepam and traces of oxycodone."

"Heavy stuff."

"Whoever clunked Leo wanted a slow-moving target. Looks like Leo was behind his desk, drinking a glass of wine. Probably wobbly when he got up. Chair was pushed back, some papers on the floor. He came around and whack. Killer dragged him by the shirt, drove him straight into the clock." Harry returned to the notes on his desk. "Now get out, Lisbon. You won't be getting any more unauthorized information from me."

I quickly stood and put the files back on the chair. "Thanks, Harry," I called as I scurried out the door. I think he grunted in return.

Poor Leo. The killer drugged him, clobbered him, and shoved him head first into a grandfather clock. He never had a chance.

EIGHT

Island Memorial Hospital was tucked in a plaza across from Oyster Cove Plantation, so I made it home in less than ten minutes. It took another ten to change into shorts and a tee, then hit the beach for a long walk in the late afternoon sun.

Sun-bleached shells, starfish, and the occasional jellyfish peppered the hard-packed sand along the shoreline as the tide lapped gently at my feet. The warm air smelled briny from the sea foam. I passed groups of tourists and locals, getting in the last rays of sun before heading home. Little children ran into the sea, then ran back out screaming when they got wet.

I walked along and thought about Jane. It bothered me she wouldn't give up her alibi. Either she *was* at Leo's, or what? A thought hit me and I laughed out loud. A booty call? Well, you're all dressed up, drinking on a Saturday night, it's close to midnight...if you're not headed home, then let's face it, you're headed to a booty call.

"Was it that simple?" I said aloud. A girl reading a book looked up at me and I smiled.

Was Jane too embarrassed to admit she'd had a date? She shouldn't be. Single, over fifty; it's a free country. Hell, I wouldn't mind my own booty call. It'd been a long time. A really long time. The closest I'd come in months was Ransom in the library.

But what about the actual murder? The crime scene, the mess, the GHB cocktail. It felt personal, a vendetta against Leo. I ruled out burglary. That's a lot of trouble to go through to shut up a homeowner just to rob the place. I considered some strung-out kid looking for drugs, or maybe searching for prescription bottles. But who drugs a guy just to steal more drugs?

No, this was love or money with maybe reputation, pride, or ego tossed in. It was personal, and judging by the ripped furniture and smashed glass, they were pissed.

Back at the cottage, I grabbed a lager, and then speed-dialed the Golden Dragon. My dinner arrived right when my friend, Matty, returned my call, so I ate while we caught up. I told him all about Leo and Jane and life at the Ballantyne, and he told me about students and teachers and life at Seabrook Prep. He invited me to the oyster roast at the Tidewater Inn on Thursday. Said a bunch of our friends were going, did I want a ride? I accepted.

Halfway through my egg-drop soup, Bebe Hirschorn called. She said she was flying to New Jersey on Thursday with Leo's ashes for his memorial, could we meet next week? She asked about the new fund for Leo; I told her if we met the next day, I could tell her all about it. She agreed: two o'clock at her hotel.

After finishing the latest Carl Hiaasen, I flipped out the lights. I slept like the dead until Zibby Archibald crashed into my bedroom with a pith helmet on her head and a bazooka in her hands. She demanded I stitch safari vests on a solid brass sewing machine while Jane polished a pair of sparkly ruby shoes in the bathroom. I blame the cashew chicken.

I woke Wednesday to clear Carolina blue skies and a mostly clear head. Until I checked the clock and realized my meeting with Mumbai Humanitarian was in twenty minutes.

Shortening my morning routine made me feel uncomfortable and uptight, like wearing a scratchy wool suit two sizes too small. But I had no choice.

I threw on a skirt, an organic tee, and leather ballet flats. I switched my goods from my hipster to a messenger bag, along with my notes, portfolio, and the Mumbai packet and zipped out of my driveway at half-past eight.

With no time for cereal, I squeezed in a drive-thru McMuffin and a Coke, scarfing it down while I sped to a mid-island office complex off Miller Lane. It may seem indulgent to detour for breakfast, but trust me, no one wants to meet with me when I'm starving.

The letter board in the lobby directed me to a suite on the second floor. I took the stairs to work off the McMuffin and found Mumbai Humanitarian at the end of the hall. I entered a small office with flecked Berber carpet and eggshell walls. A friendly receptionist greeted me, a Shania Carter, as stated on a small brass nameplate. Her desk was neat as a new pin with only a telephone, message pad, and a heavy leather-bound novel. Very staid and cerebral. The gold inlaid title was rubbed into obscurity, so I couldn't read it. But I did see a Sudoku puzzle sheet sticking out from between the pages. "Good morning. May I help you?"

"Elliott Lisbon. I have an appointment with Reena Patel."

"Ms. Patel is expecting you, she'll be right out. Can I get you a coffee or something?" she asked as she picked up her reading glasses.

"No, thank you, I'm fine."

She opened her book as I sat on a low sofa. "Did you know your shoes don't match?"

I glanced down at my feet. One leather slipper was orange, the other red. Same style, though. I pushed my hair out of my eyes and tried to look confident. "I'm trying something new."

I leaned forward to examine the magazines on the small coffee table. Back issues of *National Geographic* and *Time*. I read the covers, but no way was I picking one up. The jumbo jar of hand-sani in my office isn't the only one I own. I keep mini bottles in my pockets, purse, car, and bike basket. I'm not a germaphobe, more like germ conscious. Who knows who's coughing on the magazines, wiping their germy fingers on the glossy pages? I studied the artwork instead.

Two black and white photographs hung on either side of a large original painting. The photos depicted miles of metal shanties resting on a tower of garbage. The crooked shacks looked one cardboard box away from collapsing into a landslide of despair. An artist recreated the grim conditions in vibrant color in the center painting. At the base of the mountain of slimy trash, in a narrow muddy road, sat a little boy in tattered clothes holding a rusted can of green beans.

I gripped my hand-sani and blanched. Those people saw more germs in a single day than I'd see in my entire lifetime.

"Shocking, isn't it?"

I looked up at a stunning Indian woman. A Bollywood socialite in a sleeveless silk tunic dress with delicate appliqués. Her necklace had turquoise and polished wood beads. It probably cost more than my whole outfit. She wore her long hair loose and I recognized her even without the Hot Damn! dress. Ransom's date. So this is what his league looks like. She wasn't as tall as I remembered from the party. She was petite; her four-inch heels brought her even with me.

She held out a slim hand. "Reena Patel."

"Elliott Lisbon. Nice to meet you," I said, except it wasn't all that nice to meet her. I swallowed a twang of jealousy at this sultry creature who drove away with the ex-man of my dreams.

"Shania, hold my calls please," Reena said.

"Yes, ma'am," the receptionist replied without looking up, sneaking a pencil from the desk drawer.

I followed Reena into her private office. It was intimate. Dim and cool, almost refreshing, with an undertone of exotic spice like orange and cloves. There was a balcony across from the door with velvet drapes framing the long windows. Heavy bookshelves lined the left wall while Reena's desk dominated the right. A black sawhorse desk with masculine chairs covered in smooth black leather. We faced each other across the wide desktop.

"I'm sorry we didn't get a chance to meet at the party," she said. "Such a magnificent house."

"Yes, it is. I'm afraid I didn't see you until you were leaving with Ransom."

She arched an eyebrow. "Ransom? You mean Nick?"

"We're old friends. We go way back," I said with a smile. "Dated in college."

She matched my smile like a bet in a poker game, then raised me: my history for her present. "He's a lovely man. Strong, intelligent, kind. It's interesting he never mentioned you. Not even when he tells the most wonderful stories of his time in college."

"That is interesting." Not as interesting as the kiss he laid on me, I thought. She looked all self-satisfied as if she were holding aces and I the Old Maid. I decided to fold.

I opened my portfolio and put her application packet on the desk. "Why don't you tell me about Mumbai?"

"Of course. The art on these walls illustrates the Dharavi slums in Mumbai. An estimated sixty percent of the Mumbai population, over seven million people—almost twice the population of the entire state of South Carolina—live in this filth." She leaned forward as she spoke, passion vivid in her voice. "Poverty isn't an ugly enough word. No running water, a toilet for every two thousand people. My country is being drowned in human waste."

I looked at the pictures on the wall, and they came to life. "It's so tragic. How does Mumbai Humanitarian help?"

"We provide education for the children. When we can convince them to attend. The parents, and the children, too, are unable to grasp the necessity of education. We set up schools, but they're different from the ones here in America. Ours have cramped classrooms without desks, kids sit on the floors. We supply books, pencils, lunch if we can, inoculations if we're lucky."

Reena sat straight behind her desk, hands folded on top. Her posture perfect, her long hair clean and shiny. I hadn't showered and my shoes didn't match. I skimmed through her application. Fancy Ph.D., generous with her time and her loads of money. Perfect. I'll probably get to watch her sip champagne on Ransom's back porch. I flipped past the personal bio. "How did you choose the Ballantyne Foundation?"

"Research. The Ballantyne Foundation demonstrates a willingness to serve international causes. It seemed an excellent match.

After I checked your references, of course. Then a colleague in Mumbai phoned last week, absolutely charmed by Mrs. Ballantyne." Reena smiled. "Apparently they share a love of orchids. He told her about the application we submitted many months ago, and things have been moving rapidly ever since."

"You checked *us* out?"

"Of course, we cannot afford to be associated with a questionable organization. Though the recent violence with your board is quite disturbing."

Questionable organization? I flipped through her packet with growing irritation and found a surprising detail on the last page. "You received a Lafferty Grant?" It was one of the most difficult grants to receive; their application process can take years.

She straightened her back and shot me cool gaze. "Again, of course. We are very reputable and I resent the insinuation in your tone. Perhaps you should read the information I have provided. It might allow us to move forward without wasting time."

My face flushed with embarrassment, which only rankled me further. So maybe I should have, but she didn't need to be so snotty. "Just crossing my T's," I said as I skimmed the rest of the packet, pretending I knew it all by heart. "That about wraps it up, then. I will let you know when we make a decision."

Her phone buzzed softly. "My next appointment."

She waited patiently while I gathered up the stack of paperwork and shoved it into my portfolio. It didn't fit properly with all my shoving and I had to slap the top to get the clasp to snap. Then the strap caught on the chair and I nearly tipped over sideways.

"*You* are not actually on the board, correct?"

I swear I'm a total professional, but right then, I really wanted to pull her hair. I smiled instead and calmly walked out of her office and right into Ransom.

"Hello, darling," Reena purred. She kissed Darling right on the lips and placed a possessive hand on his arm.

He squeezed her hand in return, but spoke to me. "Hello, Red. Staying out of my investigation?"

"Investigation?" Reena asked. "What are you talking about?"

"Elliott is conducting a discreet inquiry into Leo Hirschorn's murder, trying to get Jane Hatting off the hook. Quietly, of course."

"Not with all your blabbing," I said.

"Oh, is this a side job to earn extra money? How odd," Reena said. "What can you possibly do, you're not even a professional."

"I'm working on that," I said and tucked my portfolio in my bag. "So I guess I'll see you tonight, neighbor," I added as I slipped out the door.

"You live next to *her*?" I heard Reena say as I walked down the hall.

"What kind of detective. Doesn't understand. Words like quiet. And private. And discreet!" I shouted as I drove back to the Big House. I swerved around a slow-moving sedan and slammed the gas. "I mean, *come on*. A side job? Oh, for shit's sake!"

Traffic moved from leisurely to you've got to be kidding me, and it really really really frustrated me. Usually I'm okay with it. One-third of the island population is over eighty and can't see above the steering wheel, and another third consists of temporary residents trying to figure out how to get to the Bi-Lo.

After a brief detour to my cottage to rectify my shoe mistake, I skidded into the drive at the Big House at twenty past ten. Parked right out front and ran into Chas Obermeyer in the foyer.

"Nice hours, Elliott, glad you could stop by. Tod said you'd be here an hour ago," he snapped. "When's the next board meeting? I've got a busy schedule. You can't just pussyfoot around Jane all summer and keep the rest of us waiting."

"Good to see you, Chas. We'll have a new meeting in two weeks, three tops." I took a breath and forced a smile. "Which reminds me, Leo was starting a new project called the Shelter Initiative. I have a solid proposal. You haven't chaired a committee in a while. Would you like to hear it?"

"No," he said. "But tell me when you set the board meeting. I have to run. I've been waiting for you all morning and now I'm late for an important client."

I bet, out at the first tee, I thought as he turned his back to leave. "Wait, Chas. Do you remember anything about Leo from the party Saturday?"

"Just the fight with Jane. Her telling Leo to shove that trophy up his ass. He was pretty pissed. But other than that, I didn't know him very well." He walked off without another word.

That trophy was going to be tabloid nirvana. Forget blunt-force trauma and enough rage to slam his head through a clock. Tate Keating would salivate when he heard, probably sprain his fingers typing the headline so fast: Jealous Killer Jams Humanitarian Trophy Up Victim's Ass.

I pitched into my chair. I needed different evidence. Something more than the nothing I had or the busybodies would pollute the jury pool before Jane was in handcuffs.

NINE

I called my good friend Sigrid Bassi. She was tapped into the island gossip network tighter than a shampoo girl at a downtown salon. We set a lunch date for Thursday, noon at O'Grady's. She promised to dredge every nugget in the mine regarding Leo and Jane. In this town, no one knows more than the retireds and the realtors. Sid runs with both and doesn't mind sharing the gold.

I also needed to work on my pitching skills. I was oh-for-two on finding someone to carry on with Leo's legacy project. Maybe I wasn't explaining it in enough detail. Or maybe I just needed to ask someone nicer than Chas.

Before I could scoot out for a quick bite, Carla, the kind soul from the kitchen, brought me lunch at my desk—without me asking. Thin sliced roast beef on rye with Swiss and Russian dressing. She dolled up the plate with cups of coleslaw and pasta salad, both homemade.

"Carla, you're an angel straight from the blue sky," I said after I took a bite and grunted out a thank you. Carla was hands-down the best chef on the island. Oh crap. I forgot about Chef Carmichael. I wondered if she'd snatch away the sandwich if I told her about him now.

"Um, Carla," I said. I gripped the sandwich in one hand and the plate with the other. "I need your help on a small matter with Zibby Archibald and the Wharf."

"Is that why Carmichael's called me five times?"

"Impatient little bugger," I muttered. "I leveraged the Gatsby lawn party to release Zibby from a lifelong ban of The Wharf."

She put her hand on her hip. "What did the old gal do this time?"

"Skipped the last part of the dining experience, the one that involves the check. Accidentally, though. The price of bail was a co-catering assignment with you." I scooped up some creamy coleslaw before the cup disappeared.

But Carla's face lit up, her eyes wider than the smile dancing on her lips. "Well, aren't I the lucky one!"

"Seriously? You're not mad?"

"Oh no, Elliott. What a proposition, Carmichael taking orders from me." She drifted out the door. "I know just what to serve. Shrimp gumbo!" She laughed all the way down the hall.

I groaned. I'm pretty sure Chef Carmichael wasn't going to work *for* Carla. He would probably barely work *with* her. I decided to worry about it later. I dug through my Rolodex and found the number for Whitney Tattersall.

"Hi Whitney, it's Elliott. I hate to bother you, but I noticed you were seated at Leo's table on Saturday. This may sound silly, but did he bring a date? Perhaps the hot mama Jeremy mentioned at the meeting?"

She laughed. "No, no date that I saw. But there were lots of pretty girls all dressed up at the party. Everyone at our table was accounted for. I never even noticed Bebe wasn't there."

"Did you notice anything different about Leo?"

"Not really. Same old Leo. Talked non-stop through dinner." She paused. "Wow, I never saw him after that. Hard to think he'd be dead a few hours later."

"I know. If you think of anything else, please call me."

"Sure, Elliott. You take care," she said and hung up.

I might need to speak with other party patrons, but so far Leo's night seemed normal for Leo: talk incessantly, argue with Jane, dance with all the pretty girls. I was hoping Bebe could fill in the more important blank: what happened *after* the party.

I carried my plate to the kitchen, then hopped into the convertible for the short trip to the Tidewater Inn.

The Tidewater was a boutique hotel located mid-island on six acres of prime oceanfront property. Only two stories tall, most of the rooms were spread out casita style with patios and balconies near the sand, gardens, and a free-form pool.

I parked with valet, stuffing the stub into my bag, then crossed the lobby. The concierge directed me to the Princess Suite at the north end of the property. I found the door and rang the bell.

Bebe answered wearing spandex leggings, high-heel slippers, and a smock covered in paint and glitter. She wore her hair big and teased and it was a color not known in nature. Something between rust and a brass trombone.

"Oh, right," she said. "I forgot you were coming. Hurry in, don't let Ivana out."

I glanced down at an enormous seventeen pound white Persian cat at my feet. She eyeballed the door, but kept walking with her fluffy white butt high in the air. Smart cat. Cleopatra never had it this good. I'm not sure Leo did, either.

The suite was nicer than my house. Designer furniture and a compact kitchen dressed in granite and stainless. Potted palms manned the entrance to an expansive patio with views of a garden blooming with mock orange trees. All the fragrance without the fruit.

I followed the sound of Bebe's clicking heels to the dining area. A long mahogany table sat beneath a twelve-arm chandelier, pushed directly under a picture window. It smelled like pungent paint and kindergarten paste.

Probably due to the menagerie of craft supplies spread all over the table. Scissors, stickers, beads, stamps, inks, markers, puff paints, glitter, and shoeboxes overflowing with photographs covered the entire surface. There may have even been a Bedazzler and a glue gun in there.

Bebe offered me a chair, then sat down across the table. "Lemonade?"

She poured me a glass of pink liquid from a crystal decanter without waiting for my answer. It was the Tidewater's own delicious raspberry lemonade, plus a bonus. One part raspberry, one part lemonade, and two parts rum. Unfortunately I'd already taken a nice big gulp when I figured out the recipe.

"You a scrapper?" Bebe cut into a piece of orange construction paper with fancy scissors, the kind that make the edges look like curly cues. "This one here is from our trip two years ago to Coney Island."

"I'm not really crafty." The last homemade thing I made was a ceramic handprint in the first grade. It didn't turn out so hot. I ended up with clay in my hair and paint up my nose. "But thank you for seeing me at such a terrible time."

"Oh, it's not that terrible. My massage isn't for another half hour. I'm just putting this together in the meantime."

I nodded and pretended to sip my drink. "I actually meant Leo. You mentioned on the phone his funeral is Saturday?"

"Memorial, no funeral. He's in his Cookie Corral now." She nodded toward a brown ceramic pot sitting on the sill.

"Cookie Corral?" I leaned over for a better look. It was a squat cookie jar from the forties with raised ranch fencing, a fading decal of a man and his horse, and a fat knob on top.

"That's a genuine Hopalong Cassidy Cookie Corral. It's his favorite. We're holding the memorial at St. Anthony's in Jersey City. He loves that church. Same one we were married in. You should see the memory book I made. Leo calls it our Happily Ever Hoedown." She handed me a stamper and a piece of pink paper. "Here, try it. It's easy. Just stamp along the edges and make a border. It's a self-inker, so you don't have to worry about an ink pad."

I stared at the paper and my inner perfectionist started to whine. How could I get each stamp impression perfectly placed? At the same exact angle? Spaced uniformly, equidistant from the next? I noticed Bebe was staring at me, so I decided to fling away my doubts and stamp with abandon. Stamp stamp stamp stamp stamp. That *was* fun!

I managed to get ink on three fingers, two photographs, and the table cover. Bebe reached over and took away my stamper supplies.

I cleared my throat. "Will you be in New Jersey long?"

She rifled through an egg crate filled with miniature jewels, sorted by size and color. "Well, not long enough. We've got so many friends to see again. But Travis graduates in a few weeks from Seabrook. So you know, bad timing..." Her voice drifted and she grabbed her drink.

Swigging a bit greedily, I thought. Drowning her sorrows or her guilt?

I waited until she resumed her cutting. "Do you mind if I ask some questions?"

"About the fund you mentioned? Like to help us with expenses?"

"Not quite. Leo put together a very thoughtful proposal for the Ballantyne to fund the Shelter Initiative. Easily the most compassionate local program we've had in years. I'm going to personally find the perfect board member to take it up in Leo's honor."

"Oh. I guess that's nice. So what questions?"

I started with the easy stuff. I pulled out my notebook and discreetly poised my pen. "Tell me about your life with Leo."

"Well, me and Leo married eighteen years ago. Had to, you know what I mean? But we loved each other, had a nice duplex in the neighborhood. Leo opened his first Buffalo Bill's in Hoboken right after Travis was born." She finished cutting out the orange frame and started applying glitter to the outer edges. "Never seen anything like it. Everyone loved that store. Most people never even seen a horse up close and Leo brought one out every weekend. You ever ride one at the store here?"

"No. But I hear they're very popular with the kids." And the tourists. The Buffalo Bill's parking lot was jammed every Saturday during season. Chili cookouts, hot dogs on the bbq. A real hoedown. You know, in an asphalt corral with a grill manned by a TV salesman.

"He grew the company from one store to twelve. Put his sights on expanding to the South. One vacation to Sea Pine Island and his mind was made up. Dragged me kicking and screaming outta Jersey, but Leo wanted it so bad, I finally gave in. He moved the headquarters, including Joseph and the tramp." She laughed bitterly and snatched up a bottle of blue puff paint.

"The tramp?"

"Leo's assistant, Cherry. Can you believe that? Cherry Avarone. Don't know what he sees in that tacky little tart. It's his business and good help is hard to find, he says." She squirted out a row of blue dots on top of the glitter.

Obviously a sore subject based on the velocity of the paint shooting out of the miniature bottle. Blobs and splats landed around the table in big gloppy mounds. "You ever worry something went on between Leo and Cherry?"

"Leo would never cheat on me. He knows he has it good. Besides, Cherry doesn't like men, plays for the other team."

"You mean she's gay?"

"Yep. But she's still a tart and I don't like her," she said. "Wears short skirts to the office. It's a respectable business!"

"How was business?"

"Business is good, real good. Leo's got a new summer campaign for the store, filming a commercial for it soon."

Bebe kept referring to Leo in the present tense and I was beginning to wonder if her demeanor was more denial than guilt. She refilled her glass and I hoped I wasn't going to hell for taking advantage of her loose lips. She picked up a stamper, so I kept going.

"I heard Leo might be having financial trouble."

"Not at all. He's been talking about getting a boat. A big one. After he builds me a new art studio above the garage. Built-in cabinets, light table, the whole works. And next month a cruise out of Miami. A balcony cabin."

"Did Leo have any enemies? Anybody holding a grudge?"

She dropped the stamp and pointed her finger at my face. "You know who. That bitch Jane Tatting."

"Hatting."

She glared at me, then waved me away. "Whatever."

Her outburst startled Ivana the cat. She hopped off the chair and onto the floor, settling on my feet, then kneaded her clawless paws into my shins; it was like getting punched with cotton balls.

"Listen," Bebe said. "Leo worked hard to get on that board, but that woman just can't stand someone more successful than her."

"Was there a specific incident or merely animosity?"

"Jane called here twice last week. It got really bad the last call, but Leo handed it right back at her, taunting her about the trophy. He won it fair and square. Jane was jealous as a monster and acted like it."

"Is that why you didn't go to the party?"

"I don't care about Jane or the stupid Foundation party. The board members are snobby and I don't like them." Bebe stuck her chin out. "No offense."

"None taken. I'm not a board member."

Bebe placed the sparkly orange paper frame over a picture of Leo. He wore his ten gallon hat and rode on a colorful carousel horse. She slowly stamped a proper border on the outer edge of the page. The stamper shook slightly, but she didn't seem to notice. She finished the page with a satisfied nod.

After she dusted glitter from her fingertips, she picked up my glass and the pitcher and carried them to the kitchenette.

I figured my time was running out. "So, were you at home last Saturday night?"

"Oh no, I was in Savannah for a Scrappers weekend," she said, then added, "It was our annual weekend retreat."

"Really? How fun. Where do you guys meet? Maybe I'll join you next year."

She hesitated, no doubt imagining me in a room full of craft supplies, but in the end my winning smile won out. "I guess. It's the Island Scrappers and we always stay at the River Street Inn."

"You guys go up on Friday or Saturday?"

"Friday morning. I came home on Sunday. Early." The doorbell rang and she sagged with relief. Bebe smoothed her smock and fluffed her big hair. "Sorry to rush you out, but my masseuse is here."

She clicked over to the door, opening it to a young man in a tight tee and floppy surfer hair. He carried a portable massage table. "Good afternoon, Mrs. Hirschorn. In the bedroom?"

She rushed him through a door on the other side of the living room, then turned to me. "It's such a mess out here, I can't possibly move my scrapper supplies every time he comes over, right?"

I smiled sweetly and waved her way. "Of course not. Could I use your powder room? I drank two glasses of lemonade and I'll never make it home."

"Sure, you just see yourself out, then?" She slipped through the bedroom door before I could agree.

I did a quick check for prescription meds after I availed myself of the facilities. No diazepam or oxycodone. Worth a shot. She probably had a private bath full of pills in the bedroom. I did score some dental floss, though. Apparently I'd conducted the entire interview with a poppy seed stuck between my top two choppers. You think she would have said something.

I went to grab my handbag from the dining room and noticed it sat on a massive glob of puff paint. The entire back side was soaked in blue and stuck to the table. Like dried macaroni on a pencil cup. With a solid yank, the purse came loose but my elbow cracked into the Cookie Corral. It toppled to the floor, hitting the wall on its way down.

Holy shit and OH MY GOD.

Dust floated everywhere and covered everything. The carpet, the drapes, the table, the wall. I started to choke. Air and sound battled for release. Breathe or scream? Breathe or scream? Panic crept from my toes to my fingertips. I stared at a large broken shard covered in Leo dust.

My fingers shook. I couldn't think and I couldn't look away. The dust on the floor wasn't dust. It was Leo. Literally Leo.

Ten seconds slid by, then twenty. I stared in horror, torn between doing the right thing and the wrong thing. Only I had no idea which was the right thing and which was the wrong. Other than Bebe simply could not find out about this. Nor could Mr. Ballantyne. Or any person I ever met, saw, or even thought about.

Ivana the cat brushed up against my leg. I jumped back and nearly kicked her.

She started to creep forward. One fluffy clean white paw, then another.

"No kitty, bad kitty," I said and shooed her away.

She hopped on the couch, circling in from a different angle. She squatted on the arm and watched me.

I glanced at the clock by the window. Bebe wouldn't be massaging forever. There was a glue gun plugged into the wall. A large spoon near the jewel box. I threw my handbag back onto the craft table and snatched up supplies. I emptied out a clear baggie of sparkly foam letters and grabbed the spoon.

"Okay, Leo, I have to say, I'm pretty freaked out right now," I whispered as I scooped him into the baggie. There was so much more than I ever imagined. "But I guess you're not too pleased, either."

I scraped the carpet to get as much as I could. When I stirred up more dust than I could handle, I gently set the baggie on the table along with the pieces of the cookie jar. I used the glue gun to stick them back together. I got wispy glue strands in my hair and on my blouse, but I did okay with the jar.

I checked the clock. Twenty-two minutes had passed and I wondered how long massages take. Or how long gun glue takes to dry.

The jar seemed solid enough, as long as no one touched it. I poured Leo back into his Corral. Popped on the lid and stuck him back on the sill. Snagged a paper towel from the roll and doused it with water. "So so sorry about this Leo," I said as I soaked him up from the carpet and walls. "I swear on all things mighty, I will make this up to you."

I tossed the towel, snagged my purse, and headed for the door. I reached for my keys and saw dust on my fingertips. I stopped breathing. Don't freak out, I thought. You made it this far. Just walk over to the sink and wash it off. Think of it as sprinkling his ashes in the sea. One step, then another, just like the kitty. I slowly made it to the sink.

"Who are you?"

I jumped a foot off the ground and splashed water on the floor. I was shaky and teary and nearing a breakdown, but good Lord in Heaven, my hands were clean.

A teenaged boy stood in the kitchen doorway. He looked fresh from the beach in bright blue swim trunks. His dark curly hair was wet and he had a towel on his arm and an iPod around his neck.

"You must be Travis. I'm Elliott with the Ballantyne. I just finished talking with your mom, and was washing up, um, from our crafting."

He looked around. "Is she here?"

"Masseuse."

He nodded so slowly, and looked so sad, I wanted to hug him. "I'm sorry about your dad."

He nodded again and walked into the living room. He sank onto the sofa, spraying sand all over the pretty floral fabrics.

I leaned against the edge of the sofa. "I know how you feel. I lost my dad when I was about your age."

"Really? Was he murdered by a lying bitch, too?"

He stared at the blank TV screen and I said nothing. I knew the pain of death, but not the red hot anger that accompanies it when it arrives at the hand of someone else.

He picked up the remote, but didn't click the buttons.

"We don't know who killed him, Travis. But we'll find out," I said softly. "At least you weren't home when it happened."

"I'm so lucky." His bottom lip started to shake.

He really was lucky. He could've been collateral damage. Unless, of course, he was lying about it. Great. Now I needed to ask where he was on Saturday night. But how? I just stood there, racking my brain for a decent way to be an indecent human being. Considering I just wiped up his father with a paper towel, I decided it was too late for that.

"Were you with your mom at her Scrappers weekend on Saturday?"

"Are you serious?" He wiped his nose on his sleeve and flipped on the TV. "I was with my friend Derek, spent the night at his house. Dinner at Cheeseburger Paradise and a movie afterwards. Here's his number, call if you want." He rattled it off while I jotted it down. "Is the interrogation over now?"

I nodded and slunk out before Bebe emerged.

The Hirschorns stayed on my brain for the rest of the night. I settled onto the patio and ate cake for dinner. Double-layer chocolate fudge with enough devil's food frosting to soothe my soul. I felt bonded to Leo; a new obligation to make things right. And while Travis's grieving touched me on a visceral level, his alibi was too handy. Why offer up every detail of his Saturday night on the first question? Especially to a stranger who had no right to even ask. He gave me places, times, and a phone number without hesitation or argument and that bothered me.

And Bebe's altered reality made me uneasy. Though she sure snapped back for Jane and Cherry. Called one a bitch and the other a tacky tart. I agreed with her on the first count and planned to find out about the second.

TEN

Buffalo Bill's headquarters sat just at the edge of Summerton, a straight shot from Cabana Boulevard, which runs across the island, over the bridge, through Summerton, all the way to I-95. From there you can go north to Augusta, Maine or south down to Miami, Florida and all points in-between.

A giant animated cowboy sign flashed me as I pulled into the drive. "We MISS you Leo!" (flash) "Super Sale Saturday!" (flash) "Come On Down!" It's exactly what Leo would've wanted.

The lot was about half-full, but not so many cars that I didn't notice Ransom's slick silver racer parked up front. I chose a spot at the end of a far aisle next to an abandoned haystack. It was only Thursday morning, so no bbq or ponies outside, just a lone cowboy wrangling loose carts.

I entered the store covertly and sidled up to a young clerk. A jittery kid. He needed to dial down to half-caff or his heart would give out before he hit the legal drinking age. He wore a brown vest over a blue gingham shirt tucked into blue jeans. The name on his sheriff's star nametag spelled out Brandon in a font that resembled rope.

"Howdy, ma'am, lookin' for a deal today?" he said with a timid smile.

"Hi, Brandon. I'm actually lookin' for Cherry Avarone."

"How do you know my name?"

"It's on your shirt."

"Oh. Sure. Well, Cherry's not a salesgirl, ma'am. Maybe I can show you something?"

"I'm not here to buy anything. This is personal."

"Oh." He glanced around nervously. "We're not supposed to have personal calls or visitors, ma'am."

I glanced around, too. A row of checkout counters was set up like horse stalls with wide plank fencing and saddles to hold shopping bags. Wood aisle signs hung over rows of appliances, the text burned into the wood like branding. I didn't see any managers, but I did spot Ransom talking to a salesman. I edged over two large steps, behind a checkout counter, blocking myself from Ransom's view.

"Cherry won't get into trouble. I'm a friend of Leo Hirschorn's. Do you know where I can find her?"

He lowered his voice. "A detective from the police came in when we opened. He wanted her, too."

"Thanks, Brandon, I'll see if I can't find her myself."

I snuck to the back through the music department. Two dozen speakers poured out the same Carrie Underwood song. Some blockhead stole her happy and made her cry. Wants her future, but he can't have it. I hear you, sister.

With one eye on Ransom, I made my way to a door marked Office. He was still tied up with Cowboy Bob, probably getting the pitch on a brand-new Frigidaire. I knocked softly on the door and turned the knob. "Hello, Cherry?"

"Yes?" a voice said from behind me.

I turned as a girl in her late twenties approached carrying a muffin and a coffee cup. She was the spitting image of Bebe (back in the day), but with big black hair and knockers the size of footballs. She wore her pants tight and her fingernails red.

"Hi, Cherry, I'm Elliott Lisbon, a friend of Leo's from the Ballantyne."

"Sure. He talked about the Foundation all the time." Her eyes were red-rimmed and swollen, but also dressed in eyeliner and mascara. Someone both sad and optimistic.

"Hello, Red," Ransom said. He blocked the office door with his body, his arms crossed over his chest. Years of training clearly kept his temper in check, but his eyes were so dark, they didn't look blue.

"Hello, Lieutenant."

He put his hand on my arm. "Now you're beginning to interfere."

"What? A girl can't buy a toaster? I ran into Cherry here, thought I should offer my condolences." I turned to Cherry. "You doing okay? Maybe we should talk."

Two large tears tracked down Cherry's face. "Sure. I'm doing okay, I guess, but it's hard."

I pushed past Ransom and held open the office door. "It'll be just us girls. Wouldn't you like the detective to wait outside?"

Cherry nodded. I smiled at Ransom and slammed the door. Then twisted the lock in case he got frisky.

I followed Cherry down a short hall into a posh executive suite. The larger office on the left must have been Leo's. A massive desk dominated the room with a cowhide rug on the floor and matching cowhide accessories sprinkled around the room: chandelier shades, switch plates, and a furry blanket over an iron and leather sofa.

Cherry walked into the other office on the right, smaller, about half the size, but exactly the same, down to the iron sofa. It was much more comfortable than I thought it would be. But Cherry was no neatnik. Tchotchkes covered the table with more pens scattered around the top than in the pencil cup. She had salt and pepper shakers, a tiny horseshoe, a ceramic cowbell, and a square planter, all bright red against the black and white cowhide décor.

"Cherry, I am so sorry about Leo."

"Thanks. He was a great boss, you know. Nice to everyone at the store, never too busy to talk."

I smiled in agreement. "Leo was the same with the board, loved to talk." I didn't mention that half the board wanted to stuff his cowboy hat right down his throat so he'd shut up. Even if you could slip in a sentence or two, he'd interrupt and barrel right over you.

"He couldn't wait for Monday's meeting to get his seat renewed another year," Cherry said and set her muffin on the glass-topped table between a jotter box and a stapler.

"How about here? Things going well at headquarters?"

She laughed, but the sound was sharp and bitter. "You've been talkin' to Bebe. God, I hate her. She's the only one who calls this a headquarters. Does this look like a freakin' headquarters?" She waved her arms around the room in exasperation. "It's an office. Leo left the headquarters in Hoboken, he runs the executive stuff outta here."

"You must have a pretty good job to leave Hoboken behind."

"Oh definitely. I'm Leo's marketing assistant. I help with promotional ideas, advertising. I was a graphics major at the community college. I design all the posters and flyers."

"I hear Leo wanted to film a commercial."

Her eyes sparkled and she really smiled. "We've been workin' on it for two months. We're usin' real actresses as models. We're gonna do the commercial like that game show, The Price is Right. Show the appliances like prizes, real classy-like." Tears pooled in her eyes and spilled down her cheeks again, leaving two fresh streaks of black mascara.

I handed her a tissue from the box on the table.

"Thanks," she said and blew her nose. "It was gonna start shootin' next month. Now what'll we do?" She stared into Leo's office across the hall. "He's just gone. What am I going to do without Leo? Who would've done this?"

I was wondering the same thing. I leaned in conspiratorially, girl to girl. "How close were Leo and his family?"

"We're more of a family than his crazy wife. I don't know what he saw in her. Woman's got one wheel loose and the other's dragging." Cherry blew out a long shaky sigh, then lifted herself up, shoulders back. She threw her crumpled tissue into a cowhide wastebasket. "They fought all the time. She spent money faster than he could make it. On stupid crap, too. Some nutty new hobby, re-decorating the house. Again."

"Any arguments in particular, especially recently?"

"This time it was some stupid cruise. Leo couldn't go because of the commercial, so she said she'd go alone and take the cat. The cat! I thought, fine, go. Give Leo some peace." She checked her face in a round lighted mirror on her desk and opened a clear makeup bag. It was stuffed with more products than a department store cosmetics counter.

"Bebe told me you were gay."

Her hand froze midway through the bag search and she slowly looked over at me. "What?"

"I asked if she thought you and Leo were having a thing, and she said you played for the other team."

Cherry squirted foundation onto a well-used makeup sponge, then swiped her cheeks, blending the new coat over the old. "I've been called a lot of things, but gay isn't one of them."

"Interesting, though, right? I mean, why would Leo tell her that? Unless you were having a thing."

"No 'thing.' Bebe's nuts, probably made the whole thing up."

"So Leo wasn't having a thing?"

She glanced at me. "Well, I don't want to gossip, you know, with Leo being gone and all..."

"No, not gossip. We're just talking, trying to figure this out."

"Right. Well, Leo went on and on about some gorgeous look-er. He tried to hide it, but you know Leo, can't shut up to save his life." Her eyes filled again. "Oh God. I didn't mean that."

I squeezed her hand. "I understand. Do you know who the looker is?"

"Some lady named Dee. A customer, maybe? I never met her and I don't know if anything went on between them. Like I said, he tried to hide it."

Maybe the hottie Leo swung around the dance floor. I made a mental note. I didn't want to use a notepad and look like a reporter on an interview.

"I met Travis yesterday. Seems like a good kid, pretty distraught over his father."

"More like guilt from treating his dad like trash. Leo wanted him to work here, earn his own spending money instead of mooching off his old man. Travis wouldn't step foot in this place. Called it Barfalo Bill's. This place pays for his private school and his car and his weekends with friends. What a little shit."

"A little shit, indeed. Says he had big plans that night. Though I guess I did, too. How about you? You're young and single, bet you outdid us both."

"Hardly. Home alone, where else?" Her shoulders sagged and her voice dropped. "I didn't even know he was dead until Monday. No one even called me. I heard it from the receptionist when I came to work."

I tried to remember my conversation with Bebe, anything else I could ask Cherry since she was being so chatty. I was beginning to think a notebook on my lap might be helpful. "Who's Joseph? Bebe said he moved down here from New Jersey, too."

"Well, sure, Joseph is Leo's partner. They started it together." Cherry applied a rosy powder to her cheeks with the precision of an artist. "You know, you should try wearing makeup. A little color would brighten you right up." She tilted my chin and brushed blusher on my cheeks. I tried not to make a face. I didn't want to protest and break her rhythm.

"How well did Leo and Joseph get along?"

"Like best friends. Loved each other like brothers. They were talking about opening a new store, a second one here in Summerton, near the river." She leaned in close to study my face. She zeroed in on my eyebrows. "Ever think of plucking those? I gotta waxer. I could bring it in, shape 'em right up."

I touched one of my brows. I liked my thick eyebrows, and I wanted to keep them that way. "Thanks, Cherry, but I'm good."

She took the rest of me in: my wavy hair, my simple cotton shirt, my full set of plain nails.

"Why no color?"

A movement just above my sightline caught my eye. Ransom walking away, toward the office in back. By his stride, I bet he'd pound on the door and demand entry. Cherry would love that.

I checked the home theatre department, but Joseph was gone. Cowboy Bob had wrangled the yuppie couple and Brandon was standing alone two aisles over. I waved at him. "Can you help me?"

He glanced at me nervously, then joined me. "I don't know anything."

"Is Joseph still working?"

"No. He just left. Real fast," he said and lo[oked] [over his] shoulder. "I don't want anyone to see me talki[ng]

I smiled a real charmer. "I'm jus[t] special. Can you tell me about it?"

"Um, sure." He n[odded] ally is a great TV."

"It looks like it. Doe[s] maybe just one quick ques[tion] speaking with the detective?"

He looked around for th[e] Leo Hirschorn, not Joseph Hirs[chorn] shot at sales, so I feel like I owe hi[m] heard what Mr. Hirschorn, Joseph[,] lying. It doesn't have a box, but you g[et]

"Lying about what? What's this a[bout]

He picked up the remote and flipped the channel over to The Price is R[ight] watched this every day. See the clear pict[ure] Aspect ratio is the width." He clicked throu[gh] picture zoomed in and out. "Mr. Hirscho[rn] Hirschorn, Leo, fought a lot. They did not get al[ong]

"Let's call them Leo and Joseph, just for [fun] why they argued?

"The new store, I think. It was really bad the [day] Leo died. Joseph threatened him."

"I like them natural. Low maintenance." She arched one of her thin brows. "Well, sure, slap on a coat a clear. You could catch a man easier if yo[u] little effort."

"I'm not looking to catch a man."

She laughed. "We all are. Besides, I saw you lookin' at th[at] hot detective. You'd be the competition if you gave it half an effort."

I blushed. "Okay, then. I think that's it for now. Be careful with the hot detective. He's a handful."

"So am I." I let myself out and quietly tiptoed through the That she was. I scanned the store for Ransom; he had to be lurking somewhere. He probably grabbed Joseph while I household appliance section. Who needs all that? dices, slices, purees, and shreds. I wanted to switch.

I crept around a pyramid of food processor boxes. It chops, sequestered Cherry, now I followed the strong trail of sandalwood and ginger, I picked up Ransom's scent in the home theatre department.

Literally. I followed the low rumble of their con- keeping my head low. He stood with his back to me, making notes and speaking, he looked like Leo, only taller.

es. If I squinted, I tiptoed closer. A dozen TVs played six differ- Inch by inch, I heard the low rumble of their con- versation. I peeked over a row of small flat panels. They stood about ten feet away. I could almost read Joseph's vest was real suede and his same uniform as the sales clerk only his name tag. He wore the hat real felt.

"...cousins. Me and Leo grew up on the same block. My p[arents]

"You have a nice store. Looks kind of slow, though. No many cars in the lot."

"Best friends since we were kids, like brothers."

"So you were close, then?"

devastated."

"It's only Thursday. We get a full boat on the we[ekends.] Things've been good, real steady." He spoke with his hand[s]

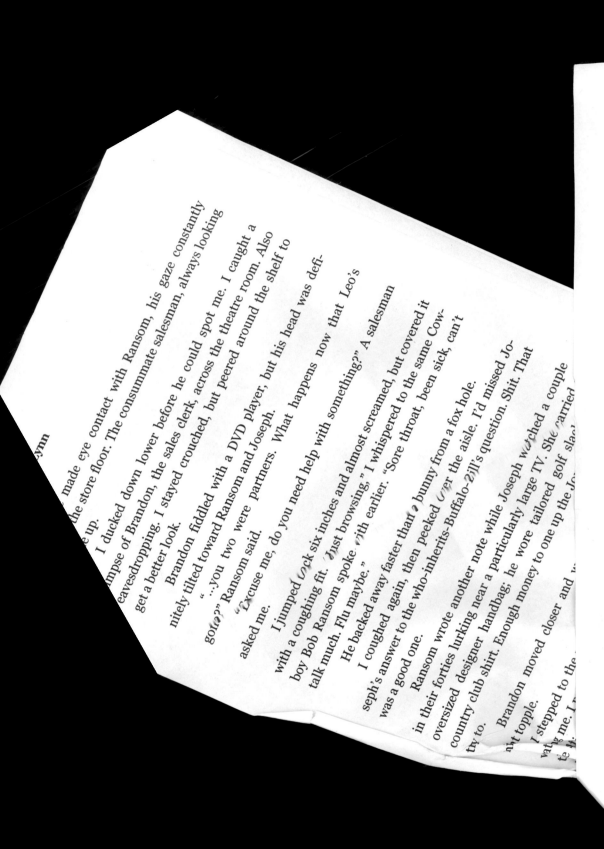

"Are you sure? Does anyone else know about this?"

Brandon clicked off the set. We both noticed Cowboy Rod at the same time. He had stepped closer to us in an effort to give his yuppie couple space while they huddled in decision mode.

"I'll take it, Brandon," I said. Time to upgrade the TV in my bedroom. It was so old, it still had a tube in it.

"Really?"

I nodded and he unplugged it. He handed me a Ziploc with the manuals and the remote, then carried the set over to checkout.

"I'll take it to your car for you," he said.

He carefully covered the TV in plastic bubble wrap while I paid. I wondered if I could charge it back to the Foundation. The price of information was $299, plus tax.

I took my plastic bag of manuals and Brandon followed me out the door. Ransom's car was gone. "Did you tell the police about their argument?"

"Me? No. No one asked and that detective didn't look very friendly." He looked over his shoulder and lowered his voice to a whisper. "What you asked before? A lot of people heard them fighting."

"Even Cherry Avarone?"

"Sure, she was in there with them. And ma'am, it got ugly."

He gently placed my new TV in the back seat, and I thanked him.

I climbed in and drove out of the lot. So Cherry and Joseph were lying about this whole best friends, like brothers routine. And Cherry didn't offer up an alibi either.

It was interesting, but sad, too. Before this week, I only knew the one side of Leo. The big mouth that grated on everyone's nerves. Over the last two days I met the other side, the people who loved him and now mourned him. To them, Leo was a husband, father, friend, boss. Of course, that also gave them more motives for murder.

ELEVEN

I drove over the bridge onto the island shortly before noon. Mounds of oyster beds stuck up from the sea floor as the water receded, the tide slowly heading out into the Intracoastal Waterway. Just like it does every other day. Life continuing on. Whether or not Leo Hirschorn was murdered. Whether or not I figured out why.

After I dropped my new TV at the cottage, I took Cabana Boulevard to Palmetto Plaza, a shopping center at the north end nestled behind pines and oaks. It housed a Sam's Club, a Bi-Lo grocery, a rehab center, various gift shops, and four restaurants, including O'Grady's, where I was headed to meet Sigrid Bassi, the secret weapon in my investigation.

I opened the heavy oak door and the familiar pub smells greeted me. Grilled steaks, deep-fried potatoes, and beer on tap. Vinyl booths and square tables were on the right side and a long wood bar was on the left. Framed photographs of sports teams in various stages of victory and defeat dotted the walls, the largest being from the last game of 1984 NBA championship series: Celtics vs. Lakers. The players wore their shorts short and their socks tall. Nothing like athletic hot pants and knee socks to bring the crowd to their feet.

I saw Sid in a corner booth. She resembled a pro on the beach volleyball circuit. Six-two, toned, and light brown hair bleached from the sun. I first met her at a ladies lunch and fashion show five years ago. We were both someone else's guest and neither of us ever joined the women's club that sponsored the show. Sid worked in one of the top real estate agencies on the island, managing to cling to the edges when the plug got yanked out and the housing market began circling the drain.

"Hey Sid." I leaned over and kissed her cheek. "How are you?"

"Good. Busy. You?"

I slid into the booth across from her. "Good. Busy. Who isn't?"

Our usual waitress greeted us. "Getcha Pepsi, Elli?"

"Yep, and I know just what I want for lunch."

"Me, too," Sid said.

What's the point of being a regular if you don't get your favorites every time? I ordered the spinach salad with grilled marinated chicken and tangy bacon dressing, Sid the steak and bleu cheese salad, and we split a basket of hot homemade potato chips with a side of zesty ranch dressing.

"Are you going to the roast tonight? Matty said you might be," I said.

"I was, but Marco caught a bad cold from a patient at the hospital. He passed it on to Marco, who's probably half as sick but twice the trouble. I think I'm supposed to play nurse tonight."

She stuck her hands out. "But I'm clean. No buggy cold germs and I used a bucket of hand-sani when I sat down."

I love my friends.

I spent the next fifteen minutes catching her up on my current life goal: trying to out investigate Ransom and solve the case myself. Prove I'm an investigator worthy of the Ballantyne and its board. Then our lunches arrived and we dove in with the vigor of those who diet often and were pretending salads drowning in dressing wouldn't count against us.

"Did you find out anything about Leo?" I asked.

She sliced into her steak salad. "Yes, sweetie, and you're not going to like it. A neighbor saw Jane leaving Leo's house the night he died. Late."

"What?" I almost spit out a mouthful of spinach. "Are you shitting me?"

"I shit you not. Saw her 'fleeing the scene with her hair on fire' is what I heard."

"Is it reliable?"

"Definitely. I got it from the retireds' network. You know those folks, it's like a senior citizen phone tree. Solid as an oak."

When Sid isn't selling real estate or dating hot doctors, she somehow squeezes in eight hours a week at the Carolina Hospice Thrift Shop. She sorts clothes, runs the register, and serves on the board.

"Well, crap. You're right, I don't like it. Did you hear anything else I won't like?"

"Tate Keating thinks he's struck gold, Pulitzer material, I'm sure. Nothing like a charity full of killers and suspects to capture an award. I think you're on the wrong side of this investigation."

"Seriously. It's been two days since Jane spoke with the police and the whole island has her in leg irons."

"She might be guilty, sweetie."

"Don't even say that. Mr. Ballantyne would be heartbroken and I can't live with that. So no one is arresting her," I said and put my fork down. "Is that it?"

"I did hear something about the Foundation. Came from only one gal at the shop; I asked around, but it's just a whisper at this point. Have you ever heard of wine futures?"

"No. What are they?"

"I have no idea. Probably why it's so quiet. No one knows what they are. Apparently someone on your board is putting together an investment group to start a new venture in wine futures. It's very hush-hush. You know those investment types, don't want to dilute the market. It might be about Leo, but I didn't get any names."

"Sounds vague enough to warrant a little snooping. Also, it looks as though Leo wanted to open a new Buffalo Bill's location in Summerton, somewhere near the river. Can you find out where?"

"Sure. Commercial's a small community. Can't lease a single Starbucks without every agent in town sniffing around. A property the size of a new Buffalo Bill's would bring out every suitor in a fifty-mile radius to try on that glass slipper."

The waitress cleared our plates and asked if we wanted anything else. We both declined, though their cinnamon roll bread pudding with rum sauce was worth riding my bike an extra three miles a day for the next week. But not today. Not after this news.

I plopped my credit card down on the check. "On the Foundation today. Thanks for the info."

"Sure, sweetie. Sorry it sucked. I've got to run to a closing. I'll call you when I know more about the new Buffalo Bill's." She pecked me on the cheek and left.

Well, shit. Jane was at Leo's the night he died? How far behind am I if everyone on the island knows about this witness? But it's basically gossip-based. Might be nothing. Also might be what convicts Jane and humiliates the Ballantynes. Or worse. Ransom ends up right. I needed to track down this neighbor witness and hear it for myself.

I calculated the time. Matty wasn't picking me up for the oyster roast until seven-thirty—five hours from now. I paid the bill and scooted out to my car.

I rummaged through my glove box and found the gate pass for Harborside Plantation, good for two weeks. A happy little break.

The guard waved me through when I reached the plantation gates. I again wound around the golf course to Ravenwood and approached Leo's house. Without the emergency vehicles, it looked deserted. Wide strips of yellow police tape blocked the front door down to the garage, marring the neighborhood of attractive homes like a black marker streaked across the canvas of a Monet.

I parked across the street and studied the neighborhood. Since I was using gossip as my information source, I didn't actually know which neighbor saw Jane. Allegedly. Ravenwood ran north to south with Leo's house dead center. The south crossed at Sparrow Road and the north curved into the golf course. I counted seven houses with a direct visual of Leo's: two on each side and three across the street. Not many neighbors, as each house was situated on a wide lot. The homeowners association probably mandated one acre minimums with extensive berms and landscaping plans for maximum privacy.

I grabbed my notebook, a pen, and a handful of business cards. I started at the first house to the south, on the corner of Ravenwood and Sparrow. Nobody answered, but I saw a woman through the sidelight. She watched me while I smiled and waved, then she turned back to the TV in front of her. I wrote a short note on the back of my card and slipped it into the doorjamb. No one answered next door either, but at least this time I didn't have to watch them ignore me. I left another note and moved on. I passed Leo's house, then approached the house adjacent on the other side.

A man of about sixty answered my knock. He wore neat slacks, a crisp oxford, and wire-framed glasses. "Yes?"

"Good afternoon. I'm Elliott Lisbon with the Ballantyne Foundation. We're assisting the police with the Leo Hirschorn case," I said with confidence. A stretch, but it was better than leading with I heard from a friend who heard through her gossip network that you might be a key witness in a high profile murder and I'm trying to get that alleged-murderer off the hook.

"Yes?" he repeated.

"I understand you were witness to some suspicious activity on the night in question," I said, using my best police-like words.

"Yes, I was. But I've already spoken to two detectives. A man and a woman. I don't know who you are."

I quickly pulled out my Ballantyne credentials, the ones I carry to philanthropy summits. They look very official and government-sanctioned. I held them face up so he couldn't see the coupon for a buy one get one free appetizer stuck in the back. "That would be Lieutenant Ransom and Corporal Parker. We're working together. Would you mind going over it with me?"

"I would mind, actually," he said and started to close the door.

I placed my hand on the door and talked faster. "Sir, I understand your reluctance. Honestly, I do. But a man is dead. It's important we speak. I won't take up much time. Just one quick question and I'm gone."

His face pinched, but I could tell his ingrained sense of duty prohibited the snappy dismissal he was itching to spout. He waited a beat, but I stood firm. I really needed his information and official police types don't back down.

"Fine," he finally said.

He stepped outside and I followed him down the drive.

"What did you see on Saturday night?"

"I was walking Sophie, my lab. We were on our way to the corner." He pointed to the south end where Ravenwood crossed Sparrow Road. "That's when Jane Hatting sped by me like her hair was on fire."

Ah, the right neighbor witness. I wondered how many times he'd repeated this story. "What makes you think it was Jane?"

"I recognized her. My wife purchased antiques from her gallery last year. Jane often visited here to assist in choosing the most appropriate pieces." He turned to me. "Jane was driving her black Sebring when she raced past me on Saturday night. The top was down and she had a pink scarf over her hair like she always does."

"What time was this?"

"After midnight. Maybe twelve-fifteen. My little Sophie's getting on in years. She sleeps better if I take her out a third time."

"I see. But it must have been very dark out here. It was late, you were busy with Sophie..."

"And I know what I saw. This is a quiet neighborhood. Mostly seniors who eat dinner at four-thirty and go to sleep before the sun goes down. If there's a car driving around at midnight, I'm going to notice it."

"Did you notice anything else? Anything odd or different?"

"Not really. She sped past me. I talked to Sophie as we walked." He stared down the street. "Wait. Jane came back. That was different."

"She came back?"

"Yes, now that I think about it. She swung around Sparrow, made a wide U-turn, and sped back down the road. I remember thinking she must have forgotten something."

"Did you actually see her at Leo's house or only driving in the street?"

He shook his head and walked over to the mailbox. "No, only driving. I didn't look back; I wanted Sophie to make it to the corner, her favorite spot. I didn't want to stay out all night. I never saw Jane after that."

I wrote a few notes in my book, including his address on the mailbox. I didn't want to ask his name, a detail someone assisting the police would already know.

"So how was Leo as a neighbor?"

"Leo was a rat bastard." He snatched his mail out of the box and his electric bill fluttered to the ground.

I quickly stepped forward and picked it up. "Harsh words about a dead man."

"Leo was an obnoxious s.o.b. who went out of his way to be a jerk. He'd throw his junk mail in my box. When I complained, he blamed the mailman. And then continued right on doing it." He walked up the drive and pointed at his lawn. "See these patches? His disgusting dog. He walked him over in my yard so I'd get these yellow spots instead of him. I didn't wish the man dead, but I'm not all torn up about it either."

"Thank you, Mr. Dobbs," I said, courtesy of the fallen electric bill made out to Owen Dobbs. I handed it to him, along with my business card. "If you think of anything else, please let me know."

I walked down the street, up Leo's driveway, and into his backyard. I crept around the deck, peeked in the back windows. The furniture was still broken. The dishes were shattered and the place was in shambles, but someone had cleaned up the spilled food. Something bothered me. A wispy notion fluttered in the back of my brain, just out of reach. I scanned the kitchen again, but nothing registered.

I went over to the same dusty patio set from Sunday and plopped into a chair. So the killer raged through the place with Leo dead in the clock and no worries about being interrupted. Took her time. Must've known no one was home, even came back. But *why* did she come back? Forget something? Maybe in her hysterical raging frenzy she dropped something. An earring, her purse?

Why am I saying "she?" It cannot be Jane. Can it? As damaging as it was to Jane, at least I found the witness. He seemed reliable, solid, unimpeachable.

There had to be more than this. "What am I missing, Leo?" I looked across the shabby lawn. Something big, something obvious. It clicked and I sat straight up.

Where's the dog?

I didn't remember seeing a dog on Sunday, nor anyone talking about a dog. I went up to the patio doors and peeked in again. No dog dish in the kitchen. Since someone cleaned up the spilled food, I'm sure they would've noticed a dog prancing around. Maybe they called animal protective services, or whoever takes in pets when dad's been murdered.

I pulled out my cell and dialed the Island Police department.

"Hi Parker, it's Elliott. Did you happen to notice a dog at Leo Hirschorn's on Sunday?"

"I didn't, but let me check," she said.

I heard papers rustling in the background.

"Nope, no animals in the house. A cat dish, but when we spoke to Mrs. Hirschorn, she told us the cat was with her. Why?"

"Leo's neighbor mentioned a dog, but I don't see one."

"It could've died or run away."

"It's possible. I'll keep digging. One more thing, do you have a Dee on your list?"

I heard the papers shuffle again.

"Nope, who is she?"

"A customer, I think. I only have a first name"

"Sorry, Elliott. No Dee, no dog. It doesn't sound like much, but keep me posted, okay?"

"Sure," I said and hung up.

I agreed it didn't sound like much, but it was something. I called Bebe at the hotel, but it rolled into voicemail.

"Hi Bebe, it's Elliott Lisbon. I have a quick question. Could you call me when you get in?" I left my number and clicked off. She was probably already in New Jersey. For all I knew, she put the dog in a kennel or he's been at the vet getting dipped for fleas.

I dusted off my pants and went back to Owen Dobbs' house.

"Sorry to bother you again, Mr. Dobbs, but when did you last see Leo's dog?"

"He peed on my newspaper last Saturday morning."

"Are you sure about the day?"

"Always on Saturdays, like clockwork." He started to close the door. It ricocheted off my foot wedged in the doorway.

"What kind of dog is he?"

"English Bulldog. A disgusting, slobbery, smelly bulldog named Donald," he said and nearly slammed the door on my foot.

I settled into my car and made notes. I started a fresh page for Donald the Bulldog. It was a big loose end and it didn't make sense. Especially since female dogs usually leave yellow urine patches, not males. So either Donald was a female or the lawn problems were caused by another dog.

Enough about the dog. Jane was at Leo's the night he was murdered and the police could prove it. I decided I'd better question the rest of the residents on the block before I left. The way the case was shaping up, one of them probably saw Jane kill Leo—caught it on video with surround sound and special effects.

I hit the first house across the street from Leo's. A gentleman of perhaps seventy-five answered. He had a full head of jet black hair streaked with white, and his skin was tan and wrinkled from years spent hunched over a golf club.

"Good afternoon. I'm Elliott Lisbon with the Ballantyne Foundation. I'm assisting the police with the Leo Hirschorn case."

"I'm afraid I can't help you. We've been in Wisconsin. Got home on Tuesday." He nodded to Leo's house. "It was already sealed up with tape by then. We were sorry to hear about it, though."

"Were you friends of the Hirschorns?"

"Not really. Enough to wave when we passed, say hello at Publix, that kind of thing."

I handed him my card. "If you think of anything, please call me."

He stopped me before I left the porch. "If you're headed next door, they've been in Martha's Vineyard since the first of April. Won't be back until September. But now Mrs. Jones on the other side, she's always home. Stays up late, too."

I put a card in the doorjamb next door in case they had popped home over the weekend, then headed to the last house near the corner.

A little lady answered the door, not a day over ninety-nine. And when I say little, I mean tiny. I could've picked her up and put her in my pocket. She wore a pretty pink sweater set with pearl buttons and a long skirt covered in pink and lavender flowers. She carried a large shiny black pocketbook on her arm.

"Hello," she said. "May I help you?"

"I hope so. I'm Elliott Lisbon with the Ballantyne Foundation—"

"Oh yes," she interrupted. "I recognize you. My sister, Marge, brought me to a tea party last fall at the Big House. It was delightful."

"The Wonderland Adventures, one of our most successful events. I'll have to make sure you receive an invitation to this year's party."

She lit up and clapped her hands. "Really? What a lovely surprise." She opened her door wider. "I'm Mrs. Olivetta Jones. Do come in, dear."

I gestured to her purse. "Are you on your way out? I won't be but a minute."

"Oh this? I always carry it with me, that way I don't forget where I set it down."

She showed me into the front room and I entered a Victorian dollhouse. Wallpaper with hearty pink roses and celadon stripes covered the walls and soft pink carpet covered the floors. Petite end tables, I counted nine, were placed around the room with Limoges boxes and figurines on top.

A child's rocker sat in the corner with a porcelain doll in the seat. Several more dolls sat around the room. All had hand-painted faces and elaborate dresses. I examined the blonde doll in the rocking chair. "She's beautiful, Mrs. Jones. Did you make her yourself?"

She flushed. "I did. All of these. I painted their faces, except for the eyelashes. Marge is much better at those. I sewed their dresses, too. Even that one with handmade lace on the collar."

I put the doll back on her tiny chair and joined Mrs. Jones on the sofa, a mauve loveseat facing a picture window dressed with silk drapes in pink plaid.

"Would you like tea, dear? I was just about to have some." She pointed to a tea set, matching bone china in a delicate chintz pattern.

"I would love some."

She scampered to the kitchen and returned with a cup and saucer for me, plus a three-tiered tray with cookies, crustless sandwiches, and miniature scones. Mrs. Jones took her tea seriously. "We're having Assam today. I hope you don't mind."

"It's perfect." It was stronger than steel wool. If I drank the entire cup, I wouldn't sleep for two days. I sipped slowly. "I'd like to ask you about Leo Hirschorn if I may."

"Of course, dear, what would you like to know?" She buttered a scone and gently broke it in half.

"Were you home last Saturday night?"

"Oh yes, the night he was murdered. I definitely was. I don't go out much anymore. Marge takes me to lunch once a week, but we never go at night. Neither of us can drive after dark."

"Did you happen to see anything strange that night?"

"Nothing strange, I would say."

"Were you up late Saturday night?"

"Yes, I find it difficult to sleep. I worry in the dark, you know. I feel safe with the guards here in the plantation, but I keep an eye out for myself. We all try to, a Neighborhood Watch of sorts." She pointed to a baseball bat in the corner. "In case I need protection."

"Of course." I nodded solemnly. If she swung that thing, she'd topple over like a toddler. "So nothing out of the ordinary. No cars or people?"

She set her cup down. "Well, now, like I said, nothing strange."

I leaned forward. "How about ordinary. Did you see something ordinary that night?"

She smoothed her skirt and folded her hands in her lap. "I know how this looks, with the big window and me staying up late at night. I'm not a Nosy Parker. I've lived on this island thirty-two years, and I know how folks in a small town get to gossiping. I'm not like that."

I refilled her tea cup. "I would never think you a gossip, Mrs. Jones. I'm sure you don't wish to tell tales out of school. But in this instance, you could be assisting me with Mr. Hirschorn's murder."

She fiddled with her pearl buttons. I ate another scone (raspberry white chocolate, either homemade or bakery fresh) while she debated with herself.

"This is confidential, whatever I tell you?"

I did an internal fist pump and back flip. "Absolutely. And you may be confirming what I already know."

"Okay, then. I saw a red Volkswagen Beetle parked in Leo's driveway on Saturday night."

"Are you sure about the make?"

"Definitely. It's been there before. See? Nothing strange."

"You're right, very ordinary. Do you remember what time?"

"Definitely after eleven, maybe eleven-thirty. I was watching a movie on TV. It ended at eleven. I made a late snack, a slice of warm banana bread and hot cocoa. Helps me sleep. I came in here to check out the neighborhood. That's when I saw it, parked in the drive."

Could this be a line on the elusive Ms. Dee? Sounds like a mistress-type situation. A car parked in the drive late at night while the wife was away. I surreptitiously took one more sip of tea and finished the last scone on my plate. "Did you tell the detective about the red car?"

She set her cup on the tray. "Of course. A nice young lady detective came by."

"Thank you, Mrs. Jones. For everything. The tea was lovely." I stood and she walked me to the door, her pocketbook on her arm.

"I appreciate the company with my tea. So much nicer for two."

"Indeed. I will make sure your name is on the invitation list for the Wonderland at the Big House." I handed her my card. "If you think of anything else, please call me."

"I will. You're welcome anytime, dear."

I practically skipped to my car. Jane may have been with Leo the night he died, but so was someone else. Who's to say the neighbors remembered the timing correctly? Maybe it was the other way around. Jane was there first and the red car came second. Jane may have even seen the driver.

TWELVE

I stopped at the gatehouse on my way out. I watched dozens of cars zip through an automatic gate while I waited for the director on duty to step out of the hut. The car line was so long, the reflective arm rarely went back down. I listened to the high-pitched whistle of air escaping from my clever balloon of a theory about a killer forced to stop for a gate pass.

The security director joined me on the curb. She was my height and had lots of gear on her utility belt.

"How does the auto-bar work?" I asked after I introduced myself, one director to another.

"A resident buys a clicker through the association. It speeds them through so they don't have to wait in line with the visitors and tourists."

"But it never goes back down. Can't a car simply slide in behind?"

"It's against the rules."

"But it happens," I said.

"A resident risks a violation if they're caught."

I glanced at the cars whipping past the upright security bar, then back at her. "What about paper passes? Do you keep an official logbook?"

"I can't give out that kind of information, ma'am."

I put my hand on my chest and leaned in conspiratorially. "Look, I appreciate having rules, I really do. You wouldn't believe the rulebook for the Foundation, thicker than a dictionary. But Leo Hirschorn was such a beloved member of our board, and one of your residents, certainly you can tell me something about the night he was murdered."

Her shoulders relaxed. "No logbooks, no databases. We had no names or descriptions to give to the Lieutenant, either. I'm sorry." She nodded to the auto-bar. "Like you said, it happens."

I thanked her and left. With my theory balloon sufficiently deflated, I returned to my office at the Big House. There were two notes on my desk. The first from Carla. Chef Carmichael would meet us on Saturday at eleven-thirty to plan the party menu. I definitely needed to be here for that. Probably should bring helmets and padded vests. The second note was from Tod inviting me to a luncheon at Reena's. A grantee mixer with board members and donors the next afternoon. He left the address with a P.S.: "If I have to go, so do you."

I stuck the address in my purse and called Jane. After a three minute wait, I finally heard her voice.

"Jane Walcott Hatting," she said.

"Hi, Jane, it's Elliott. Do you have a minute?"

"No, Elliott, I don't."

"Great. I spent the afternoon with Leo's neighbors. It seems you neglected to mention you were at Leo's house the night of the murder."

"Are you still pretending to be an investigator? I'm going to talk to Edward. You have too much time on your hands."

"You didn't answer my question."

"You didn't ask one, Nancy Drew. Care to try again? I should warn you, I may hang up at any time."

I spoke slowly. "Jane. Why didn't you tell me. You were at Leo's. On Saturday. After the party?"

"Because I wasn't there. If you'll excuse me—"

"No, I won't excuse you. Leo's neighbor saw you, Jane. Saw. You. Black Sebring, scarf in your hair, speeding away from the murder scene. A witness."

"That's ridiculous. That police detective tried to pull this same stunt at the station. The neighbor is obviously lying. I wasn't there. Period."

"Then where were you?"

"Look, Elliott, I'm not interested in playing this game with you."

"It's not a game. I'm trying to help you. I'm the *only* person trying to help you."

"You'll have to try harder than this," she said and hung up on me.

No shit, I thought. I spent the entire day running around picking up scraps of information Ransom already had. Hell, he questioned Jane on this three days ago.

I flipped through my book and decided to follow-up on Travis's alibi. A woman answered the phone.

"May I speak with Derek, please?"

"He's not here. Who's calling?"

"I'm Elliott Lisbon with the Ballantyne Foundation. I wanted to talk to Derek about a new project we're working on with Seabrook Preparatory."

"Oh, how nice. I'm his mother. Derek's with his dad for a long weekend, fishing. They'll be back late Sunday."

"I'll catch him next week then. By the way, do you happen to know Travis Hirschorn? He's next on my list."

"Sure, they've been friends since freshman year. Nice boy. Tragic about his father."

"Devastating," I said. "It must have been hard for you to tell him."

"Me?"

"Wasn't he at your house over the weekend?"

"No, he hasn't spent the night in months," she said.

"Oh, my mistake. I heard he was at friend's house and assumed. I'm sorry."

"No problem. These boys are always at one house or another."

"Anyway, I'll call Derek next week about that project. Thank you," I said and replaced the receiver.

At least my instincts were working. But why would Travis provide such a flimsy alibi? Simple naïveté, assuming I'd take the word of his best bud? Or did he want to get caught?

I made a quick list of people I had interviewed and who had lied to me: Jane, Cherry, Joseph, Bebe, and now Travis. Yep, that's everyone so far.

But who was lying about murder?

Matty arrived at my cottage at seven-thirty wearing his usual summer uniform: khaki shorts, faded surf tee, and his Oakleys on his head, tucked into his soft curly hair. "Hey, El, you ready?" he said with a light kiss on my cheek.

"Almost." I slipped on my tennis shoes, then locked up the cottage. We walked to the drive where his truck was parked, an old sixties Land Cruiser FJ40 with the hardtop off. He held the door while I climbed into the cab.

"What's with the moving boxes?" Matty asked. "Mr. Wallaby cleaning out the garage?"

"He sold the place, maybe two weeks ago," I said as we drove away.

"Meet your neighbor yet? Maybe he'll be friendlier than old Wallaby."

"Um, yep. I've met him. Semi-retired, took Sully's place at the department. Not sure about friendlier, though." Not many people knew about my history with Ransom, including Matty, even though he knew just about everything else about me. I wasn't ready to share this. At least not yet. I needed time to figure Ransom out for myself first.

"You get some sun today?" I asked. His nose was sunburned, dark pink and covered in freckles.

"Tide was out so I went fishing down off the Sound. Took my kayak out from Sandhill Beach and caught two red fish. You should join me sometime." He reached over and squeezed my hand, sensing the fret face I was about to make. "Don't worry, I throw them back. You won't have to eat them."

"I'm less worried about that than the kayak. Don't those things flip over a lot?" I did not want to land in the creek. Matty took me snorkeling once. I did fine until I stuck my face in the water and saw all the creatures swimming around. I nearly walked on water to get back to shore.

He laughed. A low sweet sound with a big grin. "Not in my kayak we won't."

The sun was near setting when we walked to the back deck at the Tidewater where fifteen or so tables with white linen toppers were arranged between the hotel and the ocean. Pretty blue china settings with painted lobsters decorated the tables and colorful paper lanterns dangled above, crisscrossing the patio.

Matty spotted his brother near the jazz band. Pete was two years older and looked like the fireman he was. Athletic build with daredevil looks and the body of Mr. October in some sexy firefighter calendar. His wife, Kyra, was his perfect match. Cheerleader-pretty with the temperament of a yoga instructor. They had two girls at home and another on the way—in about ten minutes by the look of her.

"Kyra, you look ready to pop," I said after a round of hugs and kisses and handshakes.

"If only. The little bean's been giving her mama a hard time. And I've still got six weeks to go."

Matty rubbed her belly. "Don't you listen to her, little bean. You act any old way you please." He pulled his hand back. "Hey, there, she kicked me. Gonna be champion swimmer, I bet. Maybe a surfer, too."

"Already got her a board, brother," Pete said as he grabbed his plate and headed for a long buffet spread opposite the band.

We settled into the dinner with plenty of beer (juice for Kyra) and several trips to the buffet. The evening progressed rapidly while the brothers Gannon cracked, shucked, and slurped oysters—

steamed, fried, and raw on the half-shell. An oyster roast is so much more fun if you like oysters. Or shellfish. Or seafood of any kind. Which I don't. Especially the kind you eat raw. That's just gross.

But I did just fine with a filet, sliced thick with sides of bleu cheese potatoes, baked beans, and a basket of pecan cornbread. Plus, the view was spectacular. The ocean was on my right beyond the sea grass and the sand dunes, and the band played a jazzy tune beneath the dangling lights and rising moon.

As dinner moved into its second hour, I slipped into a reverie watching Matty with his family. He was thirty-five to my forty. I think his biological clock may have been ticking like a time bomb, whereas my clock didn't even have batteries in it. Matty needed a real date. Find himself a wife, have a little bean of his own.

Small slivers of pain sliced through my belly. Guilt at keeping him to myself or jealous he might want someone else? Or perhaps too many helpings of bleu cheese potatoes? I was leaning toward the potatoes when a flicker of brassy blonde hair pulled me from my ruminations.

Bebe Hirschorn. She walked across the patio with a handsome man by her side. He was no New Jersey cowboy. More like a Wall Street shaker, and not one on the desk. The guy had the easy, confident stride of a man running the floor, wearing casual slacks and a tan Tommy Bahama. They were having a pretty friendly conversation by the looks of it. She put her hand on his arm, he smiled in return.

"Taking up voyeurism?" Matty asked me.

"Do you know who that man is, the one talking to Bebe Hirschorn?"

"No, but she doesn't look happy."

And she didn't. Their friendly conversation must have turned decidedly unfriendly because Bebe spun on her heel and hurried toward the hotel.

"Excuse me, I'll only be a minute," I said to Matty.

I crossed the patio and into the lobby, catching up to Bebe at the base of an elegant staircase leading to the second floor gallery.

"Bebe, wait, it's me, Elliott."

"What are you doing here?"

"I'm at the oyster roast. But I could ask you the same thing. I thought you were flying home."

"Tomorrow. We had to wait for Joseph. He couldn't leave the store."

"Who was that man you were speaking to?"

She glanced around. "Who? Milo Hickey? He's nobody."

"Didn't look like nobody."

"He's nothing. A guy from some stupid poker game on Saturday nights. A linebacker crab game Leo goes to. Trust me, he's a nobody." She fluffed her big hair and the bracelets on her arm rattled. "I don't trust him. Gambler. What does he know?"

What *does* he know? "I left you a message earlier, but you didn't call me."

She shrugged.

"Where's your dog?"

"I don't have a dog, and Leo finally got rid of his. Filthy dog was a nuisance. Look, I gotta go." She turned to click up the stairs in her high heels.

"Wait. Do you know a Dee? Someone who drives a red VW bug? Often parked in your driveway late at night?"

Bebe paled, leaving only two splotchy spots of orange blusher. "I have no idea what you're talking about," she said and marched up the stairs.

Now why didn't I believe that?

"Did Mrs. Hirschorn offer up any scraps to clear your client? A stolen necklace, a jealous lover?" Ransom asked from behind me.

I turned around. "Nope. Just saying hello."

"Liar."

"What are you doing here? An oyster roast seems lowbrow for a gadabout like you."

He smiled. "Just enjoying the scenery, taking in the local color." He stepped closer. "Like you, Red. Your cheeks have pinked up two shades since we've been standing here. Care to try for a third?"

"I don't think your girlfriend would approve."

He smirked. "Probably not. But I find you kind of irresistible. Like a peach."

"A peach? Who's the liar now? You just want to know what I learned from Bebe Hirschorn."

He stepped even closer, so close I could count his eyelashes. As if I could pull off that kind of concentration with his breath on my face and his lips within kissing distance.

"I'm not lying," he said. "Though if I was, you could never tell. Unlike you."

"Ha. I'm a great liar."

"Your face is a movie screen playing out every thought in real time. And God help me, I can't resist the show."

I placed my palm on his chest to push him back. I met a warm brick wall covered in silk. "Stop. We're not doing this here."

"Doing what?" Matty asked, walking up to us.

I dropped my hand, startled. "Hey Matty."

Ransom remained two inches from me, but stretched out his hand to Matty. "Lieutenant Nick Ransom, Island Police Department, former Special Agent FBI. Ex-boyfriend and new neighbor of Red's."

"Mattias Gannon, Headmaster of Seabrook Prep," Matty said. "And a very close friend of Elli's."

They shook hands. They held on too long. The men were nearly the same height and their eyes locked together tighter than their hands. Seconds ticked by, then they finally released.

"Well, I'm glad we cleared that up," I said.

It was kind of interesting, actually. To see men stripped down to their natural competitive instincts. Both vying for the top prize. Which I think was me in this bizarre scenario, considering neither man actually wanted me. Matty and I weren't even dating and Ransom had a girlfriend.

I put my hand on Matty's arm. "We should be getting back." I wanted to get out of there before the tension swallowed me whole.

Ransom tipped his head. "Of course. Have a good night."

I felt his eyes searing into my backside as I steered Matty through the lobby and over to our table. The waiter had delivered fresh pots of coffee and slices of pineapple upside-down cake while we were gone. A perfectly centered pineapple ring and cherry topped each one. Pete and Kyra had already finished; only crumbs remained on their pale blue saucers.

"You failed to mention your new neighbor is your ex-boyfriend," Matty said. He chopped off a slice of his cake, but didn't eat it.

"He's not my ex-boyfriend, Matty. We spent one night to-gether. Maybe five. Well, not like the whole night, every night. We kissed, made out, rounded a few bases." *Jesus, Elliott, what are you saying?* I stuffed a piece of cake in my mouth.

Matty wouldn't even look at me. I felt my cheeks pink up. Which made me think of Ransom, which made them pink up an-other shade. Five more minutes and my head would explode.

"What did you mean by 'we're not doing this here'?"

"I didn't mean anything, Matty. He's probably on a *date* for Pete's sake."

"*You're* on a date for Pete's sake."

A date? The stomach slivers returned. How did I miss that signal?

I saw Kyra elbow Pete, then give him a look. "Honey, it's late. I told the babysitter we'd be home by ten-thirty."

Pete protested. "Kyra, she's there as late as we want, you told her—"

"We're leaving, hon. The baby's kicking up a storm. Didn't like that last glass of lemonade, I think." Pete helped her up. They kissed us both and scurried off.

"We know how to clear a table," I said.

Silence.

"I don't understand why you're so upset, Matty. We're not on a *date* date."

"I picked you up, I'm paying for dinner, I'm driving you home. That's a date, Elliott."

He ran his hands through his hair and sighed. The music grew louder. Couples danced close, swaying to the sultry beat in the soft glow of the lanterns. Matty leaned over. "Let's get out of here."

He paid the check. I hadn't felt so awkward staring at a dinner bill since my first date in the tenth grade. Sometimes Matty and I split the check, sometimes we don't. This seemed like one of those don't times. I didn't want to make things worse by offering up my share of the ticket after he made such a point of it, so I sat in silence until the waiter returned with the receipt.

Then we walked in silence to the front of the hotel. Then we stood in silence while the valet brought the truck up. Then we drove in silence all the way home, pulling up to the cottage without saying a word.

Ransom's porch light glared like a spotlight and he had parked his car sideways in the drive as if it was on display in a showroom. Great. Batman had an ego.

"Matty, Nick Ransom was twenty years ago. Now he's just the police lieutenant working on a case I happen to be involved in," I said quietly as we sat in the truck.

He didn't answer. He leaned back and looked up at the sky.

I looked up, too. It was black as pitch with millions of stars glittering in the sky like rhinestones on velvet. A warm breeze carried the scents of pine and briny sea spray and the sweet smell of wood smoke from a distant fireplace.

He put his hand on my arm. "Wait here," he said and climbed out of the truck. He walked over to my side and opened the door. He took my hand to help me out, then shut the door behind me. "This *is* a real date," he said and kissed me.

His lips were soft and warm and unexpectedly sweet. His tongue met mine and the heat cranked up from steam to sizzle.

I wrapped my arms around his waist and pressed into the side of the truck as Matty pressed against me.

His hand slid down my chest, then under my shirt. I felt his fingers on my ribs, his palm against my skin. Hot and smooth. His hands and his body.

Oh boy.

He dipped down and kissed my neck, then whispered in my ear. "I guess it's time I got in the game; rounded some bases of my own."

"But we've always been more friends than lovers," I whispered back.

He kissed me again and I thought I might just melt it was so damn delicious. When he finally pulled back, he pressed his forehead to mine. "We've never been lovers, Elli. Not yet." He reached past me to grab my handbag, hat, and sweater. He handed over my stuff. His other hand was still up my shirt, his thumb slowly stroking my ribs. "Wasn't sure how I felt until I saw your hands on another man. Maybe I waited too long, but I'm here now."

I nodded slowly in the moonlight.

"Goodnight, El," he said with a low smile. Then he walked around to driver's side and climbed in.

I watched him back into my driveway, then down the street. I walked to my front door, touching my lips. They were swollen and tingling.

Oh my.

Then Ransom's porch light snapped out and I was left standing in the dark.

THIRTEEN

A combination of knocks and doorbells woke me. I pried open my left eye: 6:13. In the morning. I rolled over with the quilt wound tightly around my head.

More knocking. More doorbell ringing.

I flung back the quilt. Uttered a swear word or three. Slapped on a pair of sweats and marched downstairs.

Another knock.

"Stop it already," I shouted. "I'm right here."

I peeked through the peep hole. I may be cranky, but I'm not crazy. I can't just open the door for some whacko killer and then yell him to death.

Ransom stood on my doorstep.

I swung open the door. "Are you kidding me? What are you doing here?"

"Look, I brought coffee," he said. He pushed past me into the kitchen.

"I don't drink coffee."

He stared at me. I could almost see his mental wheels whir-ring, like a projector in reverse. "Pepsi, right? You still do that?"

"I'm sure you are very proud of your coffee purchase, but why are you here?"

He set two paper cups with plastic tops on the counter. "I'm interviewing actresses today. I thought you'd like to come."

"Actresses?"

"From Leo's commercial. It's a long shot, but I've spoken to everyone in town, now I'm heading to Savannah."

"I'm in. Don't move. Drink your coffee, drink my coffee. I'll be down in a minute."

I took the stairs two at a time and ran into the bath. I knew the actresses wouldn't net much—which is why he offered to include me—but I was sure I could get him to spill other details along the way.

Plus, I wasn't ready to think about Matty and that kiss. And what it meant to our relationship. Things would be different now and I didn't know if I wanted that. I liked being friends. But I also really liked that kiss. Too much to think about at the crack of freaking dawn.

I showered quickly. As quick as I could, anyway. I do things a certain way and it makes my skin itch if I change in any way. All very reasonable and not in the least obsessive. And not for everything, just certain routines. Like showers. Everything done in a particular way, in a particular order. Shampoo, body wash, rinse. Conditioner, shave, rinse. Face wash, face scrub, rinse. Done.

I made up some time with a fast blow-dry of my hair. We both drove convertibles, so either way I needed a hat. With my wavy hair, I don't worry about hat head.

Forty minutes later I popped downstairs to an empty room. "Hello?"

I found Ransom on the patio with the two coffees and a newspaper. The rising sun painted the sky pink and seagulls flew low over the ocean searching for their version of scrambled eggs and ham.

"Shall we?" I asked.

He gathered up the paper and cups and tossed them into the trash can on the side of the cottage. "Mine or yours?" he asked.

We both knew he was only being polite because there was no way we would be driving to Savannah in the Mini Coop. Not when he had air conditioned lumbar seats and a kickass sound system. A girl has to live while she can.

Ransom helped me into the snug seat. The color was a smooth combination of Cabernet and tobacco. The car still smelled new, rich leather with the undertone of Ransom's cologne.

I belted myself in with my bag and hat tucked by my feet.

"Hungry?" Ransom asked.

"Starved."

I thought we might stop at the Squat and Gobble in downtown Summerton, but he flew by it. He pressed the gas pedal, opening it up as we hit the straightaway stretch of the highway. It was exhilarating.

Put the top down on the Mini, it's all about adventure. Go where you want, when you want, and have fun getting there. But the McLaren was all thrill ride. Strap in, hang on, and feel the power beneath the soles of your feet as you rocket over the open road. Fabulous.

Ransom turned off at Poplar Grove, an elegant private community on the May River. The gate guard handed Ransom a day pass for the village five miles down a winding road. It felt as if we had traveled back in time. Tall flickering gaslight lanterns lined the streets. Climbing wisteria blanketed the trunks of towering oaks—forests of them for over twenty-thousand acres. I glimpsed rolling golf course greens and horse stables with black ranch fencing through the trees.

We passed over an iron and stone bridge into the village. Set on a square, quaint shops and restaurants served as the town center for a hundred homes built close together like a town in Cape Cod. They had their own post office and a one-room church facing the dock. A couple rode a tandem bike down the brick road, ringing the bike bell as they passed us.

Life at my parent's summer house was not like this. It may have been only a few miles up the road, but it was at least one entire class division away.

Ransom pulled around the circle drive of the Grove Inn. An antebellum plantation house with white columns and floor to ceiling shuttered windows.

After the valet took the keys, we crossed the long lobby to the restaurant entrance. The hostess sat us at a table for two against the window overlooking the river. A fireplace burned behind us to vanquish any lingering morning chill.

I studied the linen menu, eventually choosing the lemon soufflé pancakes with raspberry puree. Ransom ordered their signature eggs benedict with blue lump crab cakes.

The server arrived with our meals a quick fifteen minutes later, beautifully arranged on creamy porcelain plates. When I tasted the pancakes, a burst of lemon blended with the sweet raspberry sauce and I nearly moaned. I reminded myself to eat slowly. It's not polite to scarf when dining on real china in the presence of others.

"How's your investigation going?" Ransom asked after the server walked away.

"So now we're going to share, are we?"

"You show me yours, I'll show you mine."

"Ah, but you don't play fair. And you like to gloat. It's quite unattractive."

He put his hands up. "No gloating. I'll even go first." He leaned forward and dramatically looked around for eavesdroppers. "Jane's the killer."

I sipped my Pepsi. "You can't think Jane did this. It doesn't fit."

"Have you met Jane? She's a nasty person."

"She's unfriendly. There's a difference," I said. "This is messy and Jane doesn't do messy. What else do you have to offer?"

"Plenty, Red. But let's stick to the case." He sipped his coffee. "I'll give you this: Leo was taking cash, weekly withdrawals, and meeting someone. I don't know who—yet—but it wasn't his wife. I'm thinking Jane's involved."

I nodded. I was thinking a poker game and a woman named Dee was involved, but I kept that to myself. It's not like he was sharing everything with me. He sure didn't mention the red veedub in the driveway. I traded something easy. "Leo's son, Travis, wasn't at Derek's house that night, like he said."

Ransom looked up from his eggs. "Really? I spoke with Derek and the two other friends they met at the movies."

"I spoke with Derek's mother. Travis hasn't slept over in months. The whole dinner and a movie line was just a ruse." I tried not to look smug, but I was definitely sparkling on the inside.

Ransom speared a fresh raspberry from my plate. "Interesting. I hadn't given junior much thought."

"Exactly. Look around, Jane is but one of many."

"But Jane fits perfectly."

"That's why I don't like it. What about a jealous wife? Or maybe a crazy wife who kills her husband to make room for the hunky masseuse? Bebe was only in Savannah. It's less than a thirty minute drive."

Ransom watched me while I spoke. The interest in his eyes made my stomach flip. He leaned forward and wiped my cheek with his finger. "Raspberry sauce."

"Thank you," I whispered as the waitress arrived to clear our plates.

"You and Gannon been together long?"

I didn't see that coming. I started nodding like a bobble head doll. "Year and a half. Not dating. Friends. Good friends. Best friends." I thought of Matty's soft lips on mine, his body pressing against me. "Well, we're dating now. Maybe. You know, he's in the game. After last night."

Ransom watched me babble and squirm. His eyes were hard, but his lips were all smirky and amused.

"Whatever, Ransom. Just pay the lady and let's get out of here already."

We didn't linger and within twenty minutes, we were screaming over the Talmadge Bridge into downtown Savannah.

"Who are we interviewing?" I asked.

"Brooke Norman and Jenna Hopper," he said. "They both auditioned for Hirschorn three weeks before he was killed. I'm wondering if maybe they heard or saw something while they were in his office."

"Like the fight he had with Joseph over the expansion."

"Like a fight he had with Jane over the board."

He turned onto Jones Street near the Savannah College of Art and Design. A row of walkups lined the street with small iron fences and gates trimming the properties. Large oaks and magnolias provided shade against the summer heat.

"They're on the second floor," he said and I followed him up the iron staircase on the outside of the building, a converted turn of the century home chopped into compact apartments. We entered a small foyer with chipped black and white tile flooring.

He knocked on apartment 2A. "I do the questioning. You are only here to observe."

A young girl answered. She was maybe twenty-two with a dozen long blonde braids held back with a scarf housekeeper style. She wore leggings under a jean skirt and a men's plaid suit vest. She greeted Ransom with a smile. "Hi, you must be the detective?"

Ransom showed her his badge. "Jenna Hopper? I'm Lieutenant Ransom, this is my associate, Elliott Lisbon. May we come in for a minute?"

"Sure. Like I said earlier, I have a class at ten, so I can't talk long."

She led us the two feet into the living room. It was furnished in early garage sale, a chapter of college life I remembered well. Lumpy tweed sofa, two mismatched chairs (one vinyl, one dining room with a rip in the seat). An old Magnavox was perched on a plank of wood held up with cinder blocks. Stacks of books, some opened with papers scattered around, sat off to the side.

"You wanna sit?" she offered. Jenna sat in the recliner, leaving us to the sofa.

"What can you tell us about your meeting with Leo Hirschorn?" Ransom asked.

"It's been like four weeks ago, I guess. Brooke and I, she's my roommate. We went together, but she's not here now. She's at her boyfriend's up at UGA, she'll be back next Wednesday, I think. Anyways, we drove to Summerton, only about thirty minutes if you go highway 46. My sister thinks I-95 is faster, but that's only because the speed limit's higher, right? But it's so the long way around." She hitched her thumb toward a galley kitchen at the back of the apartment. "You guys want some coffee? I drank the rest of the pot, but I can make another. I usually grab a large cup on campus, but it adds up, you know?"

"No, thank you," Ransom said. "Please go on. You were saying about Buffalo Bill's?"

"We were there about an hour. I spoke with Mr. Hirschorn for about fifteen minutes, Brooke for about forty-five. He definitely really liked her. But she's much more serious about the whole acting scene. It just doesn't pay the bills. I'm a waitress nights, but I pick up modeling jobs when I can. Helps with tuition. I'm a student at SCAD."

Ransom took out a slim notebook. "Did Mr. Hirschorn talk to anyone while you were there?"

"Besides me and Brooke? His assistant, I think. Gal with big boobs and red nails? He spoke to her, too." Jenna got up and started putting books from the cinderblock shelf into a worn backpack.

"Do you remember what they discussed?"

"Mostly the commercial. What dates for shooting, how many models he needed. The receptionist interrupted for an inventory question. A special closeout price on blenders, I think."

"What did you and Mr. Hirschorn talk about?" Ransom asked.

"Usual audition stuff. My experience, my other jobs, any speaking roles, that kind of thing. Oh, and could I talk with a Texas accent."

"Could you?" I asked.

"Why, sure thing, darlin'. Y'all come back here now," she said with a perky western twang.

I laughed. "It's perfect!"

"Hey, thanks! I thought so. Brooke and I practiced in case he asked."

"Leo found you through the production company?" I asked.

"They have a database of on-air talent, headshots, videos, voiceovers. Client flips through, chooses who he likes, they send us out to audition. Brooke and I are in at least a dozen talent books in the South, but so are a thousand other girls, you know. It's a lot harder to get a part than it sounds." She zipped up the backpack and slung it over her shoulder. "What happens now with the commercial?"

Ransom stood and I followed. My butt hurt from the lumpy sofa with wobbly springs. "I'm not sure," I said.

"Man, Brooke'll be so bummed if they cancel it now."

"Did she get the part?" I asked.

"No, but I bet he would've given it to her. You know, if he'd lived."

Ransom handed her his card. "Will you ask Brooke to call me when she returns? And if you think of anything, please let me know."

"Sure," she said.

I smiled and handed her my card, too. Just in case.

Jenna locked the apartment behind us and clamored down the metal stairs ahead of us. She moved at a pretty good clip with that heavy pack strapped on her back. She was down the sidewalk and around the corner in ten strides.

"Well, that was a bust," Ransom said as he helped me into the car. He shut the wing door and climbed into the driver's seat.

"Except for the sale on blenders," I said. "I always did want one of those."

"You don't have a blender?"

"I don't even have a toaster. If I have to use an appliance to make it, I'm not eating it. Microwave excluded, of course."

"Of course."

He started the engine and the McLaren sprang to life, humming like a jet engine. "I'll have you to the Big House before eleven. The way you sleep in, no one will even know you were gone."

"Funny. Look, while we're all the way out here— "

"All this way."

"Exactly. Let's swing by the River Street Inn and confirm Bebe's alibi. I'm telling you, she could've driven to the island, killed Leo, and been back before the Scrappers even missed her."

"This may surprise you, but I checked Bebe's alibi."

"And?"

"And she didn't leave the hotel all weekend."

"Did you actually go to the hotel and speak to the clerk in person?"

"No," he said slowly. "That I did not do."

"Well, then. We're like five blocks away. Isn't that why you drove out here? It's much better to talk in person, remember? Phone calls can be so unreliable, isn't that what you said this morning?"

"I'm sure I didn't use that tone." He tapped his fingers on the steering wheel and his phone rang. "Ransom," he said. Then five seconds later, "What did it say?"

He glanced at me and mouthed "stay here." He slid out of the car and shut his door tight.

I tried to read his lips, but he saw me and turned his back. A minute later he hung up, then made another call. Two minutes after that, he got back in the car.

"What was that about?"

He ignored my question and pulled away from the curb. He turned left on Montgomery, then a right on Bay Street. "You think you can get information out of the hotel staff?"

"Absolutely."

"Well, this should be fun," he said and parked near the hotel, a brick building reminiscent of a warehouse with tall windows overlooking the Savannah River.

Ransom let me take the lead as we approached the front desk. "Let's see what you've got."

"Good morning. May I speak with the manager, please?" I asked a trim man in a gray suit. His name tag said Philip Feeney and he stood in front of a computer terminal and keyboard. Ready to check us in, I presumed.

"I'm the manager. How may I assist you?"

"We're investigating a homicide on Sea Pine Island." I elbowed Ransom. "Show him your badge," I whispered.

Ransom pulled a slim leather case from his pocket. "Lieutenant Ransom, Sea Pine Police."

"The victim's wife, Bebe Hirschorn, was a guest at your hotel last weekend. We need confirmation as to her whereabouts."

He looked down his nose at me. "I'm not sure I can help you. Our guests are free to come and go as they please. It hurts business when we lock them in at night."

"Cute. Here's the thing, Philip. I'm the director of the prestigious Ballantyne Foundation. Perhaps you've heard of us?" I handed him my business card.

"Of course. I didn't realize."

"I thought not. A very distinguished member of our board was bludgeoned to death in his own home, possibly by a guest at your hotel. News like that could also hurt business, yes?"

He nodded slightly.

"I understand discretion. I would never breach confidentiality, from one prestigious organization to another. If you would be so kind as to confirm Mrs. Hirschorn was indeed a guest, with a little cooperation, this matter will practically resolve itself."

He flicked a glance at Ransom, who simply smiled.

Phillip picked up my card. "Of course, Ms. Lisbon." He began typing on the keyboard, his fingers flying with the speed and randomness of a ticketing agent. "Here we are. Mrs. Bebe Hirschorn, checked in last Friday, checked out two days later on Sunday early afternoon. She ordered two meals from room service and brought a cat."

"Does your hotel track guests with their electronic room key?" I asked.

"Yes, but for that you'll need a warrant. I'm afraid security handles those logs."

I stiffened my back. "I see." I turned to Ransom. "A warrant can be so..."

"Public?" he said.

"Exactly. But if we must..."

Phillip's fingers again flew across the keyboard. "Wait. This may help. Mrs. Hirschorn had a roommate. A Ms. Gina Beckendinga." He rattled off the address while I took notes. "Perhaps you can extort some cooperation from her."

I smiled. "Perhaps I can. Thank you, Phillip." I was elated. No warrant necessary. And thank goodness, because I'm pretty sure no one would give me one. I tucked away my notebook and walked away.

"Any other favors, Lieutenant?" I heard Phillip say behind me.

I kept walking, not stopping to hear Ransom's answer as I crossed the lobby. I whirled on him when he joined me on the curb in front of the hotel.

He smiled and said, "Not bad, Red. I'm impressed."

"What did he mean about favors?"

"Don't worry about it."

"What kind of favor? Like talking to me?" I studied his face. His grin was a shit-eater and I remembered the second phone call outside Jenna's fifteen minutes earlier. "Did you call the hotel and tell them we were coming in?"

"It's no big deal, just a head's up."

My face flashed red with hot blood and embarrassment. "What about Gina Beckendinga? Was that even real?"

He didn't seem to notice the change in my demeanor. Or that my face now matched my hair color, tone for tone. He either didn't notice or didn't care. He smiled wider. I think he was going for charming, but all I saw was gloating. "I got her name from security and spoke with her three days ago. Bebe's alibi is solid."

"But you said you didn't talk to the hotel."

"I said I didn't speak to the clerk. I spoke with security, then the Scrappers coordinator, and then with Ms. Beckendinga."

"You are such an asshole." I turned on my heel, and marched down the street mortified. I blinked back tears. My emotions run very close to the surface. Anger, hurt, humiliation, bliss. All launch the waterworks whether I want thcm or not.

Foot traffic on the sidewalk was heavy, crowding the narrow walks as lunchtime closed in. I turned down one street, then another. I slowed near a row of antique shops and a sidewalk café.

"Elliott, wait," Ransom said. He touched my arm to stop me, then stood in front of me. "Hey, don't overreact."

"You set me up to make a fool of myself, Ransom."

"It wasn't like that."

"Of course it was. Did you enjoy my amateur interrogation? Get a giggle watching me sweat the old hotel clerk? I thought you at least respected me. Why did you even bring me? To see how big an idiot I can be? Well, you hit the jackpot."

A tear escaped and rolled down my cheek. "Shit," I said and sat on stool at the café. "Honest to God, this just keeps getting better."

"I didn't mean to hurt your feelings," he said and put his hand on my arm.

I slapped it away. "I'm not hurt, asshole, I'm pissed." And embarrassed. I should've recognized it right away. Ransom looking all smug as if he was doing me a big fat favor while I questioned the hotel manager.

"Elliott, stop. You're making too much of this. You wanted to talk to the hotel, and I didn't see any harm in letting you. So I gave him a heads up. No big deal."

Letting me? "I should've known you would never let me lead if you weren't up to something. I overestimated our relationship and I underestimated you. It won't happen again."

He ran his hands through his hair. "This isn't what I wanted."

"I can't help you with that."

I stood and walked down the sidewalk not waiting for him to follow. I stopped at the window of an small antiques shop. It wasn't the fancy kind like Jane's gallery, but the other kind, with retro collectibles and chic vintage kitsch: a matching tin canister set in faded mint green from the thirties, a genuine Brunswick bowling pin from the forties, a black and white houndstooth coat from the fifties.

"Are we still friends?" Ransom asked. He stood close and put his hand on my elbow.

Matty's words about friends and lovers came rushing back. "We were never friends. Apparently we're not even colleagues," I said, without turning from the display.

He tapped the glass window. "See the red pen in the cherry wood case? That's a Parker Duofold from the 1920s. See? No arrow on the nib."

"You shop antiques?"

"Now and then. I collect vintage pens, clocks, things like that."

I studied the window a few minutes more, then walked toward Bay Street where the car was parked. Ransom walked by my side.

"Elliott, about the hotel. I admit, you asked the right questions. But I've got this investigation covered. I'm very good. You're not going to uncover anything I don't already know."

He may have been apologizing in his own Batman I'm-the-hero way, but all I heard was the clanging sound of a gauntlet being thrown down.

FOURTEEN

We sped back to the island in twenty-six minutes. That's from downtown Savannah, over the Talmadge Bridge, along the two-lane highway, through Summerton, over the Palmetto Bridge, and to my cottage door in twenty-six minutes. Since we didn't waste time on scenery or pleasantries, I had plenty of time to get ready for the luncheon at Reena's.

I took another shower. I wanted to start my day over. It was already lousy and only noon. I was still ignoring the implications of Matty's kiss. I was cranky from being dragged out of bed at dawn. I was embarrassed from my humiliating interview with the hotel manager. I didn't want to go to Reena's, who I simply did not like after meeting her a total of one time. And it all circled right back to Nick Ransom, who was probably going to be at the party. I hadn't asked; I didn't want him to think I cared.

Forty-five minutes later, I dressed in a floral tunic over white cigarette pants and slipped on a new pair of strappy slingbacks. I styled my hair and even wore makeup like a big girl.

Reena Patel lived off-plantation in an enclave of homes directly on the water in South Pebble Beach. A tourist beacon of restaurants, shops, and plenty of public access. Several hotel chains bordered the plaza. Their pools were packed during the day and their bars took over the night.

I turned on Ocean Boulevard, then made a right on First Street. Reena's house was about a mile and a half down, enough distance from the tourist hub to afford privacy. Or at least lessen the risk of a family of five parking their beach chairs, umbrellas, coolers, fishing gear, boogie boards, pails, buckets, and beer three feet from your million-dollar deck.

Cars lined the street around her house, but I squeezed into a spot right in her driveway. My left tires rested on the front lawn, but I doubted she'd notice and I didn't care if she did.

Reena answered the door carrying a platter of canapés. She wore a leaf-green sundress with twisted spaghetti straps and her hair hung loose with an orchid tucked behind one ear. She looked like a Hawaiian princess.

"Elliott? What are you doing here?"

I've never been greeted by a hostess quite that way before. "Tod invited me," I said.

She relaxed. "Oh, good. You're late, though." She stepped aside so I could enter.

She thrust the canapé platter into my hands. "The guests are either on the terrace or the deck by the pool. When you've finished passing these, check the punch bowl, it might be low." She tossed her hair over her shoulder and clacked away in her super high heels.

I should've shoved the tray back at her, but I didn't want to create a scene. Instead, I carefully stepped across the expansive marble floor. Miles of marble floor: sleek, shiny, and slick. And I wore new shoes.

The house was fresh from the pages of a magazine. The first floor was practically one open space. The living room, dining room, foyer, and kitchen blended together with only furniture to define the rooms. Like a fancy furniture showroom, it was nice to look at, but I wouldn't want to live there.

I met Tod in the kitchen. "Apparently I'm serving the hors d'oeuvres," I said and set the plate on the black granite countertop. "Your note failed to mention I'd have to work for my lunch."

Tod arranged shrimp and cocktail sauce on a crystal tray. "Do I look like I knew?"

I glanced at his outfit: gray slacks, linen shirt, and a smooth black belt around his slim waist.

"It's Armani, Elliott. Armani. Apparently Reena sees this as a Ballantyne function, so naturally, we're the help. But we're only supplementing. She hired two uniformed servers to help us."

"She's too kind." I admired the catered spread. Trays of canapés, hors d'oeuvres, and sandwiches covered the granite island. A heavy, cut-crystal punch bowl with dozens of matching cups worked as a centerpiece for the array of desserts in the living room. I helped Tod place the shrimp on a bed of ice cubes.

"Why do we do this?" Tod asked.

"We're doing this for the children of Mumbai. I can pass salmon puffs for a prima donna princess because our organization will help her organization keep those families from sleeping in the trash."

"And it fills us with a secret superiority. He who controls the food rules the world."

"Amen." I lowered my voice. "I, for one, plan on glomming information about Leo. Someone here knows more than they're telling."

I looked out to the open room beyond the kitchen island. A white sofa with matching chairs and rug made up the living room straight ahead. It faced an enormous glass wall, forty feet of windows overlooking a long terrace, brick deck, swimming pool, and the Atlantic. The ocean sparkled in the sunlight as a thin white line of surf gently rolled to the sand.

"Pretty nice view," I said. "Where does she get the money?"

"Did you even read her application packet?"

"I may have skimmed." It was still tucked in my messenger bag. The only time I actually cracked it open was during the meeting with Reena.

"Daddy's money," Tod said.

I finished with the shrimp and washed my hands twice, then dosed them with hand-sani to get the shrimp smell off. It almost worked. "I thought her people were poor, living in slums."

"Not quite. It seems in Mumbai, you either live in a slum or a palace. No bothersome middle class to confuse things. She is of the palace people. She wanted to give the family money to help the poor, daddy did not. This is their version of a compromise."

"Donate somebody else's money to the poor."

"Exactly. It's the way of the wealthy. Daddy sets her up with a house and an allowance while she gathers grant money to give away." Tod picked up a tray. "Shall we earn our keep?"

"I live to serve." I picked up a platter and followed Tod to the patio where the guests mingled on the multi-level deck, several holding Mumbai Humanitarian brochures.

A sight Mr. Ballantyne would enjoy. He liked to work with local groups. It allowed board members and loyal donors to meet grantees, learn about their causes and how they can help.

"Why Elliott, don't you look pretty!" Zibby Archibald said. She had dyed her hair to match her blouse, a lovely shade of turquoise.

"Walnut chicken summer roll?" I offered.

She took two for her plate. "I can't thank you enough for your help with the Wharf, dear..."

Her voice faded out as I met Ransom's eyes. He was sitting behind Zibby on a lounge chair near the pool.

"...the best meal yet. The chef even stopped by my table," Zibby finished.

"I'm happy for you, Zibby. If you have any more trouble, you call me." I said. I turned my back to Ransom and served the guests to the west of the most annoying man at the party.

Ninety minutes and five tray refills later, I was down to my last three puffs. I spotted Whitney Tattersall at a bistro set in the corner. "Moroccan salmon puff?"

She smiled. "I don't eat seafood."

"Really? Me neither." I joined her at the table, setting my tray down and putting my feet up.

Whitney was what you might call big-boned, or a plus-sized gal. Though I imagine most of her childhood nicknames were much crueler and included some version of the word fat. She had creamy smooth skin and pretty soft brown hair that fell in curls past her shoulders.

She was drinking a bottle of water and offered me one from a galvanized tin on the deck behind her. "Thanks," I said as I twisted off the cap.

A uniformed server came by with a tray of petit fours and sliced vanilla cake. We both declined, but the girl raised her eyebrows and asked Whitney again before she walked away.

"What was that about?" I asked.

"Shock that I passed up dessert. People think fat folks eat cake for breakfast and cream pies for lunch. Sure, I wish I weighed a hundred pounds less. I've tried—still trying—exercise, diet, low-cal. Haven't eaten processed sugar in ten years. It just won't come off. Big-boned, metabolism, whatever. People are so afraid of being fat, they'll suck it out, the riskiest form of surgery. It's nuts. All the while we tell ourselves inner beauty is all that matters."

She set her water bottle down and laughed. "I don't know where all that came from. Sorry to unload. I'm passionate I guess."

"You have a right to be. The server was rude."

"People can't help being judgmental. They see you eat a cheeseburger, they think nothing of it. They see me? They think I'm an oinker scarfing down my third one. Nothing subtle about the ridicule either. People figure I deserve it."

"Well, sure, what with eating all that cake for breakfast," I said.

She laughed. "Exactly. You know that server is just waiting for me to sneak over and stuff a piece of cake in my mouth when no one is looking."

"Or shove some in your handbag for later."

"Five bucks says she comes back by." She took a sip of water. "Listen, I've been thinking about Leo ever since you called." She looked around. We were tucked away on the top deck. Everyone else was either down by the pool or inside the house. "I'm sure it's nothing, it's so small."

"Any little thing might be important. Honestly, even something totally innocuous."

"Well, Leo was really happy at the party, like I said. But more than normal. He was sure his seat would be renewed."

"The meeting was on Monday," I said. "Most seats are automatically reassigned. Maybe he was just being positive."

"I don't know, Elliott. He was certain. He said it was *guaranteed*. I laughed at the time, said we still needed to vote. But he patted my hand, said he might even be vice chair."

My antenna went up and I leaned forward. "We don't have a vice chair position."

"I know, right? That's what's bugging me. He was so certain."

The same uniformed server swung by with a fresh platter of cake, asking if we were *sure* we wouldn't like some cake. We declined again, and Whitney stood to leave.

"One last thing," I said. "Leo put together a fantastic proposal for an innovative homeless center. It's called the Shelter Initiative and it will have the full Ballantyne support. Could you chair the committee?"

"Sorry, Elliott. I'm swamped with work right now, I just don't have the time. But I bet anyone else would love to take it over."

You'd think so. "Thanks for the info on Leo at the party, I appreciate it." I stood and picked up my nearly empty tray with the now wilted puffs. "Don't forget to stuff your purse with cake."

She laughed. "Right. It'll go great with the chocolate pie I'm having for dinner."

I slowly walked down to the pool. I gathered empty plates and glasses from the short side tables next to teak chaise lounges and reclining chairs. Very few guests remained; most had left while Whitney and I chatted.

I thought about Leo. What was he up to? How could he *guarantee* his seat on the board? Especially when the board chair absolutely despised him.

"Is bussing part of your director's job?" Ransom said from behind me, leaning on the porch rail.

I was lost in thought and hadn't noticed him. "According to Reena it is. Serving, bussing. I'm sure I'll have to scrub the floors before I'm allowed to leave. I'm not an important board member, you know, just the lowly director."

"She can be slightly snobbish."

"That's one way of putting it." The tray in my hands grew heavy as I stood there. "Well, okay, then," I said and stepped away.

"Wait. Elliott. I meant what I said earlier. You handled the hotel manager really well. I was impressed."

I slowly turned back and looked at him. He wore the same snug crewneck shirt and tailored trousers from our trip to Savannah. He looked good. Confident, assured, charming.

"I suppose I should say thank you."

But I couldn't. It still stung like a fresh slap and the embarrassment rushed back. I gripped the tray so tight, I feared the handles might snap off.

I saw Reena approaching even though my eyes never left Ransom's. I smiled wide and raised my voice. "I'm so sorry I ran out of the hotel this morning. You were a devil, but I really did have a wonderful time with you. Breakfast was divine."

A flicker of confusion touched his face and I winked and stepped right into Reena. "Oh. Reena," I stammered. "I didn't see you there." I shot a worried glance at Ransom and scurried away.

Take that, asshole. They totally deserved each other.

"What are you smiling about?" Tod asked when I set the tray down in the kitchen.

"Oh, just a little petty vengeance. Petty and satisfying."

Especially when I peeked and saw them in a heated discussion.

By now everyone had left except Tod and me, Reena and Ransom (who probably wouldn't be leaving), and Jane, who was in her own deep discussion on her cell by the pool.

"I guess we're on clean up duty as well," Tod said.

"We're not washing dishes. I draw the line at crusty plates. She may be our newest grantee, but I don't like her and I'm not doing her slimy dishes."

I walked over to the dessert table. "We'll just gather up the rest of the dirty plates and leftover food and get out of here."

The heavy, cut-crystal punch bowl I admired earlier from across the room was actually plastic and not so heavy. So I used way too much strength when I lifted it. Throw in my sassy attitude and a pair of new shoes on a slick marble floor and this is the result:

I tipped back, launching a bowl full of bright red punch into the air. Then in an effort to right myself, I slipped on the marble and threw the punch bowl away so I could break my fall. It didn't work. I landed on the once-white rug, flat on my ass, covered in punch. Just as Ransom walked through the door with Reena by his side, carrying a platter of sliced cake.

"What are you doing?" Reena gasped. "My sofa, my rug."

Tod rushed over. "Elli, are you all right?"

"Yes, I think," I said and held up my hands. "Be careful. The floor is really slippery."

"Slippery? You spilled punch on everything!" Reena cried. "You ruined a fifteen-thousand dollar rug."

I looked at the rug. Fifteen thousand? It looked like one of those shaggy Flokati things you get at Bed Bath & Beyond.

But ruined is ruined. I scrambled to my feet. I was dripping in punch, my white pants splattered and stained. My embarrassment deepened and I didn't know what to say. "It was an accident."

"An accident? Are you out of your mind? Your job is to clean up the messes, not make them. You...you did this on purpose." She came closer with a mad scowl on her face.

I stepped forward. "On purpose? Why would I do this on purpose?" I threw my hands in the air and caught the edge of her tray. Two pieces of cake plopped onto the floor.

"Don't you dare come after me!" She flung the entire tray at me.

Cake went everywhere.

A piece of vanilla cake with rich chocolate frosting hit me square in the chest and slid down my shift into my bra.

"You're so jealous, you can't stand it," Reena said. "I saw you drooling over my boyfriend. As if a man like that would ever settle for a glorified lackey like you."

I saw red. I scooped a fistful of petit fours from the dessert table and flung them at her perfectly made up face. "Boyfriend? What, did he give you his letterman's jacket and ask you to the prom?" Then I threw a thick slice of cake and it smacked her in the head, knocking the orchid from her hair.

She wiped away the icing and flicked it at me, then grabbed her own slice of cake and hurled it at me with the speed of a major league pitcher. "You throw like a girl. With such an inappropriate name, you should at least try to live up to it."

Within twenty seconds, Reena and I had completely decimated the dessert table, trays, and scraps from the floor.

"Have you lost your mind?" Jane said. She slammed the sliding glass door behind her. "Jesus, Elliott. *You're* the one helping me beat a murder rap?" She turned to Ransom who was grinning in the corner next to Tod. "You might as well take me now, Detective."

"Oh stuff it, Jane," I said.

"Get out of my house," Reena said through clenched teeth. "I will be calling Edward Ballantyne to immediately withdraw my grant application."

I stuck my chest out, my chin up, and strode to the front door. The frosting on my palm made it difficult to turn the knob, but it finally twisted. I made sure to slam the door hard enough to shake the house.

"Son of a *bitch*," I said as I stomped to my car. I ripped my shoes off and tossed them on the grass.

"Elliott, wait," Tod said. He came out of the side gate. "Here, take these." He handed me a beach towel and laid another one over the driver's seat.

My hands shook so badly, I dropped my shoes twice trying to wipe them off. "Thanks."

"I'll give you points for originality. She now has a hell of a lot more than dishes to wash."

I climbed into the Mini, careful not to smear icing on the door. "The funny thing is, Tod, this wasn't even my most humiliating moment today."

He pulled a chunk of cake from my hair.

"Okay, maybe it was. But not by much."

"To live in your shoes for a day," he said wistfully.

He looked at me with such pity, tears sprang into my eyes. He went to pat my goop-covered hand, and settled on a small spot on my left wrist. "I'll talk to Reena about her grant. She won't call Mr. Ballantyne."

"Did you see her, Tod? She's furious. Rip-off-my-head, get-me-fired furious."

"Yes, well, furious or no, she'll never pass up the opportunity to lord this over you for the rest of your life."

"Perfect."

I backed out before anyone else came out of the house. I took First Street to Ocean, then cut over to Palmetto Drive. As I sat at the light, hot tears streaked down my cheeks. I touched my beautiful shift, now splattered with punch and chocolate and raspberry sauce. It was ruined. My pants and shoes, too. No amount of soaking or dry cleaning could save them.

It broke my heart. I checked out my face in the mirror. The tears left matching tracks of mascara, pudding, and sticky sauce on my cheeks. What a disaster. I had destroyed my best clothes. Ones I couldn't afford to replace.

"I'm a fool," I said as I passed through the Oyster Cove gate. I had hoped Ransom would be at the party. I wanted him to see me as a professional, not an amateur to be toyed with. Now he'd never consider me a colleague to be taken seriously. I made a fool of myself again. While he watched, laughing at me in the corner. Not to mention hurling handfuls of petit fours at his girlfriend.

That bitch made fun of my name. Who over the age of twelve makes fun of someone else's name? I didn't choose my own name, for shit's sake. Having been told they were having a boy, my parents chose the name Elliott. When I popped out a girl, they decided not to hassle with choosing something different.

I parked in the garage, but walked around the outside to the patio. I didn't want to add insult to injury and ruin *my* rugs, too. I unlocked the sliding door and grabbed a towel from a shelf behind the quilt rack. I also grabbed my robe. I kept them there in case I needed an outdoor shower. Usually from a day at the beach, not a food fight.

I carried them to the side of the house. In the center of the walk, attached to the house, was a lava rock shower larger than a decent walk-in closet. The walls were only six feet high and the top wide open to the sky. It was blocked from view by a high hedge along the back and side lot lines, and a gate at the front.

After hanging the towel and robe on a hook, I stripped off my sticky clothes, and took my third shower of the day. I kept the water turned on hot. I washed the pastry from my hair and the frosting from my cheeks, but couldn't do anything about the humiliation in my heart.

I cried for the first half of the shower. Mourned my beloved floral shift and fabulous red slingbacks. Poured out my sorrow for the Batman hero who crushed me, letting me interview a hotel clerk as a joke. Who laughed at my humiliation. Tears of frustration over a woman who launched a tray of desserts at me and threatened my life at the Ballantyne, whom I hated but was stuck with for years to come.

But man, that last custard tart slapped her right in the nose. My tears turned to laughter for the second half of the shower. I giggled and enjoyed the freedom. Of being naked under a warm sky. Of kicking ass with that hotel clerk—I so got the information I wanted. And for letting the cake fly. She definitely had more than just dishes to wash.

"Fifteen thousand dollar rug, my ass. You better get yourself on over to Bed Bath, & Beyond, babe. I should've slung a little cake at Batman. See what you think of that!"

I danced around until the water cooled. I put on my robe and snuggled on the back deck with a six pack of Dos Equis and a hot dog. I updated my notes on the investigation, omitting the unlady-like incidents, of course. The day wasn't a total bust. I had glommed one interesting piece of information on Leo: his confidence on keeping his seat. Not sure if it was worth getting pudding up my nose, but it was something.

FIFTEEN

I spent Saturday morning cleaning the cottage. The last week had been messy. Both emotionally and literally. I took stock of my life with a wet sponge in one hand and a can of gritty cleanser in the other. My verdict: who cares about a few embarrassing moments? I can't possibly be the first person to hurl a pastry tray during a luncheon.

And it doesn't matter that Ransom witnessed both of my downward spirals. He even caused one of them. He's an ex-crush. A man, no, a boy, I once knew. Once loved. Who made my heart pound and my insides tingle. Stop it. I have a fabulous cottage on the beach and a fantastic wardrobe. Both of which are equal in value, by the way. I don't wear the fancy dresses every day and I don't have much money left over, but I don't need it. I ride my bike to work. I have friends who love me. I live on an island. Who doesn't want to be me?

So I scrubbed, vacuumed, washed, and mopped the entire place from baseboard to ceiling fan. It was cathartic. It restored my balance to physically scrub my life clean.

I showered and dressed for my meeting with Carla and Chef Carmichael. I tucked a bottle of water into my bike basket and rode the two miles to the Big House. Ten miles of bike paths wound through Oyster Cove Plantation, skirting the landscaped roads and golf course greens from the Big House to the beach cabanas to the country club clubhouse, and all paths in between.

I parked near the side door and entered the mudroom. The aroma of fresh-brewed coffee drifted over me. I may not drink it, but I do love the rich nutty smell of roasted grounds.

Walking into the kitchen, I faced the battle of the seafood soup: she-crab bisque vs. shrimp gumbo. Fighting for team bisque was Wharf head chef Paul Carmichael, two-time award-winner. In the other corner—or on the opposite side of the steel island wielding a butcher knife—was renowned Ballantyne chef Carla Otto, holding her own for the survival of the gumbo.

"It's my kitchen and I decide. I'm all for sharing the love, Carmichael, but I've decided on gumbo," Carla said.

"I'm co-catering, Carla, so I get to co-decide. My name is attached. The guests will be expecting my signature bisque."

"Attached to what? The party's in four days. No one even knows you're here. You can co-decide the salad. Maybe I'll let you choose the dressing."

"Hi guys," I interrupted. "Getting the menu worked out?" I walked around the island until I stood with Carla on my left and Chef Carmichael on my right.

"I am," Carla said.

I held up my hand before Chef Carmichael could speak. I came prepared for this particular standoff, considering it's the same one they launched three years ago.

"Picture this," I said. "It's summertime. Late afternoon, outside on the lawn. A bright sun still blazing like a red devil in a blue sky. Now I ask you, why are you serving hot soup?"

Carla opened her mouth, then shut it. A full minute of silence followed. "Well, huh," she said. "I guess crisp salad greens might make a better first course."

"Maybe not salad greens. I'd serve spinach leaves with wine poached pears and applewood smoked bacon," Chef Carmichael said.

Carla started scratching notes on the pad in front of her. "We could go Southern lowcountry. I've got a fantastic blackened catfish with Carolina dirty rice."

"It needs my habanero chutney," Carmichael said.

"Don't forget us non-seafood folk," I said.

Carla snapped her fingers. "Buttermilk fried chicken."

"With collard greens and cracked pepper biscuits," Carmichael added.

Carla pulled a bottle of wine from a wine cooler beneath the counter. The Ballantyne has a large wine cellar, but Carla keeps the kitchen stocked with her favorites. For cooking, and for drinking while she's cooking.

Carmichael examined the bottle, then exchanged it for a different one. He started to uncork the sleek black bottle, using a complicated silver corkscrew thingy while Carla grabbed a crystal decanter with a fat base and skinny neck.

"Okay, then. My work here is done. I'll be in my office if you need me," I said, but they weren't listening. It seemed as if they were finally able to work in some sort of harmony.

"Pecan pie for dessert, I think," Carla said. "With bourbon caramel."

"Too blasé. My apple cobbler with brown sugar ice cream is much more impressive."

"Blasé?" Carla snapped back.

So maybe not harmony, I thought as I walked to my office. But at least I didn't have to hide the knives before I left.

The Big House was quiet. Yellow sunlight streamed through the windows, warming the empty rooms. It was peaceful with no one around, almost lazy. Until I reached my office. I had six messages from varying media outlets, from the Atlanta Journal-Constitution to the Miami Herald. All wanting quotes regarding Jane's imminent arrest. I jotted down phrases about Jane assisting the police as opposed to being wanted by them.

On the bright side, I had only a single piece of mail. An invitation to Jane's sewing machine auction on Tuesday, addressed to Mr. Ballantyne. I sank into my chair and stared out the window, watching a butterfly and a bumblebee jockey for position on a pink daisy.

I needed progress on the case, and soon. I couldn't avoid the press or Mr. Ballantyne or Reena Patel's threat to tattle. But I had no answers. Just random tangents with nothing to tie them to. Ransom liked Jane as the killer, but I wasn't so sure. Though maybe he wasn't either since he hadn't arrested her. What was he waiting for? More evidence?

He had the trophy and Jane's flip words for Leo to shove it up his ass. Not exactly a death threat. He also had the ripped form for the committee Jane swore she'd kill, and at least one eyewitness saw her at the scene. Well, near the scene. There's certainly a difference.

Maybe the red vee-dub stood in Ransom's way. A late night visitor actually at the murder scene was stronger than one driving a block away. Since he so dramatically confirmed Bebe was not home, the car belonged either to a friend of Leo's or Travis's.

Was it the mysterious Dee's, Leo's lover? It fit. But who was she? A customer, a member of the country club, a local vendor? What kind of business associate stops by at midnight? The kind who sells more than appliances, I bet. Drugs? Sex? A truckload of stolen toasters?

And why not a high schooler? Travis was out with someone, it just wasn't Derek. Maybe Travis has a girlfriend. She could've zipped him over there. Travis argues with his father, then kills him. Travis lied about his alibi, why not the murder?

I flipped through my notebook. Something else Ransom said. The weekly withdrawals. I connected them to the weekly poker game, but what about the deposits? Even a mediocre player wins sometimes or at least breaks even. Why wasn't Leo putting the money back into his account? Either a) he was spending large chunks of cash on something each week or b) he sucked at poker.

I looked up Milo Hickey's address in the phone book. According to Bebe, Milo hosted the game on Saturday nights. I checked the map on my wall. It listed every street on the island, even color coding each plantation. I found his address in Haverhill Plantation. Very swank.

My desk phone rang. No more stalling. I took a deep breath and picked it up on the third ring. "Elliott Lisbon."

"Elli, my dear!" Mr. Ballantyne shouted into the phone. "So glad to catch you!"

"Yes, sir," I shouted back, then lowered my voice to normal. "Just getting ready for the Gatsby. Looking forward to having you home."

"Indeed. Which is why I'm calling. I fear we've been away too long. I've received disturbing news from the Charlotte Observer. Seems our Jane is at the heart of a scurrilous article."

How did they track him down in freaking India? Scoundrels. I grabbed my earlier press notes and starting scribbling. "I'm composing a statement as we speak, sir. Nothing to worry about. I'm working with several media outlets, expressing Jane's cooperation working with the police to find those responsible for Leo's death."

"On that front, too, Elli. I thought you would've made more progress. He deserves justice, he deserves everything we've got."

"Agreed, sir. I'm making serious headway. Discreetly, of course."

"Discretion! The school board fears this murder investigation will overshadow their participation in the Gatsby, and I must say, my dear, I do worry."

The school board was an ally we couldn't afford to lose. "I'm on it, sir. I'll work with the coaches, make sure we have plenty of students on hand for the Gatsby celebration. It will be fantastic."

"Very good, my dear. Very good!" Mr. Ballantyne hollered, sounding relieved. "Just what I wanted to hear. Anything else you need to tell me?"

I stopped pacing and stared at the phone, quickly debating about Reena. Should I tell him I got in a food fight with the head of his pet project? Wrecked her rug, destroyed her desserts, called her names? I hated being indebted to that nasty woman, but Mr. Ballantyne was already stressed at the state of the Ballantyne. No sense worrying him needlessly. Better to wait until things eased up.

"All's well, sir. Just looking forward to having you home."

"Tally-ho!"

"Tally-ho," I said and clicked off.

I immediately called the coach at the middle school with invitations for the entire softball team plus their parents. Then armed with my freshly scratched out statement and a pitch for a fabulous photo op, I grabbed the stack of press messages and started dialing. I slapped a smile on my face so my voice would sparkle with confidence and grace. An hour later, hassled and drained, I hung up with the last out-of-state reporter. My hand cramped and my ear burned, but I felt pretty confident the media was on my side.

Three minutes later, my phone rang.

"I knew you'd be working," Sid said.

"A friendly voice. I'm so grateful, I may never hang up."

"Listen, I only have a minute. But my darling Dr. Marco canceled for tonight and I don't feel like staying home. Care to come out for margaritas? I made reservations at the Mariposa for eight."

"I'd love to. But awfully presumptuous to assume I'd be free."

She laughed. "Of course you're free. What else would you do on a Saturday night? It's not like you're going out with Matty on a date night."

"How little you know, Sigrid Bassi. Matty's changed the rules."

"Ooh. I like the sound of that."

"I'll tell you all about it tonight, my dear. See you at eight."

But I was going to need more than margaritas to explain about Matty and my twin breakdowns with Ransom. Definitely sangria or tequila shots.

Sangria? I flipped to the last page of notes. Wine futures. Sid didn't know which board member was involved, but it wasn't a stretch to connect it to Leo. A big hush-hush investment scheme and a murder. Quite a coincidence for one small board.

Leo could've invested his weekly poker take on wine futures. Maybe a deal gone bad? Do wine futures deals go bad? I didn't know what they were, but I knew two wine-drinking chefs who might.

I hit the kitchen hoping for lunch and information. I wasn't disappointed on either front. Carla asked me to set the table in the solarium, a bright square room behind the kitchen. It had floor-to-ceiling windows on three sides and a flat glass ceiling. It overlooked the vegetable garden. Metal Folk Art chickens pecked in the dirt between tall leafy bell pepper plants and garlic going to seed. In the distance, the gardener scooped a lone frog from the pool. Every night a battalion of tiny green chorus frogs no bigger than walnuts dove into the pool. They swam. They frolicked. They got caught in the filter. By morning, they clung to the side tile, unable to make it over the lip of the pool, waiting to be scooped out and set free.

Chef Carmichael poured the wine (white for me, red for them) while Carla served plates of sliced beef tenderloin with grilled grape tomatoes. She added a loaf of crusty French bread and an almond-fried brie topped with cranberry chutney. The filet was so tender, it practically melted in my mouth. I needed these two to fight all the time. I love eating like royalty without doing any of the cooking.

"What can you tell me about wine futures?" I asked.

"I'm afraid you got me there, Elli," Carla said. "I've never invested in them."

"Neither have I," Carmichael said.

"But you can explain them?"

"Sure," Carmichael said. "Wait one moment." He left the table and returned with an empty red wine glass. He poured a small amount from the decanter. "Here, taste."

"It's nice," I said.

It wasn't really, not to me anyway. But only because all red wines taste like communion wine to me. Although maybe it's not so bad to have little reminders of faith. But I didn't think that's what Chef Carmichael was going for.

"This bottle of Punto Final Malbec was grown in 2010, the vintage year on the label," he said. "But that's not the year it was bottled, it's the year the grapes were harvested. Simply put, after the harvest, it's made into wine, then stored in wooden barrels to age. At that stage, the wine is young, not fully developed. Vintners bring investors in—connoisseurs, retailers, and collectors—to taste the wine from the barrel."

He swished the wine in his glass, then slowly inhaled the fragrance. "These investors purchase the wine right then, at the barrel tasting, before it's bottled."

"What's the advantage?" I asked.

"Price and availability. Say you buy a case at fifty dollars a bottle. Two years later when it hits the shelves, it's at two hundred dollars a bottle. You receive your case at the same time as the stores, but you've paid almost two thousand less. Also, some vintages produce fewer bottles, which means less availability. Good old-fashioned supply and demand. More demand, the price rises again. If you purchased two, three, five cases, your investment pays off in spades."

"And the disadvantages?" I spread a layer of brie on a chunk of bread and popped it into my mouth.

"If the wine doesn't improve with age, basically it's not much better than when you tasted it two years earlier. Its shelf price is fifty dollars a bottle or less. Even if you break even, you end up with cases of wine crowding your wine cellar, wine you could've bought by the bottle at your local liquor store."

"Can investing in wine futures be dangerous?"

"It can certainly be risky. It started in the Bordeaux region. They've been doing it for centuries, but it's relatively new in the U.S. Very few wineries even offer wine futures. One or two in Santa Barbara, Napa. You must choose highly reputable, established wineries. With any investment opportunity, you must watch out for sleazy ventures. Worst case scenario, you invest thousands of dollars in wine that's worth less than hundreds."

I tasted the red wine again. It made me wonder. Did Leo stumble onto a phony wine futures scheme? Or was he running one?

SIXTEEN

After we cleaned up lunch, I rode my bike home and spent the day at the beach recharging my batteries and crafting a plan. But two hours of sun netted me nothing but a splotchy burn. I sketched out seventeen theories on Leo's murder and damn it if every last one didn't end with Jane in handcuffs. Thank God there were margaritas in my immediate future.

The Mariposa was located mid-island in Locke Harbor, a one-hundred boat marina with shops and restaurants overlooking the Intracoastal Waterway. I parked near the center entrance. A band playing Beach Boys favorites entertained a small crowd around an enormous statue of Poseidon. I cut to the left, walking along the boardwalk. A miniature amphitheater faced the harbor to my right where folks gather on Tuesday nights for a colorful fireworks display.

A hostess greeted me, but I spotted Sid at a table to the right of a massive bar and joined her. High-backed barstools surrounded it on all four sides with a take-out section at the far end.

"Hey, sweetie," I said. I kissed her cheeks and plopped into an empty chair. A fresh frozen margarita in a cobalt blue glass awaited me. I handed her a bag containing my cake-stained tunic and pants. "I need your help with a small stain. I spilled punch on my new outfit and I'm hoping you can salvage it."

"Oh, a little punch shouldn't be hard." She pulled the tunic from the bag. It was crumpled and deep red splotches and colorful cake smears coated the once bright white background topped with brown flowers. "Elliott, sweetie, what in the world did you do?"

"Just a minor mishap involving a punch bowl and a platter of petit fours. I may have taken a wee tumble." I snorted out a laugh. "You should see the other guy."

"Tell me you're kidding."

The combination of her shock and awe made me rethink dishing up the details. I had a feeling they were actually worse than she imagined. "Um, not exactly. But I changed my mind. I really don't want to talk about it."

"Cleaning this will take a miracle," Sid said. "But if I succeed, you're going to tell me everything. You got me?"

After I agreed, we spent the next hour and a half eating enchiladas and catching up on life. Sid bemoaned the problems on the board at the hospice. But since no one was murdered or accused of murder, my board troubles trumped hers. For now, anyway. And she sold two houses this month, which in this economy is like finding a golden nugget the size of a gumball in your pan two years after the Gold Rush ended. You didn't strike it rich, but it was enough to keep you in pans and picks until you did.

"Speaking of real estate," Sid said. "I found the new Buffalo Bill's location. Five acres in Summerton near the river, just like you thought. I can take you to see it this week if you like."

"I like," I said. "Anything special about it?"

"Depends on who you ask. In real estate, one man's paradise is another man's money pit."

"Worth a peek. I'm not making much progress with anything else. And the media is killing me. I've called in every favor I ever earned to keep Tate Keating calm. The last article dragged out every Ballantyne scandal back to when the senior Mr. Ballantyne wore short pants on the golf course."

Sid scraped the last of her enchilada from the colorful plate and cleaned the spoon. "So not going well, huh?"

"I have no faith in Jane Hatting's innocence and Nick Ransom doesn't play fair."

"What's the deal with you two anyway?"

I took a long sip of my melting margarita and my tongue tingled as I thought about Ransom. "Pure chemistry. He picked me up for our first date, but we never made it to the restaurant. From that night on, we spent every minute together. All talking and touching and kissing and dreaming. Then he was gone. Like Keyser Söze into the night. Now when I see him, I'm torn between the desire to hate him forever and the desire to finish what we started."

"Geez, sweetie, that's a lot to carry around."

"Tell me about it. And then there's Matty. He gave me a toe-curling, throw-me-against-the-truck, hand-under-my-shirt good-night kiss that said I don't want to go home, I want to go inside. One more minute, I would've dragged him ass over teakettle into the back seat of his cruiser, Ransom be damned."

"Matty did that? Holy shit. Definitely a game-changer."

"I know! And I think I *like-him*, like-him, and I never even knew it. As if someone turned the kaleidoscope one click and now everything's all sparkly and bright. And my emotions are running super high. I'm all awkward and blurty and inappropriate." I took a gulp of margarita. "Hence the pudding pants."

"Well, there's nothing wrong with getting a little dirty." She patted my hand. "Just load up on the sanitizer and stay in the game. You might have some fun."

"I don't know. Even one of them is more than I can handle. Matty doesn't appreciate Ransom and Ransom doesn't appreciate my investigative efforts."

"Be careful. The killer may not appreciate them either," Sid said. "Remember the shoes? That ended badly, Elli."

"She was crazy, Sid."

"Murder's crazy. The gal only stole shoes. You're investigating a killer. They won't like your poking around and they might let you know it."

"I'll be super careful and stay away from dangerous situations," I promised.

Sid glanced at her watch. "We should get the check. It's late."

"Good idea. There's a guy at a secret poker game I need to question. I think Leo was involved in something."

Sid stared at me.

"What?"

"Can you even *recognize* a dangerous situation?"

"It's just poker."

"Those games are dangerous. Guns, Elli. *Guns*. Lots of cash lying around. The mob runs secret poker games. They draw all kinds of unsavory characters."

"Uh-huh."

"Listen to me. It's no place for a girl like you. You can't go driving around in that kind of neighborhood alone," Sid said and leaned across the table to grip my arm. "Who knows what type of slimy lowlifes will be there."

"It's in Haverhill Plantation. I'm pretty sure it's a safe neighborhood."

"In a house bought with illegal gambling money," Sid argued. "Filled with desperate gamblers risking their paychecks. What happens when they lose? They see a pretty little thing like you, way out of her element?"

I pictured Milo Hickey in his beige Tommy Bahama. He didn't seem so desperate. But I relented. "Fine, I'll skip it. I can't get in anyway. I'll meet with Milo in a nice public place. Maybe the cereal aisle at the supermarket."

"You'll thank me later," Sid said.

I excused myself to go to the ladies room and heard her mutter behind me, "When she's not lying in the gutter from a gunshot wound, then she'll thank me."

On the way back to the table, I spotted her boyfriend, Marco, at the take-out window at the bar. He was dressed in tan slacks and a loose linen shirt. He spun his keys around his finger while he waited.

I slipped into my chair and whispered, "Isn't that your date?"

He was handsome in a movie star way with thick brown hair and bright green eyes. He had a rakish mole on his cheek. I met him two weeks earlier over dessert. It was supposed to be for dinner, but he and Sid didn't make it on time. Something about an emergency surgery, but I figured it was an operation of a different kind, judging from Sid's mussy hair and glowing cheeks.

"Why did he cancel on you tonight?" I asked.

"Sick mother. I guess she's been ill for a while now. This is his second cancellation this week."

We both leaned forward to the center of the table with our heads low, instinctively ducking beneath his sightline. Though he had no interest in the dinner crowd. Not with a young barmaid in a tight short skirt standing next to him.

"He's dressed awfully fancy for visiting a sick mother," I said. "And it's kind of late for dinner."

Sid didn't say anything. She just watched him, leaning against the bar, spinning his keys. "Maybe I should say hello."

"Maybe we should follow him."

She slid her gaze to me. "Follow him?"

"See what he's up to. If you say hello now, he'll obviously tell you he's going to his mother's. Doubt will stick with you like a song you can't get out of your head."

"I'm forty-five, Elliott. I can't follow him."

"Of course you can. There's no age limit." I grabbed my wallet and threw forty bucks on the table. "Every girl over the age of sixteen has the right to follow her man when he's out where he shouldn't be. It's practically expected."

"It's stalking," Sid said. "Would you follow Ransom?"

"No."

"Matty?"

"Look, woman, this isn't about me." I slung my hipster crossways over my shoulder. "It's now or never."

Marco laughed at something a cute young waitress said, then watched her walk away.

"Fine," Sid said.

We inched out of our chairs and snuck out the door. Cut through the shops, straight to the lot, avoiding the center entrance.

"That's his car," Sid said as we passed a black Porsche 911 at the curb.

"Perfect. Now we have a starting point."

Sid walked to the left, while I went to the right.

"Where are you going?"

"To my car," she said. "It's more comfortable than yours. And faster."

"And more obvious."

"What about drinking, are you okay to drive?" Sid said.

"Yep. I'm more worried about the six glasses of water I drank. Come on, he'll be here any second." We hustled to my car and climbed in to wait.

"Well, at least put the top down," she said.

"Sure, Sid. With your five feet of hair billowing around next to my bright red head, we might as well hook onto his bumper and honk the horn all the way down Cabana Boulevard."

"Well, excuse me for not knowing the proper way to stalk someone."

"Look, there he is."

Marco appeared around the corner of the last shop carrying a white takeout bag. He hopped into the Porsche. Twenty seconds later he pulled out of the lot.

"Hurry up, you're going to lose him," she said as I slid between two cars on Cabana. "Shouldn't you turn off your headlights so he can't see you?"

"A car without headlights grabs attention. Every oncoming car will flash their brights at us."

He drove south on Cabana in the left lane. I stayed one car back. He drove sedately through traffic, then punched the gas and cut to the right. He passed a mini-van on the left, then cut back over.

"Shit," I said. "Do you think he saw us?"

"No, that's just the way he drives."

The Porsche flew into the turn lane at Ocean Boulevard. He swung a U-turn and passed us going the other direction.

By the time I got to the light, it was already yellow. I floored the gas and zipped into the turnaround. "Do you see him?"

Traffic cleared and I sped north on Cabana.

"Up ahead, four cars on the right," she said.

I passed an enormous sedan on the left, trying to make up the distance as fast as the Mini would let me.

"He's turning into Sugar Hill. Hurry, Elli, the light's going to turn again."

"For someone who didn't want to follow him, you sure are into this." I hit the right curve, barely slowing as I popped onto Sugar Hill Drive.

"It's a rush," she said. "No wonder you love your investigations so much."

We approached the security hut directly behind Marco, but I kept back at least thirty feet. He rolled through while the guard waved him on.

"That's a good sign, right?" I said. "He must come here a lot, probably has a sticker. You can do that if your relatives live here."

But I didn't have a sticker or a pass or a relative and had to stop.

A guard in a tan uniform ambled forward. "Yes, ma'am?" He was ninety years old if a day and resembled Buddy Hackett.

"We're here for drinks at Molly's on the Beach," I said.

"Okay, then. Nice night for it. Let me get you a ticket," he said and slowly entered the guard shack.

"He's getting away, Elli. His taillights are almost gone."

I watched the two red pinpoints shrink in the distance. Then they disappeared. "I think it's just the curve in the road. We'll catch up." I willed grandpa Buddy to move faster. Come on, come on. My palms were sweaty from gripping the steering wheel and I had to pee like a racehorse.

Buddy finally moseyed over and held out the pass. It took the willpower of a saint not to snatch the pink paper from his grasp.

"Now, you know how to get—"

"We're good, thank you," I hollered and slammed the gas.

"He's gone," Sid said. "We lost him."

"We didn't lose him, just keep looking." I floored it, speeding around the curvy road at fifty-two with a posted limit of twenty-five.

"There, there, there," Sid said and tapped the windshield at a pair of taillights. They flashed bright red as he braked. "Might be someone else, but it looks like his lights."

"I think so, too." I reached the side street he turned onto and followed. The street was deserted. I slowed. "Look in the driveways." The homes were dark, very few had their porch lamps on. The only street light was at the corner stop sign where we had turned.

We rounded a sharp curve and I spotted his car. "On the right, Sid. Duck, quick."

"I can't duck in this car. It's smaller than a soup can."

"Well, turn around then for shit's sake."

He was just climbing out of his car as we passed, but he didn't pay attention to us. I whipped into a driveway six houses down on the left for another U-turn, then parked on the opposite side of the street, facing Marco. He carried the takeout bag to the porch and rang the bell.

"I'm going to feel like an idiot when his mother answers the door," Sid said.

I didn't say anything because I knew what was coming. Who rings the doorbell at their mother's house?

A short woman in a silky black slip answered the door. Five seconds ticked by with smiles and gestures. Then he kissed her. Passionately. Hands in her hair, then all over the slip. He pushed through the front door and kicked it shut with his foot.

"Well, shit."

"I'm sorry, Sid."

"Screw this. Let's go to the poker game."

SEVENTEEN

"Really? Are you okay?"

"Sure. I felt something coming anyway, just didn't want to see it," Sid said. "But screw him. Let's make a night of it. I'm all hopped up on adrenaline and margaritas."

I squeezed her hand, then reached for my phone to dial Tod.

"You calling the poker guy?"

I shook my head. "We're uninvited guests. We need to start with a pass to get through the gate."

"Hello," Tod said.

"Hey Tod, did I wake you?"

"I haven't been asleep before midnight on a Saturday since I was thirteen. You should try it some time."

"So it's a no, then?" I said.

"Can we put the top down now?" Sid said, reaching for the button.

I slapped her hand away. "No, Sid, not yet."

"Well, why not?"

"Because Casanova over there might see us. He may be a shit, but it's still bad form to get caught out front."

"Elli, what are you doing now?" Tod asked.

"I need a gate pass for Haverhill Plantation," I said to Tod. "Can you get me in?"

"Like I said, what are you up to? A little B and E, kidnapping a suitor, perhaps another food fight?"

"Nothing like that. Exactly. Can you get me the gate pass or not?"

"Of course. Try not to get arrested."

"I'll do my very best."

"By the way, we've had twelve cancellations for the Gatsby, and I expect more tomorrow," Tod said.

"What? Why?"

"Seems some folks don't want to mingle with a murderer. You're not doing so well on your investigation."

"Alleged murderer, Tod, and I'm working on it," I said and clicked off.

I started the car and drove to the stop sign with the headlights off. Once we cleared the guard shack and stopped at the light, I put the top down.

We drove down Cabana to Haverhill Drive, a short ride to the guard gate. Unlike our last destination with ace security officer Grandpa Buddy, Haverhill Plantation was locked down tighter than a military base, complete with an intimidating soldier defending the entrance.

A tall black man in full dress uniform, including service bars and a stiff hat, greeted us. "Ma'am?" he said with an expressionless face.

I noted the Glock on his utility belt and cleared my throat. "Yes, hello. You should have a pass for me. Elliott Lisbon."

"Identification?"

I rifled through my hipster. My driver's license was tucked in a zipper pouch. I handed it to him and he disappeared into the hut.

"How can Tod get us a pass?" Sid said.

"Shhh. Discretion," I whispered. "I don't ask, he just does."

The sentinel approached the car. "It's good for tonight only," he said. He slid a blue pass onto my dash.

"Thank you."

I cruised past the raised gate arm, maintaining the speed limit down to the mile. Massive live oak trees lined the main drive on both sides. The branches met in the middle, creating a canopy of leaves and dangling moss. Landscape lights rested at the base of every tree to light our path.

I turned right on Magnolia Avenue, then another right on Cypress Court. Each house we passed was a different architecture: Georgian, Charleston, Tudor, Colonial. The last one on the block was a sprawling French country estate with a stone front and ivy covered courtyard wall. Milo Hickey's house.

We were definitely late to the party. I counted seven cars parked in the drive. Each with a sticker price higher than my annual salary times two.

"So far the neighborhood doesn't look so bad," I said as I slowly drove past the house.

"No kidding."

I parked at the end of the cul de sac, switched off the headlights and turned to Sid. "Can you climb a wall in those shoes?"

"What are you talking about?"

"We can't just stroll up the walk. They'll never let us in. Did you see the bruiser out front? Looks like he could smash my car just by leaning on it."

"No, I'm not climbing a wall in my Josef Seibels."

"Well, flip them off, because we're going over." I shoved my keys in my pocket and my hipster under the seat. I switched off the interior light as a precaution, then slid out.

We waddled like ducks on a promenade, hunched low, following the courtyard wall. It was thick and imposing, made from heavy cobblestone. I stopped thirty feet or so from the driveway, just out of the glow of the carriage lamps.

I turned to Sid in the shadows and whispered, "Any ideas how to scale this wall?"

She grabbed my arm and stood. The top of the wall hit her shoulders. "It's more like a brick hedge." She placed her palms flat on brick tops and hopped. With a quick swing of her left leg, she straddled both sides. She reached down. "Take my hand."

I gripped her right palm with my left and she pulled. I almost screamed. "Jesus, woman, you're yanking my arm out of the socket." I grasped onto several strands of ivy growing on the wall for balance. They were thick and strong, but I still managed to rip them clean off.

"Grab my leg, Tarzan," she said. "But with the skirt, not just my skin."

Clutching her leg with my other hand, I scrambled up the side. I conked my head into her hip, knocked her off balance, and we both landed in a lump on the other side. Thank God for boxwood bushes.

"Well, that was graceful," Sid whispered.

"Don't criticize my techniques. I'm still in training." I snapped open the lid on a small hand-sani bottle from my pocket. I rubbed my palms nearly raw and pretended there was no dirt under my fingernails.

The beefcake out front took a step in our direction and we froze in place. He passed beneath a gaslight lamp. He looked even larger up close. So did his gun. After a few steps, he turned back to the front walk.

We walked a slow wide circle around the perimeter, passing a small iron gate in the wall, before coming up to the side of the house. We crept up close to a picture window and peeked inside. An oak-paneled study with three men in dark suits. They looked expensive. Polished fabrics, silky ties. All three carried guns.

"I can't believe you were right about the guns," I whispered.

"If you didn't believe me, why are we squatting in the azaleas?"

A low growl echoed to my right, toward the back of the house. A sharp bark followed, then faded.

"We should go," Sid said. "There's an alarm, I can see the pad. And this window has a shield sticker."

"It could be a fake sticker. You can get them on eBay."

"Well those aren't fake." She pointed through the glass at a very large flat screen monitor. Black and white images flicked on the screen. The outside steps. Flick. The driveway. Flick. The swimming pool. Flick.

I smashed myself against the house. "Oh shit, we gotta go."

Sid scrunched below the window sill. "Good idea. Back the way we came." The bushes shook as she crept along the side of the house.

"No, wait," I blurted out and grabbed her hand. The poker game was a real lead, and I couldn't afford to throw it away. "I have to get inside, Sid. I need information."

"What information?"

"I don't know," I said and threw my hands up in desperation. "But come on, we're already here, and this is my chance to get ahead of Ransom. No way he knows about this."

"How can you be so sure?"

"There'd be cop cars out front, not sports cars."

Another dog barked in the distance. Something rustled the pine straw beneath my feet, then scurried across my left flip-flop. I jumped back and slammed my heel into the house. "Son of a bitch," I groaned through clenched teeth.

"Probably just a lizard," Sid said.

I limped out of the bushes. "Well, I'm not staying out here."

"Fine. But let's think about this. How do these guys get in? Invitation?"

I shook my head in the darkness. "Probably not. Nothing in writing. No texts or email. Too easy to go viral, land on the wrong device."

"Okay. How about a password?"

"I like it," I whispered. "But it could be anything. Open, sarsaparilla. Open, Saskatchewan. Open, saddle soap. Open, sesame."

"Relax, Daffy Duck. I've got an idea." She fluffed out her hair and unbuttoned the top button on her blouse, then the next one.

"What are you doing?"

"We need a password. Now I'm the password. Let's go."

We crept back the way we came, along the courtyard wall to the small iron gate. It wasn't even latched. I opened it wide, then swung it closed with a bang so the guard wouldn't see unexpected shadows and shoot us.

A short path led straight to the driveway. The bulldozer met us in front of the open front door. He made the gate sentinel look like a ballet dancer. His shiny white head was attached directly to his collarbone.

Sid smiled. "Hello. We're here for the poker game."

He tilted his head and slowly swept his eyes down her body, from her silky brown hair to her shapely tan legs. She was impressive, I admit. If there was an Amazonian warrior Barbie who sold real estate, this is what she'd look like.

He whistled. "Sorry, doll, I don't know what you're talking about."

If he noticed the leaves in her hair, he didn't mention it.

Okay. Time for a different tactic. I casually brushed the dirt from my blouse. "I'm Elliott Lisbon with the Ballantyne Foundation. I'd like to speak with Milo Hickey, please."

"Not home."

"With all these cars?" I looked over my shoulder, then waved my arm for dramatic effect.

"Sorry, ladies." He started to close the door, but I slapped my palm on the raised wood surface to stop him.

He growled.

Okay. Time for a new different tactic. I knew there must be a password; I just didn't know what it was.

"Sorry. Please wait one second, I'm having trouble remembering the password," I said in a rush. What did Bebe say? A linebacker crab game? Well, this dude definitely fit that description. "Linebacker?"

His expression remained unchanged.

"Crab?"

Silence.

"I'm close, though, right?"

He didn't react, but he didn't slam the door either.

Wait, I thought. "Crabline?"

He hesitated, then stepped aside so we could pass. The foyer spilled into a beautiful living room with mustard yellow walls, arched windows, and polished walnut beams on the ceiling. Soft leather sofas faced a low mahogany table in the center.

"Definitely not a crack house," I whispered to Sid. "You must be so disappointed."

She nodded at the three security men in the hall, their backs to the flickering security screen in the study.

"This way, ladies," the bulldozer said. He led us up a wide staircase to the second floor landing. He held his hand out to the archway on the left.

Vegas had nothing on this private poker room. Fifty-inch flat screens hung on the walls, tuned to separate sporting events. A black granite kitchen and bar consumed the right corner. A full buffet stretched from the bar to the back door wall. Bowls of fresh salads sat on one end, while the other held sandwich meats. Not the thin kind served on flimsy metal trays, either. This buffet boasted a carving station with rare roast beef and honey-glazed ham.

An iron chandelier lit the room with matching sconces on the wall. The room smelled very manly: scotch, musky cologne, and rosemary crusted beef. Five men sat at a regulation poker table to the left, all holding cards and facing a dealer. Three of the men were over sixty, and one was a skinny kid who didn't look as if he'd reached the legal gambling age. Although that probably didn't matter much at an illegal poker game. The last man was Milo Hickey. Looking as debonair as an aristocrat on vacation. He rose when we entered and two beefy bouncer types strode forward to block us at the door.

"She knew the password," bulldozer said with a shrug.

I thrust out my hand. "Mr. Hickey, I'm Elliott Lisbon with the Ballantyne Foundation. This is my associate, Sigrid Bassi."

He smiled and shook my hand. "Very nice to meet you. Please, call me Milo."

He shook Sid's hand and held on for an extra beat. "We've met before. At last year's masquerade benefit for the hospital."

She smiled up at him. "Really? I think I would've remembered you."

"What can I do for you ladies? I'm sure you didn't come to join the game."

"Actually, Milo, you do have an empty seat," Sid said. "Would you mind?"

"Not at all." He raised his finger to the dealer, who nodded in return. "Five thousand dollar buy-in okay for you?"

I nearly choked, but Sid smiled like a kid at a carnival. "Absolutely." She turned to the table. "Good evening, gentlemen. I'm Sid."

"A drink, miss?" the young bar attendant asked her.

"Scotch, neat."

"And for you, Ms. Lisbon?" Milo asked.

"Nothing, but please, it's Elliott. Is there somewhere we can talk privately?"

He led me down the hall to a wood-paneled study. I spied a private bathroom through a tall door and asked to use the facilities. Five minutes later, we were sitting on a leather sofa facing a wide screen TV and a writing desk with a blank tablet on top.

"Is this the lounge?"

He laughed. "Actually, it is. Sometimes the players need to place a private phone call."

"Or shower before going home?"

"Sometimes. There's also a smoker's lounge on the patio."

"You have a lovely home," I said. "Not quite what I expected."

"And what did you expect?"

I felt my face flush. The words crack house and mob flashed in my mind. "Something less formal, I guess."

He smiled. "I'm a formal man."

He continued to smile while I racked my brain for a question. Nothing brilliant popped up, so I went with what I knew: generic party small talk. "May I ask what it is you do?"

He crossed his legs and rested his hands against his knee. He was also an elegant man. Sharp clothes, short black hair, smooth dark skin. "I'm the CEO of an asset management firm, Hickey Thompson Equities."

"I'm surprised you've never approached Mr. Ballantyne. His asset portfolio is considerable."

"Very interesting man, your Mr. Ballantyne. We met in London at a dinner for the ambassador. Now, are you interviewing me for the open seat on your board or is there something else I can help you with?"

"Would you mind answering some questions regarding Leo Hirschorn? I promise to be discreet with anything you tell me."

"Certainly. As long as I don't have any conflicts of interest."

"What type of conflicts?"

He tipped his head. "I'll let you know."

"Actually, I saw you on Thursday with Bebe Hirschorn at the Tidewater Inn. She didn't look too happy."

"No, she wasn't. I wanted to give her my condolences. She said Leo enjoyed the Saturday games. She thought maybe if he'd have gone to the game instead of the Ballantyne party, he'd be alive."

"I suppose that's true."

"I'm afraid I stuck my foot in it, so to speak. I told her Leo stopped coming months ago. I thought she'd feel better not wondering a 'what if' scenario."

"How'd that work out?"

"Not so well. Apparently Leo looked forward to the games, she said, never missed a single one."

"Ouch. So Leo stopped playing?"

"At least with us. In a way, we missed him."

I raised my brow. "Really?"

"It's more fun to take money from a man like Leo," Milo said. "He never stopped talking. Ever. Poker is a game of observation. Reading the table, not just your cards. Leo never shut up long enough to read anybody. Plus, his tell was like a loud speaker with a billboard kicker. Held a small red horseshoe in his hand when his cards sucked, and spun it around his index finger whenever he had three of a kind or better. It was like shooting fish in a barrel."

"Did he ever mention a woman named Dee?"

He shook his head. "No Dee that I remember. But if I had to guess, I'd say he had a woman on the side."

"What makes you say that?"

"Where else would he be on Saturday night?"

"Indeed," I said. I couldn't think of anything else, and I didn't want to press my luck. The gunmen still patrolled the halls. "I'll let you get back to your game. You'll probably need a new password now."

We stood and shook hands. He walked me back into the game room. Sid held cards in her right hand while she shuffled two stacks of chips with her left.

"How's it going?" I asked Sid.

"Great, Elli," she said. "You go on home, I could be awhile."

"I'll get her home safely," Milo said.

I wasn't sure. This may not have been a mob-owned crack house, but I still didn't know these people. And I'm pretty sure more than half of them were armed.

Milo must have read the skepticism on my face. "See the gentleman on her left? He's a circuit court judge," he whispered. "And the man on the end?"

I looked at the round man with a receding hairline and Ben Franklin spectacles. He looked vaguely familiar.

"Retired deputy from the Summerton County Sheriff's Department. Handled the murder of the New York couple on vacation three years ago, remember?"

I did remember. It was all over the news. The deputy personally arrested their son.

"She'll be fine," Milo said. "You have my word."

Sid stayed in the game, so I said goodnight.

Milo nodded at the bulldozer. He escorted me to my car. And didn't ask why I'd parked at the very end of the street.

"Good night, Ms. Lisbon. You drive careful."

"Thank you," I said.

Thoughts swirled in my head as I drove home. Looks like Leo really did have girlfriend. The little sneaker used the poker game as a cover while he diddled the mysterious Dee without detection. And his money management was just as sordid: bouncing checks *and* withdrawing large sums of cash. An interesting juxtaposition. So where was the money coming from and where was it going?

EIGHTEEN

Sunday started with a mission. I treated myself to the Pancake House in Summerton as a reward for my good idea. Yes, before I had the chance to see if the idea panned out. If I waited and it didn't, I wouldn't be entitled to a reward, would I? After devouring a plate-sized Big Apple pancake topped with crunchy sugar, I paid the bill and hit the road.

I headed for Pine Lake, a residential community near I-95 and the local USC campus. I turned off the highway and wound through a dense forest of scrub pine to the entrance. Pine Lake had a lovely guard shack done up Queen Anne style with a cupola on top, but no one to man it. I sailed through the open drive without having to charm my way into a day pass.

This particular development followed the less-is-more philosophy. As in less land, more neighbors. Short streets ran off the main drag, each crammed with tall Victorian houses pushed right to the curb. Tiny alleys threaded through the backyards so residents could hide their cars and their trash cans.

I found 327 Maple Lane easy enough and parked at the curb. I walked up the path to the side gate first and peeked over the fence. A dog barked wildly when my head popped into his view. A slobbery, smelly bulldog.

Beyond the fat yapper, parked under the carport, was a red VW bug. I smiled. I loved being right. Totally justified my victory breakfast, too. The adrenaline rush made me bold.

I scooted to the front door and rang the bell.

No answer.

I rang again, then knocked. "Come out, come out," I hollered. "I know you're in there." At least I hope you're in there, I thought. I'll be really embarrassed if I'm wrong and I'm pounding on the door like a showoff.

The door opened and Cherry stood with her hand on her hip.

"Hi, Cherry!" I said cheerily. "Mind if I come in?"

"You're awfully snappy this morning."

"I'm trying a new tactic. Plus, I discovered some juicy tidbits about Leo and his girlfriend. You'll want to hear this."

She eyed me warily, then opened the door wider, her guard sufficiently up. "Sure, I guess."

I followed her through the living room, past the dining room and a tidy alcove kitchen. Her decorating style was eighties music video. I think she held onto an unhealthy fascination with Devo's funky red hats a little longer than she should have, considering she wasn't even old enough to have lived it firsthand. Everything was totally new wave, in red, black, and white. Red leather sofa, black and white checked rug, red lamp shades, big plastic red lips on the wall. She even had red appliances: a shiny red KitchenAid mixer (the fancy one with all the attachments), red toaster, red blender. Actually, she had a lot of appliances. A bread maker, a juicer, a food processor, an espresso machine.

"Before you get any ideas I stole all those things you're gawking at, I paid for them. I get an employee discount. It's a perk."

She led me to a small screened porch at the back of the house. The dog continued to bark, protecting his dish of Gaines-Burgers as if I was the Hamburglar complete with a black mask, cape, and two sacks of stolen drive-thru all beef patties.

"So that's Donald," I said and sat on a metal lawn chair. A red one, naturally. "But she's a girl, right?"

"How'd you know?" Cherry lit a cigarette from an open pack next to her chair. She inhaled that sucker so long, I thought smoke might seep from her ears.

"Owen, Leo's neighbor. He said she left pee spots on the grass. Only female dogs do that."

"Huh, I didn't know," Cherry said between puffs.

"Why name her Donald?"

She smiled. "Leo's joke to drive Bebe crazy. He hated her cat."

It took me a minute, then I got it. "Oh, Ivana. Cute." I leaned back, trying to look casual. Hard to do in a chair as comfortable as a bus bench. "So, there is no Dee, right?"

She flicked ash into an overflowing ceramic ashtray with shaky hands. "Why do you say that?"

"Something I heard about Leo and a tiny red horseshoe. I remembered it from your desk the first time we met. Made me wonder why Leo would carry it as his lucky charm. Then I thought about the red car, your name's Cherry, and everything you own is red. Except for the dog."

"Listen, just because I have the dog, doesn't mean I killed Leo."

"But you were having an affair and you were at his house the night of the murder. I have to say, Cherry, it doesn't look too good."

"It doesn't mean I did it."

"It certainly doesn't clear you."

She took another long drag, then blew out a thick stream of acrid smoke. "What makes you think I was even there?"

"Because a neighbor saw your car in the driveway. And because you have his dog."

"*My* dog. Donald is my dog. Aren't you, girl?" At the sound of her name, Donald wagged her tail and Cherry opened the screen door to let her in. "Leo bought her as a gift, but my landlord freaked out. So Leo kept her for me, told Bebe she was a stray."

"What else did Leo do for you? Give you piles of money? Another part of the perk package?"

"What money?"

"Let's save a little time, shall we? I'm not here on a fishing expedition. I already have a pretty stellar catch. I know you were at

Leo's the night he was murdered. I know he gave you cash. Humungous sums of cash. But what was the money for?"

She ignored my question and stood. "I think you should go now."

Maybe bold wasn't working so well. I backtracked and added honey to my tone. "Tell me your side, Cherry. I'm very close to the lieutenant. He listens to me."

She rolled her eyes.

"You need me. He's very close to making an arrest. Seriously. Really close." Which he was, just not her. When she made no move to help me out, I shrugged. "Fine. It's your murder conviction, not mine. You might really like prison."

She plopped back into her seat and looked resigned, almost relieved to finally tell someone. "Leo helped with my expenses. The house, my car, some groceries. I don't make squat as his assistant. Buffalo Bill's ain't exactly Microsoft."

"No offense, but there's no way this place cost forty grand a month. Where's the rest of the cash?"

She stubbed out her cigarette. "I don't know what you're talking about."

I leaned forward. "I'm serious, Cherry. You're on the hook for Leo's murder. You were at his house. You have his dog. You stole his money."

She leapt to her feet. Her chair scraped against the concrete pad and startled Donald. "I didn't steal any money. I don't even know where he hid it." She snatched another cigarette from the pack.

"Why was Leo hiding money? I figure he stashed at least a hundred grand."

She barked out a laugh. "Try two-fifty."

"Jesus, Cherry, what for?"

"Insurance money against Bebe. In case she found out about us. Leo was getting real paranoid. Worried about the business, worried about Bebe taking him to the cleaners. He was expecting a big windfall, ten times what he already had. Then he'd feel better, he said." Cherry sat back down. "But I don't have it, I swear. I don't even know where it is."

"Tell me about Saturday night."

She stood again. Walked to the rail and leaned against it. "We fought. He wouldn't let me go to your fancy Foundation party and I was pissed. I mean, what the hell? It's like I never get to go anywhere with him. Bebe was out of town, no one would even care. I'm a business associate, you know?"

She leaned over and stubbed out her freshly-lit cigarette. "So I waited for him to come home. We fought. I broke it off. I left and took Donald with me."

She looked down at her bare feet. Her shoulders shook slightly and she rested her hands on her knees.

"What time did you leave?"

"Eleven-thirty or so. Maybe a quarter till." She lifted her head. Thick streaks of teary mascara ran down her face. "If I'd stayed, he'd be alive."

"Or you'd be dead."

Her hands shook as she fumbled with her cigarette pack. She emptied the ashtray into a plastic waste can, then lit a third cigarette.

"Have you told any of this to the detectives?"

"No!" She wiped her face with her hands. "They'll think I did it."

No shit. You probably did do it. At the very least, Ransom's case against Jane now had a nice big hitch in it. "Where did you go after you left?"

She wouldn't look at me. She turned and rubbed Donald's head, scratched her ears while she drooled on Cherry's toes.

"You can tell me."

"Man, this is all so personal."

"I know. I'm sorry. But I can't help you if you don't tell me."

"Fine. Call Joey. He'll tell you."

"Joey? Leo's partner, Joseph Hirschorn?"

"Yes, Joey Hirschorn. I drove to his house afterward."

"Wow, that was fast. With the dog, too?"

"Don't you judge me. I didn't move down here for nothing."

I tried to look sympathetic. "Of course not. I'll need Joey's address and phone number."

She walked inside and came back with Joseph's business card, his home info scribbled on the back. "But he's still up north. Won't be back until late tomorrow. Maybe even Tuesday."

I lifted myself out of the metal lawn chair. "If you think of anything else, call me. You need to call the detectives and tell them everything: the car, the fight, the dog. I'll talk to them, but it will be much better if they hear it from you first."

She took a deep drag on her cigarette. "Okay, okay. I'll call the detective tonight. I got the guy's card in the kitchen. He's a hottie, huh?"

"I'll see myself out," I said.

I left the curb just before eleven and sailed over the bridge to the island forty-five minutes later. I wasn't sure about Cherry. Even with Joseph as an alibi. How reliable was that going to be? One lover for another. Maybe they both killed Leo and stole his money.

My fingers tingled at the thought of the money. A huge windfall, she said. It explained the frantic state of Leo's house. Would Bebe trash her own furniture? Wreck her own possessions? For two million bucks, why not? Finds out about Leo's young buxom mistress, murders Leo, ferrets out a big stash of untraceable cash. Ain't love grand?

NINETEEN

I rode my bike to the Big House Monday morning ready to crack down on Foundation business. With the investigation as the top priority, my day-to-day duties had been neglected. I pulled the Mumbai Humanitarian file from the stack. Best to swallow the bitter pills first.

I phoned the Lafferty Foundation in Atlanta.

"Gayle Everheart," a friendly voice said into my ear.

"Hi, Gayle, it's Elliott with the Ballantyne."

"Elliott! How nice to hear from you. How long's it been? The Atlanta Symphony fundraiser last October, right?"

"You have a great memory." We caught up on industry gossip for a few minutes. Neither of us mentioned the murder, but I felt it on the line with us, like a switchboard operator dying to butt in. I quickly swung the conversation around to Mumbai. "We received a new application for Mumbai Humanitarian. It says here you awarded them a grant in February."

"Yes. Reena Patel, right? Charming lady and such a sad tale. It was an easy grant to approve, actually. My assistant personally oversaw the app package, helped walk them through the process," Gayle said. "Ms. Patel introduced us to several teachers, she showed us the educational materials, a typical day plan. She's very detail-oriented. I was impressed."

"So you'd offer a recommendation?"

"Absolutely."

"Thanks, Gayle. I appreciate the info. Mr. Ballantyne wants this to go to committee next week and I've been neglecting it," I said. "Let me know if I can return the favor."

"You know I will," she said and hung up.

I admit it, I was disappointed. I was hoping Gayle would give me a boatload of reasons to decline the grant. At least a sniff of a scandal or tinge of bad press. I would've settled for a concurring opinion on Reena's nasty personality or maybe a snarky remark about her ridiculously small feet.

My phone rang before I could deteriorate any further.

"Elli! Hello, my dear, hello," Mr. Ballantyne shouted into my ear. "Can you hear me, Elli?"

I laughed. "Yes, Mr. Ballantyne, loud and clear. You sound like you're right next door."

"Oh no, dear Elli. We're still in India, but we'll be home on Wednesday. Bringing our new friends from Australia. Did I tell you, Elli? They're wonderful people."

"You did, sir. We're looking forward to it."

"I've gathered the information you wanted on Leo Hirschorn. Do you have a moment to discuss?"

"Of course. Please, go ahead." I slapped the Mumbai folder closed and opened my notebook to a fresh page.

"He had a life insurance policy. A one million dollar payout split between his wife and son. A straight-forward certificate, signed ten years ago. Nothing hinky there, my girl."

"Uh-huh," I muttered as I wrote. "What about Buffalo Bill's? Any financial troubles?"

"You're very good. Troubles, indeed. It seems he would leverage one store to finance the next. Our Leo was in a pinch with this economic slowdown. His debts were high and his income low."

I scribbled the word "money" in bold blue letters. "And the store, sir? Who inherits his shares in Buffalo Bill's?"

"Bebe Hirschorn, she has rights of survivorship," he said. "She inherits Leo's share of the stable. But they'll need an infusion of cash to keep her afloat."

"How much cash are we talking?"

"From what the accountants tell me, I'd say two million dollars. Probably not something she has lying around."

"You never know, sir." I had a feeling I did indeed know. I underlined my money doodle. Love and money. It seems Leo stockpiled both.

"That's all I have for now, my dear Elli. We'll be home in two days. We can't wait to see you! Vivi sends her love."

"I send mine as well," I said, but he was already gone.

Two days! I needed to put Jane's new attorney in the loop. I left a message for Gregory Meade, asking him to call me back. I thought he should know about Cherry. Pretty hot stuff with Leo stashing cash to protect his mistress, and their stormy fight on the night he died which included both a witness and a dog.

I hadn't heard from Matty since the big sex kiss on Thursday. I had a feeling he was waiting on me to make the next move, so I went ahead and made it. Two minutes later we were set for a picnic lunch at Seabrook Prep the next day.

I worked until early afternoon catching up on Ballantyne business: files, phone calls, paperwork, lunch. I wanted to get the new meeting scheduled for next week, but unless the case broke, it would have to wait. Of all my top priorities, Leo's murder still ranked number one.

My phone rang at half-past two. I thought it might be Jane's attorney returning my call, but it was Sid. "Elliott, you busy?"

"Sid! You made it home from the poker game alive."

"Yes, sweetie. No gunshot wounds or mob encounters," she said. "I did try to pick up a little inside info on Leo, but I didn't get a single drop."

"Thanks for trying. Speaking of drops, how's my tunic? Any chance at salvation?"

"I'm working on it, sweetie, but keep your hopes down, okay? Listen, if you've got some time this afternoon, I can show you the new Buffalo Bill's location. There's a meeting with the developer and I thought you might like to listen in."

"I'd love to. When?"

"An hour or so. It's out on Summerton Parkway, near the Poplar Grove turnoff. You'll see a narrow drive leading to a dilapidated shack, the old Delafield House."

"Sure, I know where that is. I'll see you there."

It might not be very productive to visit a piece of land Leo might have bought had he lived, but I figured it couldn't hurt.

I cleaned up my desk so it looked as if I had put in a full day. I pedaled home in the bright sunshine and exchanged my bike for my car. I kept my raffia hat, then cruised out onto Cabana with the top down. I was over the bridge and around the traffic circle in downtown Summerton shortly before three-thirty.

The old Delafield House was actually more of a crumbling clapboard house. From what I could remember, Walter Delafield was a prominent figure during the Civil War, but his family built the small house many years later, either after he was knocking on the pearly gates or at least walking up the drive. And I thought the land was larger than the five acres Sid mentioned over the weekend. The Delafield fronted Summerton Parkway near the downtown shopping district, which consisted of tiny boutiques, old-fashioned ice cream shops, and the Piggly Wiggly grocery.

I pulled into the long drive and parked next to Jane's infamous black Sebring convertible. There were two other cars. I recognized one as Sid's and the other was a shiny black SUV. I figured it belonged to Chas Obermeyer, since he and Jane were arguing on the front steps of the house.

I greeted Sid as I stepped out of the car. "What's going on? Where's the developer?"

"Apparently Chas Obermeyer *is* the developer."

"Chas is? But why is Jane here?" I asked, but we reached the argument before Sid could answer.

"I don't care if Mr. Delafield rose from the grave and signed over the deed himself," Jane said. "As president of the Historic Society, I can assure you that no amount of huffing and puffing is going to tear this sucker down."

She and Chas faced each other on the rickety porch. The dusty planks appeared rotted and nearly broken through. I, personally, had no intention of stepping foot on them.

"This house is a dump, Jane, and you know it. It didn't even belong to Delafield. It was his nephew's kid's house. It's like you: old and decrepit with no historical value."

"Be careful. The veneer of Southern civility you've worked so hard to coat is cracking," Jane said. "It's a shame your temper is as fragile as a soap bubble. Must make it difficult to keep up appearances."

"What's going on?" I asked from the walk.

"Oh, gee, Elliott, what a surprise. It figures you'd stick your nose in the middle of this," Chas said.

"Why is that?" I asked.

"Because Leo tricked Chas into buying this property," Jane said. "He's now the proud owner of ten acres of prime historic land. Why, he could turn this beauty into a nice museum, donate it to the county. I'd approve that."

"Tricked you? What happened?" I asked Chas.

His face was tomato red. "Leo lied, according to Jane. But I don't know how reliable she is. She killed him, right? Isn't that why you're here? Ready to confiscate the broom and whisk her off to jail?"

"The property, Chas," I prodded.

"None of your goddamn business," he said.

"I'll tell her if you like," Jane said. "I do enjoy telling it."

"Leo and I had a deal," Chas said before Jane could tell her version. "I would subsidize the Delafield land for the new Buffalo Bill's location. Act as developer and owner, he'd sign on a twenty-year lease. So I bought the property, free and clear."

"But Leo was playing both sides," Jane said.

"It's bullshit and you know it," he yelled. "You won't get away with this!"

"Oh yes, he played you like a fiddle at a rodeo," she said sweetly. "You see, Leo had more than a bale of hay beneath his ridiculous cowboy hat. He signed with Chas, metaphorically speaking. You don't actually have a written agreement, right, Chas?"

She smiled while he kicked the front door. The wood splintered and dust billowed, dirtying his neat tan slacks.

"Anyhoo," Jane continued. "Leo told me all about his expansion plans for this land. I objected, of course. But we struck a deal last week. He would back out of his proposal, and in exchange, I wouldn't fight his renewal to the board, in fact, I would endorse his seat. All legal, mind you, before you get any wild ideas, Chas. I personally believe Leo never intended to go through with building on this land, but I can't prove it."

It explained Leo's mood at the party on Saturday night. And Whitney's comments on Leo, how confident he was that his seat would be guaranteed.

"Did you find out about this just now?" I asked Chas.

He didn't answer, only glared.

"Leo told him at the party on Saturday night," Jane said. "Chas overheard us finalizing our little deal out on the terrace. No Buffalo Bill's, no development fees, no recurring rent stream for Chas."

"You bitch. You're not ruining this deal. I've already contracted my home expansion. The pool, the deck, the cellar. Dammit, what am I going to tell my wife?"

"You'll see her in twenty to life? You're the new suspect, Chas. I feel fantastic, really. Nothing can bring me down now."

"Watch me," Chas said. "I'm building the new Buffalo Bill's on this land. I'll tear down this crumbling shack with the biggest bulldozer I can rent. You and your pansy-ass women's club can watch and weep, but no way you're going to stop me."

"Try it, Obermeyer. I'll own you," Jane said. "Or what's left of you, anyway. I always wanted a house in Pelican Beach."

Chas stepped toward Jane, but tripped on a knot in the wood plank. He fell forward and caught himself on the porch rail, skinning his arm in the process. "This isn't over, Jane. Not by a long shot!" He marched down the steps.

I jumped out of the way before he could plow through me and nearly knocked down Sid. Then tires screeched on the asphalt out at the road. Two police cruisers and Ransom's silver McLaren flew up the dirt driveway and parked caddywhompus behind my Mini.

"Wait, Chas," Jane hollered. "It looks like word has spread. Don't worry, sugar, you look good in orange."

Ransom nodded at Chas as he passed, but kept walking with two officers on his heels. They stopped a foot from me at the base of the steps.

"Jane Walcott Hatting," Ransom said. "You are under arrest."

TWENTY

"Is this a joke?" she asked.

"You have the right to remain silent," an officer said. He continued spelling out her rights as he handcuffed her hands behind her back.

"What are you doing?" I asked Ransom, trying to bite down the panic. "You can't do this."

He ignored me as he escorted Jane down the walk.

"What about Chas?" I yelled. "And this land deal? He was furious with Leo!"

Ransom kept walking. "Chas has an alibi, unlike Jane here. Right, Jane?"

"Moron," Jane spat out. "I didn't kill Leo. Seriously, all this time, and *I'm* the one you arrest? You can't do this. My auction is tomorrow."

"You better cancel it," Ransom said.

"Like hell," Jane said.

I caught up to Ransom. I tugged his arm and pulled him away from the other officers. "Wait. What's wrong with you? So focused on Jane, so determined to show me you're the big detective, that you ignore everything else? It's bullshit, Ransom."

"This may surprise you, Elliott, but this isn't about you. Jane Hatting killed Leo Hirschorn. There are no other suspects."

"Oh, and what about Cherry Avarone? You know she was inside Leo's house right before he was murdered. You can't seriously buy her flimsy alibi. Really solid, Ransom. One lover covering up for another."

He stopped and stared at me. "What did you say?"

"You heard me. Cherry. Was. There. At the time of the murder."

"What the fuck are you talking about?"

"The red VW bug in the driveway. The witness across the street who saw everything. Cherry who admits she fought with Leo minutes before he was bludgeoned to death. It's called evidence," I yelled. "Certainly you've heard of it."

"You've crossed a line, Lisbon," he yelled back. "You're obstructing this investigation. I should arrest you right now, right here. I told you not to withhold information."

"So now it's my fault I'm better at this than you? I can't help it if I uncovered the truth while you were out chasing Jane, come hell or high water. Not! My! Fault!"

Ransom stormed off. He got to his car and whipped his door open. "Your discreet inquiry is over. It's over, Lisbon," he shouted. "You get to the station now. I want you in my office in five minutes."

He slammed the door and sped down the driveway in reverse. He spun around in the grass, then peeled out onto the highway with the two patrol cars behind him.

"Holy crap, Elli," Sid said. "Your life is way more exciting than mine."

My hands were shaking as I walked to my car. "It's overrated." I fumbled for my keys, dropped them in the dirt. Then remembered I hadn't locked my car.

"So that's Nick Ransom, huh? He's sexier than I imagined. And more passionate."

"You mean pissed," I said and opened the car door.

"That, too. You headed to his office?"

"Yeah, I don't think so," I said. "I didn't do anything wrong. Technically. I'm going to let him cool down first. Maybe a day. Or a week."

"Sure, sweetie. Nothing will cool him down like ignoring him."

"Exactly," I said. "Thanks for the heads up on the property. I'd better get out of here."

She squeezed my hand. "You take care. Call if you need me."

I nodded and backed out of the drive, using the same patch of grass Ransom used to turn around. *Well, I'm in the muck now. Jane better not be guilty or I'll strap her to the chair myself.*

I couldn't ignore Ransom's demand outright, but I certainly didn't have to walk into the lion's den, either. I pulled out my phone and dialed the police station. My fingers still trembled and I took a deep breath.

I hit Parker's extension and said a quick thank you prayer when she answered.

"Parker, it's Elliott," I said. I was speeding down the road as I spoke. "You got a minute?"

"Are you kidding? The Lieutenant is raging mad. I mean livid, Elliott. I could barely make out every third word he said. I would not want to be you."

I choked out a laugh. I remembered my thoughts from earlier: I live on an island, right? Who doesn't want to be me? Apparently there are caveats.

"I hear you, but it's not my fault. Please say you'll meet me. I have to give you my account of what happened."

"No way. Ransom expects you in his office. He may not get to you until tomorrow, but he'll kill you if you don't show up. I should be pissed, too. You promised not to withhold evidence. I should hang up right this minute."

"Please don't," I said, whipping onto Cabana Boulevard into busy traffic. "Just hear me out. I swear I didn't withhold anything. Not intentionally, anyway. Besides, it's you or nothing, Parker. I'm not facing Ransom. So if you want to hear it, it's you or nothing."

I changed lanes and passed a motor coach hauling a trailer full of bikes. I foot-slapped the gas pedal and rocketed into the left lane.

"Fine, Elliott," Parker finally said. "But this better be good."

"Thanks, Parker. Meet me at the library, along the path by the back lot. I'll be there in fifteen minutes or less."

She clicked off without saying goodbye.

If I could sequester Parker while Ransom tangled with Jane, I had a decent chance of getting my statement on record while avoiding Ransom altogether. I wasn't about to show up at his office and have him scold the shit out of me in front of every uniform in the station.

The Island Civic Complex is on the north end of the island, close to Oyster Cove Plantation and the airport. The police station occupied the east end of the property, the county library took on the west. I pulled into the drive just as a sporty little MG roadster cut across the lot, nearly swiping the Mini. Tate Keating waved from the driver's seat and zipped out onto the road.

Oh God. The *Islander Post*.

I parked in the very last spot on the farthest end. I hopped out of the Mini and ran over to a bench tucked beneath the trees. Parker walked up as I sat down.

She opened her flip-top notebook. "Go."

"Was Tate Keating here about Jane?"

"Go."

"Okay, right. Remember when I called you about the dog? I had just finished talking to Owen Dobbs, Leo's neighbor. That's what led me to the dog. I couldn't understand where he was. Turns out he's a she, and Cherry took her the night of the murder."

"Cherry stole Leo's dog?"

"Not exactly. It's her dog—according to her. But we're jumping ahead." I took a deep breath. "So while I was in the neighborhood, I decided to see if anyone else saw anything. Someone did. A tiny lady named Olivetta Jones in the last house near the corner."

"With the doll house and the tea party?"

"Yep, that's the one," I said. "She told me she saw a red VW bug in Leo's driveway on Saturday night. And it wasn't the first time she'd seen it."

"How can she be sure it was Saturday night?"

"She watched a movie, ate some banana bread, drank a cup of cocoa, peeked out front. She was certain."

"Seriously," Parker said. "I interviewed her myself. She never mentioned anything about a red car."

"You should've drunk the tea. After two scones and some reassurances, she told me all about it." I leaned against the bench arm with one leg tucked under me, facing Parker. "I specifically asked if she'd spoken with you about the car. She said yes, Parker, and I believed her."

"Okay, so how'd you figure out it was Cherry?"

I couldn't expose Milo Hickey or his poker game. Not after he graciously answered all my questions. So I fudged. "I went to her house to ask about the dog. The car was parked under her carport and the dog, Donald, was running around the backyard."

She scribbled notes as fast as she could. "So what did she have to say?"

"After I revealed my clever deductions, she admitted to sleeping with Leo. He helped her with expenses, paid her mortgage. When he refused to take her to the party at the Big House Saturday, she flipped. Met him after the party. They argued. She stormed out and took the dog with her."

"And after that?"

"Went to Joseph Hirschorn's house."

"Well that was fast."

I snorted. "That's what I said. She called me judgy. Anyway, I told her she absolutely had to call Ransom. She promised, said she had his number and would call him as soon as I left. I swear, Parker, and this was only just yesterday."

She finished writing and looked up at me. "The Lieutenant is furious. There's no way he'll believe you weren't keeping this from him."

"I know, that's why I'm talking to you. But I have no reason to hold this back. This clears Jane, my pseudo-client. Why wouldn't I want to share that? I already called Jane's attorney."

"Elliott! You told her attorney before the Lieutenant?"

"I didn't know he didn't know." I ran my hands through my hair. "Her attorney hasn't called me back yet, but I have to tell him. You've arrested Jane, but it will never hold up with an enraged Cherry sitting on Leo's doorstep two minutes before he was killed. Unless you have more you aren't telling me?"

"This doesn't work both ways." She tapped her book against her knee. "Man. I'm going to have to tell Ransom."

"Better you than me."

"That's not funny," she said.

"Who's joking? Now what happens?"

She stood and brushed the dust from her uniform. "You're going to have to face him at some point, you know. But for now, I'll pass this along. Jane will probably be out by dinner."

"And Keating?"

"Sorry, Elliott. That cat is out of the bag and racing to meet a deadline."

"Son of a bitch." I put my head in my hands.

"Listen, anything, and I mean *any*thing comes up, you call me first. First, Elliott. Not the attorney. Me. Are we clear?"

"Yes, I promise," I said. She walked toward the police station and I climbed into my car. I rested my head on the steering wheel. My heart continued to pound, but the shaking had all but stopped. The tremble in my hands felt like little more than the result of an overdose of Pepsi and a one pound box of chocolates.

I called Tate, but he wouldn't deal, only gloat. I couldn't think of a single defense, so I ended with "No comment." I didn't dare mention Cherry's car in the driveway. Ransom might actually kill me.

I raced home and tucked the Mini into the garage. It was not yet six o'clock, but it felt like midnight. Ate a big bowl of cereal for dinner. I had no idea when Ransom would be home and I didn't want to risk take-out.

The phone rang eleven times over the next three hours. I finally unplugged it when I went upstairs.

I made sure all the lights were off. Grabbed a book and crawled into bed with a compact book light attached to the cover. An hour later the doorbell rang. And rang. Then came the knocking.

I knew I was right and I knew he knew I was right. But there was simply no way I was answering the door, because by the pounding nature of his knock, Ransom wasn't dropping by with cupcakes and an apology.

TWENTY-ONE

I wanted Tuesday morning to arrive like I wanted a pop in the nose. I woke at six, which should tell you how dreadful I felt. The morning's headline delivered the expected punch: Ballantyne Chair Arrested in Gruesome Slaying. Tate Keating opted for shockability rather than visibility. More words, smaller type. The word "gruesome" was a nice touch. He included a picture of Jane snapping at Ransom. I skimmed the article hoping for a bright spot, but naturally Tate left off the part about Jane being released or the other suspects being questioned.

After tossing the paper in the trash, I sped through my morning routine, which included grumbling every epitaph I'd ever heard. Sufficiently scrubbed, I raced to the Ballantyne to wait for the call. No matter the country, I knew Mr. Ballantyne would've heard the news by now.

Carla greeted me at the door with a very large glass of Pepsi.

"Your Lieutenant stopped by this morning," Carla said.

"Jesus, already?" I asked and swigged down a third of the drink.

"He seemed excited to talk to you."

"Excited?"

"Determined," she said with a pat on my shoulder. "He left a note on your desk."

I dragged into my office. Ransom's note sat square in the middle. He'd cleared away every other scrap from the surface, not even a pencil remained. The phone was on the floor. I peered at his message. Two words on a postie in bold marker: CALL ME.

I crumpled it in one hand and dropped it on the floor. I didn't need to hear anything from him. Parker left a voicemail earlier saying Jane's arrest was on hold, which meant two things: Jane was free for her auction that evening and the morning's headline was wrong. But much too late. The barn door was open and the chickens were roaming free.

I stared at the phone. Mr. Ballantyne had left me in charge and I screwed it all up. How did I ever trust Cherry to call Ransom to confess seeing Leo before he died? Or believe Mrs. Jones told Parker about seeing the car in Leo's drive, especially since she was so hesitant to tell me in the first place? I gulped down the rest of my Pepsi.

My phone rang at seven-thirty on the nose. "Elliott Lisbon," I said before the first ring finished.

"Elliott!" Mr. Ballantyne said. The background was noisy with city sounds and the line crackled. "We're en route home. In Paris today, but not enjoying it, I must say. Vivi's taken to her room."

"Oh no, sir," I said and sank deep into my chair. "Please don't worry. The media has it all wrong. Jane was not arrested."

"I've received a dozen calls from donors, Elli. Wanting reassurances their good names will not be dragged down by me."

Oh God. I slumped down further and I felt I might faint from shame. I thought about the growing cancellation list for the Gatsby and realized I'd done nothing to stop the exodus. "Mr. Ballantyne. Seriously. I'm on it. No dragging."

"I told those blowhards to be careful with their cancellations. They may not get another invite," he shouted into phone. "I expect you'll meet us tomorrow. Should be before lunch."

"Very good, sir," I said faintly. I cleared my throat. "Please send my love to Mrs. Ballantyne. Take her shopping on the Champs-Élysées, to the café she loves so much. Their croissants will lift her spirits." My heart ached. Things definitely weren't going well and I missed them dearly. "It will be so good to see you both again."

"Au revoir, then, until tomorrow," he said.

"Au revoir."

I set down the phone and picked up my pen. Time to clean up this mess before they got home and I needed to relocate to Alaska. The morning flew by in a whirlwind of phone calls and promises. To the press, to the school board, to a dozen loyal Ballantyne patrons. By lunchtime I was starving and ready to catch a killer.

I conned Carla into packing a picnic for my lunch with Matty. With a plastic cooler on my arm, I hustled out to the Mini. I zipped out of the drive and down to Seabrook Prep, located at the very southern tip of the island near the lighthouse in Harborside Planta tion. I parked in the lot under a shady live oak. Like most of the parking on the island, the spaces were hidden behind chunks of trees, bushes, and seasonal flowers. It was pretty to look at, but re sulted in half the spaces and double the blind spots.

I followed a brick path through a short forest to the campus determined to find a helpful student to point the way to my seventeen-year-old suspect. I focused on underclassmen, the weakest in the herd. They're still young, mostly unjaded, and eager to please. And at Seabrook Prep, easy to recognize in their white golf shirts with a logo embroidered on the front pocket. Seniors wore blue.

"Excuse me, can you tell me where to find Travis Hirschorn?" I asked a young boy who looked about twelve.

"Sure, eating lunch at his tree," the kid said, pointing at the largest oak tree in the quad where five kids sat at the base in various stages of lunch consumption.

I smiled and said thanks, then crossed the quad at a fair trot. I had no more than ten minutes to elicit information from Travis and his crew before Matty came looking for me.

Travis lounged in the middle of the group, holding court to two boys in blue with two girls in between, sitting boy girl boy girl. All wearing identical uniforms, though somewhere along the way, a tailor had altered the girls' uniforms to show off their blossoming assets and shiny new navel rings. It must be hard to scratch out your own identity when everyone at school shows up in the same outfit day after day.

"Hello, Travis," I said. "Remember me?"

He stared at me. Grief, anger, and uneasiness radiated from his very pores, but he didn't say a word. This would not be easy.

"And which one of you is Derek?"

The boy on my right nodded once in my direction.

Talkative bunch.

"Okay, Travis, I'm just following up on last Saturday night. You mentioned you were at Derek's house?"

Derek spoke up. "Yeah, he was at my place. Went to a movie, dinner, then we crashed in my room. Totally kick back."

I nodded sagely. "Sounds solid. Except for the part where I spoke with your mom, Derek. She said you and Travis here haven't had a slumber party in months."

The girls looked at each other, then at the ground. The girl on the left was white with shiny blonde hair streaked with pink; the other girl was black with shiny black hair streaked with blue. And the boy opposite Derek had a red face and a sudden flurry of texting to do on his cell.

"Hey, it's none of your business, anyway," Travis said. "I don't have to tell you anything." He stuck his chin out, then took a long swig of his Snapple. Hard to look tough toting a Snapple.

"I see. Okay, then how about we move on to Plan B?"

Travis squinted at me. "Plan B?"

"Yes. I go over to Mr. Gannon's office," I said and held up my cooler. "Which I'm headed for anyway. We're very close friends, having lunch today as a matter of fact. Then I tell him several of his students, *senior* students who would like to graduate at the end of the month, are obstructing a murder investigation. Of course, he'll be very unhappy upon hearing that news. I'll suggest we phone up all of your parents, including you two hotties here in the front row, get the police down here, and find out what exactly went on last Saturday night. Plan B."

"Wait, you guys—" she of the blue streak said.

Panic flooded the face of pink streak. She grabbed her friend by the arm. "Ashley, no. My parents will totally kill me."

"Mine will too if I don't graduate. I'm going to *Princeton.*"

Travis finished his Snapple with less snap in his attitude. His eyes bounced between the streaks, a trace of fear etched on his face.

I watched the two girls debate silently, trying to decide which fate was worse: exposing their misdeeds now or facing their parents later.

But it was Derek who finally broke. "And if we tell you where we were? You'll drop the whole thing?"

"You promise and swear?" Pink Streak added.

"Pinkie swear and cross my heart. I won't tell and will erase my memory immediately," I promised. Since I had never planned on dragging Matty into this anyhow. I rolled my hand in a let's-get-this-moving gesture. "Spill."

"Okay, look," Pink Streak said. She twirled her hair around her finger. "My parents were out of town and I maybe had some people over."

"For the night?"

"For the weekend," she said. "It's not a big deal or anything. It's just that I sort of was supposed to be staying at Ashley's. But seriously, why let the whole house sit empty, right? I mean, someone should stay there to, you know, watch over it. I was really doing my parents a favor."

"Uh-huh," I said. "And how many people helped you with this favor?"

"Just us," she said and waved at her peeps. "Maybe another couple."

"And Sylvie, too," Ashley of the blue streak said. She nodded toward the boy with the mad texting skills. "That's Drew's girlfriend, but she's out today. I think she's got the flu."

I casually stepped back in case flu germs were circulating in the immediate area. "Go on," I said, prompting Pink with another hurry-up hand roll.

"Well, Travis was with me all night. With us, all night. I swear," she said. "He didn't know about his dad's, well, um, you know, his dad until the next day."

"Do you have any proof? Other than your undoubtedly sincere and honest word for it?"

Drew handed me his cell phone. It was a fancy touch screen model opened to a photo album section listing fifteen pictures, all dated the night Leo was murdered, between ten and two-thirty the next morning. I opened one, then skimmed through the rest. Travis and Pink Streak were lip locked through most of them, as were another couple. It looked relatively tame. Less than a dozen beer bottles scattered around and a pile of pizza boxes. No hard booze or drugs that I could see.

"I'm not sure how convincing this evidence would be to a jury," I said. "But it'll work for me. For now." I'm not sure it's possible to fudge the time and date on a cell phone. I think those suckers are wired into some sort of satellite time trigger unchangeable without a top secret launch code and level five clearance. But hey, what do I know?

I handed back his phone. "Don't erase them."

"Why not? I can't keep them forever. I don't have that kind of memory, dude."

"Because, dude, it's the only thing that clears you of murder." I turned to Travis with my most serious face. "I'm off to see Headmaster Gannon. If I have more questions, I'll expect you to answer them."

I sauntered off like I meant business. I was so intent on my exit, I almost slammed right into Matty.

"Hey, Elli," he said with a smile. "Good to see you."

"Hi," I said. I didn't know if we were supposed to hug or kiss or something. We usually did both—the friend kind, not the friendly kind—but after the big sex kiss, I didn't know what to do, so I lifted the cooler instead. "Hungry?"

We walked over to a picnic table at the edge of the quad and I unpacked our lunch: three homemade honey pecan chicken salad sandwiches (with sliced red grapes and light mayonnaise), a large tub of sliced fruit (cubed watermelon, honeydew, and cantaloupe), and four chocolate brownies (with frosting, without nuts).

"The Gatsby is tomorrow at the Big House," I said. "Would you like to come?"

"Like a date?"

"You're always my date, Matty."

"How about a real date? I'll pick you up and we go together."

"Mr. Ballantyne comes home tomorrow, so I'll be there all day. But I'll let you drive me home."

"Even better." He touched my fingers with his and my stomach actually fluttered. "I enjoyed the roast the other night. Maybe next time we can dance under the stars."

"I'd like that," I said and almost giggled. Holy crap, I thought. I think I'm nervous.

I watched him arrange our lunch like a picnic. He somehow managed to look laidback in a plaid tie and faded blue button-down. Academic, athletic, outdoorsy. I imagined half the girls on campus had a crush on him. Easy on the eyes and smelled like the sea, a lively mix of clean and salty.

"So how's Travis?" he asked.

"You noticed?"

"You're the only girl on campus not in uniform. Plus, you're pretty hot in that sexy little skirt." He took a large bite of his first sandwich. "You questioning Travis about his father's death?"

"Yes, but just a follow-up question. How's Travis been lately? He seems like a kid in turmoil. More than just his father's passing."

"A little moody, I guess, but a good kid. Having a hard time. Worse now."

"What kind of hard time? Girl trouble? Problems at home?"

Matty slowly wiped his fingers on a paper napkin, one at a time. Forearms on the table, eyes slightly narrowed. A subtle shift from casual to cautious.

"I'm just trying to understand the kid," I said. "Something's on your mind."

"College. It's tough this time of year for seniors. He couldn't go to Duke. Too expensive. He was going to have to settle on his second choice."

I glanced over my shoulder at Travis who was smiling and drinking his Snapple. "Was?"

Matty finished his sandwich. He casually tossed the wrapper into the cooler. Then he picked up his second sandwich, slowly unwrapping the clear plastic wrap. He bit into the corner, taking more time to chew than recommended by nine out of ten medical professionals.

"Was," he said.

"So he *is* going to Duke in the fall?"

"Yes."

"When did this happen? Before or after his father was killed?" This could actually be something. My skin started to tingle and I ditched my sandwich in favor of a brownie.

"Elli, I don't like you questioning me about a student. Doesn't seem right. Travis had nothing to do with his father's death."

"Then it can't hurt to tell me." I licked frosting from my thumb. "Was it after?"

Matty speared a watermelon cube. Then a cantaloupe wedge. The bell rang and several students scurried by with backpacks on their backs, tossing empty paper bags into the trash bin.

"So before? How soon before? Right before?" I asked.

Travis could've found out about the hidden stash of money and cooked up a way to get his hands on it. Or maybe his mother told him about the life insurance policy. Off dear old dad and Duke U here I come.

"Okay, so he just went up a notch on my list."

"Stop, Elli. You're way off base, here."

"Hardly. He had motive and opportunity and his alibi is shaky at best."

"Alibi? He doesn't need an alibi."

"Of course he needs an alibi. He wouldn't be the first kid to kill his father. Why are you so rankled?"

"You can't come onto my campus and accuse one of my students of murder. You have no right, no authority."

"Authority? It's a free country." I tossed the fruit tub and waded papers into the cooler and snapped it shut. "I can question whomever I want. Including a spoiled brat who decided to off his dad so he could go to the college of his choice."

"Did you have lunch with me just to get to Travis?"

"You asked me to lunch, remember? You know I'm investigating Leo Hirschorn's murder."

"You can't investigate a murder. You have no business getting this involved."

No business? I flew to my feet. "You are not the boss of me." I snatched my cooler and stomped away with my head held high. Ten feet later I cracked my shin on a bench I hadn't noticed with my nose stuck in the air. I bit back a saucy expletive and kept marching.

Well, that hour sucked. I managed to both secure Travis's alibi and confirm his motive, all the while irritating the crap out of Matty for no real reason, because I actually believed Travis's alibi more than I bought into his guilt. So why was I picking a fight? Because I didn't like Matty pointing out the truth, that I shouldn't be bullying kids in a schoolyard? He was only protecting his students.

Great. I'm a terrible person.

I reached my car and my breath caught in my throat. Every tire was slashed clean through. Shredded rubber created four flats and someone had pinned a note beneath the driver's side windshield wiper. I slowly approached and lifted the top flap. I read the words scratched in sloppy black marker on a torn sheet of notebook paper: STEP OFF OR YOUR NEXT.

I looked over my shoulder, then spun around. The lot was filled with long creepy shadows and empty cars. I heard a twig snap behind me. The slow crunch of a footstep on gravel.

I clutched the cooler and my purse and ran with everything I had.

TWENTY-TWO

I ran up the path so fast, I got a stitch in my side. While I had dined on chicken salad, someone ripped apart my tires, and by the size of the gash on the front tire, they used a very large knife.

I stopped when I hit the picnic benches and pushed the hair out of my eyes. My hands were shaking. This will never do. If I sprinted into the quad in a puddle of fear, Matty would latch on like a bear with a honeycomb. The only words I'd hear for the next six months would be "I told you so."

With a determined walk, I worked myself from a hysterical panic into an irritated snit, trying to pull off an air of exasperated inconvenience. As if the violent strike was nothing more than petty vandalism. Just what us savvy investigators deal with every now and then. I sat at a picnic table, facing the parking lot. No sense being foolish and turning my back toward a knife-wielding maniac stalking me across campus.

My heart rate returned to almost normal at the same time my rationale did. Travis, that little shit. Who else held a grudge and was also on campus? And had crappy grammar? I guess he didn't appreciate my advice.

I pulled the phone out of my handbag and dialed the police station.

"Hi, Parker, it's Elliott," I said when she picked up.

"Wow, that was fast," she said. "You *are* pretty good at this."

"Thank you, I think. But what are you talking about?"

"Wait. What are you talking about? You called me, remember?"

"Right. I'm at Seabrook Prep and apparently a young delinquent slashed my tires. All four."

"Oh crap, Elliott. Anything else vandalized or stolen?"

I ran my hand through my hair. I hadn't even looked. I shot out of there as if a bomb was attached to the windshield instead of a scrap of notebook paper. "No, I don't think so."

"Okay, stay put. I'll call dispatch for a patrol car. I think Smitty is in Harborside anyway."

"Um, Parker, can you not tell Ransom about this, at least for now?"

"Sure, that's easy. He'll be tied up for a while anyway."

My ears perked up. "Yeah? With what? What's going on?"

"Don't you worry. I'll send Smitty over. Stay with your car, Elliott."

"Fine. But you know I'll find out."

"Of that I have no doubt," she said and hung up.

Now I was genuinely pissed. Something was going down and I was trapped. I quickly made arrangements for the dealership to send a tow truck and rush me to the front of the service line. Matty appeared as I hung up.

"Let me guess," I said. "No loitering on campus."

"Two teachers ratted you out in less than ten minutes."

He sat next to me on the bench and I took his hand. It felt warm on mine. I traced my finger along his thumb. His hands were tanned from hours in the sun. When he wasn't kayaking or surfing, he was on his brother's boat, a beautiful thirty-five foot catamaran. They spent many summer afternoons on the sea. I didn't join them too often. I got all green and wobbly and seasick just thinking about it.

"Before I make things worse, I'm sorry about earlier. I didn't mean to put you on the spot."

He brushed a loose strand of hair from my face. "You could never make things worse."

I cleared my throat. "Someone slashed my tires in your parking lot."

"Just now?"

I nodded.

He was off the bench in a flash. "Where're you parked?"

"Far corner to the left when you reach the end of the path."

We crossed the campus at a clip just shy of an Olympic record pace and ended up by the Mini Coop before I could catch my breath. I really needed to start exercising. That or ditch the lunch cooler.

Matty read the nasty note under the wiper, then inspected the tires. The damage was severe, but on closer scrutiny, it probably didn't take a machete to slash through the rubber. It's not as if the Mini had steel-belted monster truck tires. They looked more like large stroller wheels.

"This is because of your investigation, right?" Matty asked.

"Probably. I'm pretty sure Travis and his friends didn't appreciate my threats."

"You threatened Travis Hirschorn?"

"Well, not *threatened*, threatened."

"Are you crazy?"

"Me? Look at my car! He's the one who's crazy. You should watch that kid."

"What exactly did you say?" he asked, all tall and lean and unamused.

"My inquiries are discreet, Matty. That means I can't blab what suspects say all over town."

"The threat, Elliott."

I didn't budge, but Matty's sturdy stance unnerved me. I sighed and took a step back. "I maybe said if he didn't tell me where he really was the night his father was murdered, I would drag him and his friends into your office with all their parents and the police and they probably wouldn't graduate or go to college."

"Did it work?"

"Apparently a little too well."

He examined the jagged edges of ripped rubber. "I can't see where Travis or his friends could get a weapon to do this kind of damage."

"He looked pretty crafty to me."

"You're making a very serious accusation against Travis," Matty said. "Just the suggestion of his involvement could get him kicked out of Duke."

"I'm not going to tell the police it was Travis," I scoffed. "They'll drag my entire interrogation into the light. Discreet, remember? Besides, Ransom would pop out a kitten if he heard about this."

Matty stiffened at the sound of Ransom's name and turned back to the tires.

A black and white patrol car rolled into the lot followed by a flatbed tow truck. Over the next twenty minutes, I answered questions from Smitty while the tow truck driver hoisted the Mini onto the bed of the truck. Matty pecked my cheek and went back to his office around one-thirty.

Smitty tucked the threatening note, now wrapped in a plastic baggy, into his book and climbed into his car.

"Hey, Smitty," I called and hustled over to his door. "So is Lieutenant Ransom still wrapped up with that earlier problem? Crazy thing, right? Any updates?"

"Sorry, Ms. Lisbon, Corporal Parker warned me about you. You're on your own. Good luck, though. Smart girl like you, I bet you figure it out before the day ends."

"Me, too."

I waved as he pulled out of the drive, then climbed into the tow truck. As it turned out, I only had to wait another hour and forty minutes before I heard about the big break in the case.

I was pacing around the dealership waiting room, eating my third bag of peanut butter M&Ms when my phone rang. Pacing makes me hungry.

"Elliott, thank God you answered," Cherry cried into the phone. "Someone tried to kill Joey."

"What!"

"Yeah, tried to murder him just like Leo," she said. "The police questioned me like it might be me. You gotta talk to them. You said you'd help me."

"Where are you?"

"At the hospital. The one on the island."

"Stay there, I'll be over—" I dashed out of the lounge to the service bay, my hand over the phone. The Mini was still up on a lift.

"Hey Bobby," I yelled. Bobby and I became friends when he removed the slashed tires. It was the first assault he'd seen on a Mini. "How much longer? I have to go."

"Just finishing now, Elli," he hollered back. He wiped his hands on a stained rag and lowered the Mini.

"I'll be over in twenty minutes or less," I said to Cherry. "Which room?"

"Two-ten," she said. "I guess I can wait twenty minutes. The police are still talking to Joey anyway."

"Don't tell them I'm coming—it's important. I'll talk to the police later, okay?"

"Whatever, Elliott. Just get over here."

Fifteen minutes later I whipped into the parking lot of the hospital, sliding into a space in the back row. In an effort to avoid a collision with the police, including a particular lieutenant who was trying to track me down of late, I entered through the clinic lobby near the M.E.'s office. I breathed in the scent of alcohol—and not the fun kind. I appreciated the antiseptic nature, but not the medical undertone of sterile instruments and hygienic syringes.

I used the stairs, cut through two waiting rooms, and popped out at the nurse's station. The germy hospital made my palms itch, but seeing (and using) the giant bottles of hand-sani mounted on the walls around every corner relaxed me enough to open doors with my hands instead of my elbows. It sped things up and I finally caught my first break of the day: I saw Ransom walking away from

Joseph's room as I turned the corner. I waited until I heard the elevator bing, then snuck into the room.

Joseph Hirschorn was in the far bed. He had layers of thick white gauze wrapped around his head, a black eye, and a nasty gash on one cheek. The strings on his cotton hospital gown hung loose around his neck. Cherry sat at his side, holding his hand. She jumped up when she saw me.

"Elliott, you have to help us," she said. Her eyes were puffy from crying, her artful makeup smeared on her face like an abstract painting, all streaky and random. She sat, then stood again.

"Sit," I said. I dragged a chair over to the end of the bed and joined her. "What happened?"

She twisted her hands in her lap, shredding an already tattered tissue. "Joseph went to the office on Sunday night—"

"Sunday? You said he wasn't coming home until Monday or Tuesday."

At least she had the decency to blush. "Well, he came home early. I didn't know he was going to do that. It's not my fault he took an early flight home." She stared at her hands and plucked tissue lint from her skirt.

"So, he comes home early Sunday and goes to Buffalo Bill's..." I prodded.

She sniffed back more tears. "Yes. He stopped by the office on his way home from the airport. His flight was late so he didn't get by the Bill's until after ten."

"Why did he stop at the office so late?"

"He'd been out for a few days, wanted to see what was going on," she said without looking at me. "What's it matter? That's not the important part."

"Go on," I said.

"He heard something in Leo's office. He goes to check it out and wham, he's hit over the head. No one even knew until the next morning when the receptionist opened up the offices. She thought he was dead!" Tears spilled out onto her cheeks. She wiped them with the crumbly tissue in her hand.

"What makes you think it was Leo's killer?"

"The place was trashed," Joseph said in a low scratchy voice. "I never seen such a mess. It looked like a tornado blew through there. Tables turned over, couch cushions slashed apart, papers ripped like goddamn confetti. This was no robbery, lady. They wanted something."

"Only in Leo's office?"

"No, everywhere. The whole office, even Cherry's."

"You lied, Joseph," I said. Even though it wasn't to me, it was still a lie. "You said you and Leo were best friends, like brothers."

He struggled to sit up. "That's no lie."

"We're past that part, Joey," I said. "You've been out of it. Out of town and out cold. I know you two were arguing the week he died. Heated arguments. Care to tell me about them?"

"No," he said. "It had nothing to do with Leo's death. We worked it all out before he died. Just ask Cherry."

"So I'm supposed to believe your girlfriend? Sure, that's reliable."

"What? There's nothing going on between me and Cherry," he said all indignant as if he'd never heard such a ridiculous accusation.

Cherry held his hand. "It's okay. I told her."

"Jesus, Cherry, what'd you do that for? Bad enough we told the police, now everyone will know."

She threw down his hand. "Is it so bad everyone knows? You act like I'm a piranha."

"You mean pariah, I think," I said, though piranha was probably more accurate.

He reached out for her hand. "I'm only thinking of you, Cher. You know how gossipy everyone is at the Bill's."

She squeezed his hand and started to cry again. "What would I do without you?"

"Okay, guys, back to me," I said. "I know you lovebirds want to protect each other. Which is why you make really bad alibis for one another."

"I didn't do this to Joey. I could never hurt him."

"Not *this*, Cherry," I said. But thought, why not? "I'm talking about the night Leo was killed."

"Cherry was with me all night," Joseph said.

"See Joey, there you go lying again. How can I believe anything you say?" I grabbed my handbag and stood.

"Wait," Cherry said. She turned to Joseph. "Leo's neighbor saw my car in the driveway the night he was killed. I had to tell Elliott why I was there and that I went to your place afterward."

"Dammit, Cherry," Joseph said. "Did you tell the cops this? I've been lying all over town to protect you. Least you coulda done was tell me."

Cherry leaned over Joseph and kissed his cheek. "I'm sorry. She's gonna help us though, that's why I called her. She's gonna explain everything to the detective."

I cleared my throat. "Um, no, I'm not. I've got nothing to explain. You two could've killed Leo together. Your alibis are wafer thin."

Joseph squirmed in the bed, pulling the thin blanket up to his chest. "Look, lady. Our alibis are solid. We didn't kill Leo. Cherry came by my house at eleven forty-five."

"You're awfully specific about the time. Were you staring at the clock?"

"Kinda. I'd ordered a pizza and was waiting for the driver. Guy pulled in right behind Cherry, walked her to the door. Call Antonio's, he'll tell you. I order all the time, driver knows me."

I took out my notebook and jotted down the pizza information. "What did you and Leo argue about?"

"I'm not telling you. I don't even know you."

"Fine."

"Wait!" Cherry said. "You said you'd help."

"I can't help if I don't know what happened," I said, looking at Joseph.

He leaned back and closed his eyes. His skin was the color of putty, and the bags beneath his eyes only added to his bleak appearance. "Money," he said. "We argued about money. The store was in trouble, real trouble. Leo wanted to expand and I didn't. We fought for weeks. He finally admitted he had no intention of opening a new store, he was just scamming that chair lady to keep his seat on your stupid board. I was furious."

"But you made up? How'd that happen?"

He opened his eyes and tried to smile. It didn't quite work; the bloody gash forced his face into a grimace. "He smoothed it over the day he died. He said he was coming into some money that would solve all our financial problems."

"And you believed him?"

"I did. He was really excited. For real, you know? Happier than he'd been in months."

"Do you know where he was getting the money?"

"He said it was a new investment. Something to do with the future of the Foundation," he said and closed his eyes again.

A nurse walked in with the determination of a drill sergeant. "What are you doing in here? This patient needs his rest," she said to me and pointed at the door with a sharp snap. "Out, now."

I stood and touched Joseph's leg. "Take care."

I left the room before Nurse Ratched could admonish me further. I wandered down the hall toward the elevator, my rubber soles squeaking on the vinyl tile floors. The ransacking of the office was bigger news than the attack on Joseph (no offense to Joseph). Too much damage to be a robbery. All those TVs and they break into the office? But why bust in an entire week after Leo's murder?

I dashed back to the hospital room. The nurse was taking Joseph's vitals while Cherry slumped in the visitor's chair. I waved at her and she met me at the door.

"Who knew Joseph was out of town for the weekend?" I whispered.

She shrugged. "Everybody, I guess. There's a notice on the big Bill's sign that Leo was headed home to Jersey for his memorial. Anybody driving by would see it. You'd have to assume Joey would be going, too."

"Thanks," I whispered and walked back to the elevator.

So maybe the killer's frantic search at Leo's house resulted in a big goose egg. Had to wait until Joseph was out of town to search the Buffalo Bill's office, but Joseph comes home early. Picks the worst time possible to stop in and the killer shuts him down. Hard to believe Cherry thrashed him. She had to have known when Joseph was returning, and she could have searched the office anytime. But what was the attacker looking for?

It all went back to the missing money. Did Leo spend the money on a new investment? What did Joseph say about the future of the Foundation?

I stepped off the elevator and walked down the long hall toward the entrance. Future, I thought. Like wine futures? I picked up my pace and nearly knocked over an orderly who flew around the corner.

Chas mentioned a cellar during his fight with Jane at the Delafield House. Around here, he could only mean a wine cellar. It's called the lowcountry for a reason. Most of the land is at or below sea level. You dig under your house, you won't get a basement, you'll get a lake. Maybe Chas wasn't only upset about the land. Maybe Leo was scamming him out of wine futures.

TWENTY-THREE

I considered calling Chas to finagle an invitation to see his new wine cellar, but an invitation might be overly optimistic. Chas didn't like me. A peek through the windows and the trash would probably net more information in less time. Between a quick call to Tod for the address, and studying the island map in my glove box, I found his house.

Chas Obermeyer lived in Pelican Beach, a small plantation tucked between Oyster Cove and Sugar Hill. It took less than fifteen minutes to get to the gate from the hospital parking lot. I found an old pass in my glove box from a trip to Deidre Burch's Easter egg hunt last month.

I tucked the pass in my windshield and cruised through the gate in the outside lane, waving merrily at the guard as I passed. He was busy with a family in a mini-van and didn't notice the lapsed date typed in the corner of my pass. I zipped down Ibis Lane toward the shore, turning left on Heron Way. I passed Chas's house on the left. A neocolonial beach house with blue-gray siding and black shutters. A white van with "Domestic Bliss" written in fluffy pink script on the side sat in the driveway.

I parked one house down, then scooched down in my seat and watched Chas's front door from my rearview mirror. It was almost five o'clock. I pulled out my phone and called his office at Charter Bank.

"Chas Obermeyer's office, Ann speaking," a perky voice said.

"Hi Ann, is he in?"

"No, ma'am. He's gone for the day. Would you like his voicemail?"

"Maybe you can help me. This is Elliott Lisbon with the Ballantyne, and I really need to reach him. It's about the Gatsby lawn party at the Big House tomorrow."

"Oh sure. He just left with his wife for an early dinner party on the beach. You can probably reach him on his cell."

"Perfect, you've been a big help," I said and clicked off. With Chas gone for two hours at least, I could snoop at my leisure, assuming the Domestic Bliss crew finished soon.

They did. Five minutes later, Chas's front door opened and three women stepped out. One carried a bucket filled with typical cleaning supplies: brushes, bottles, and rags. Another carried a tall purple vacuum. The third carried a plastic bag. I twisted in my seat for a better look. She turned her back toward the street (presumably to lock the front door), then walked past the van to the side of the house. The other two gals loaded the van, then climbed in. The bag lady returned sans bag, hopped in the driver's seat, and pulled out of the drive.

I looked around. A landscaping truck and trailer were parked up the street. A tree-trimmer another six houses over, across the street. The neighborhood had more service personnel than residents. It was after five, perfect for twilight golf and early-bird dining. I rolled the Mini forward and parked another house down. The lots were large, considering properties this close to the beach were usually jammed in like a pack of PEZ, and only one house had a clear view of Chas's front drive.

I rummaged in the backseat, emerging with an official-looking clipboard in my hand. I dialed Chas's home number just to be sure no one else was inside. After a dozen rings, I clicked off.

I walked purposefully up the sidewalk to Chas's drive as if I belonged there. I'd seen this on TV, so obviously it had to work. I rang the bell on the front door. I didn't think anyone would answer, but wanted to play through the charade in case a nosy neighbor was watching the show. I pretended to write on my clipboard, then walked to the side of the house along a narrow path in the grass.

A stack of wooden crates leaned against the utility gate. I peeked around the gate, inside the utility room. More crates sat next to dual HVAC units and a pair of rubber trashcans on wheels. The crates were made from pale wood with winery names burned into the sides. The room smelled like rancid meat and rotten eggs. I changed my mind about digging through the trash. It may be another trusted TV investigative technique, but no way was I sticking my hands in those slimy cans without a hazmat suit and three layers of rubber gloves.

I closed the gate and checked around the back door for a hidden key. Took all of two seconds. Sitting alone on the grass next to a large clay pot filled with bright red geraniums was a rock. Or a fake rock, as it turned out. Very secure and not obvious at all. I slid the bottom compartment open and a square nickel key dropped into my hand. I unlocked the side door, then stuck my clipboard behind a hydrangea bush near the geranium. I didn't want to drive home and remember I left it on the kitchen table.

I tiptoed into a mudroom past a shiny turquoise washer and dryer set. The frontload Electrolux ones with Wave Touch controls and Perfect Steam drying technology. Not that I was jealous or anything. Stacks of freshly laundered towels, t-shirts, and men's boxers were neatly folded on top of a white tile countertop. The clean smell of dryer sheets was a nice reprieve from the stink of the garbage pails. I slipped into the kitchen. It held a stunning array of appliances: a six burner gas stove with double oven, two drawer dishwasher, a warming drawer, and a microwave larger than my real oven. The stainless steel sparkled in the afternoon sunlight. No clutter on the granite, not a spoon in the sink. Those Domestic Bliss gals really knew their stuff.

I wandered into a casual living room. A staircase climbed to my left, but I continued down a narrow hall. I didn't know what I was looking for. Certainly not the murder weapon, since it wasn't missing. Probably not a note detailing a confession. A dozen empty crates of wine didn't prove anything, other than the man likes to drink. I needed something to tie Chas and Leo and wine futures.

I spotted a pair of tall oak doors at the end of the hall. They opened into a wine cellar like I've never seen. I haven't seen that many, but I'm going out on a limb here to say this one was a masterpiece. We're talking seven hundred square feet, easy, with slate floors and a high tray ceiling with tiny lowlights. The walls were lined with natural redwood in diamond-shaped slots to hold a thousand wine bottles. Or more. The room was cool and smelled like blackcurrant and dry wood. Six rows of tall racks jutted into the room, three on each side of a long table in the center. A crystal decanter sat on top with a variety of wine bottles and openers.

I picked one up to examine its swirly parts when a door slammed shut somewhere in the house. I dropped the opener and it clattered on the table. Crap.

I ducked behind the first short row on my left. I barely fit. I think the edge of my left shoe stuck out into the aisle. I inched over to the right, squishing against the slots. It didn't help. I was about to make a dive for the next row over when a hand gripped my arm and yanked me forward.

"What in the hell are you doing here?" Ransom asked.

I looked up into his scowling face, only inches from my own. My heart was in my throat as adrenaline flashed through my veins. "You scared the shit out of me," I croaked out.

"This is illegal, Elliott. You can't just break into someone's house."

"You did."

"To stop you."

He gripped my other arm and pulled me closer. "Jesus, Elliott, why didn't you tell me about that damn red car?"

I wrenched my arms from his grasp, twisting and flinging until I was free. "I didn't know you didn't know," I said indignantly. "Mrs. Jones said she spoke with Parker and told her all about it. After the stunt you pulled in Savannah at the hotel, I see no reason to run to you with every little thing I find out, especially since I specifically asked Mrs. Jones if she passed her observations along to the police."

Ransom's scowl relaxed to a tightlipped frown.

"See, I can tell you already know all this, so you have no reason to scold me."

"Really? Why are you here? Stealing wine seems a little petty."

"Why are you here? Trouble getting your own information?"

"Tell me or I'll arrest you."

I wiped my sweaty hands on my skirt. I didn't want to share all my good information, but clearly I had to tell him something. I was standing in the wine cellar of a house I may have entered illegally. But I used a key in the door, not a brick through the window. That had to be worth something. "Have you heard of wine futures?"

"Wine futures?"

"Yes, where you buy wine before it's bottled."

"I know what they are, but I don't understand the connection."

"It's a little hazy. Chas was furious yesterday at the Delafield House, screaming at Jane for ruining his wine cellar expansion which was initially caused by Leo backing out of the new Buffalo Bill's development. He found out the night Leo was murdered and somehow wine futures figure into this mess."

"That's it?"

"I said it was hazy."

"What else haven't you told me?"

I thought about Milo's poker game, my slashed tires, and Leo's missing money. I shrugged nonchalantly. "Nothing, really. I'm sure you're way ahead of me."

He narrowed his eyes at me and opened his mouth to speak just as another door slammed.

I jumped back and cracked my elbow on the redwood wall. Vibrations rattled down to my fingers.

Ransom pushed me into the row I hid behind earlier, but I knew we'd both never fit. I grabbed his hand and pulled him to the last row. We wedged in face to face next to a line of upright wine bottles. Ransom smelled like his cologne, sandalwood and ginger and Cuban tobacco. I breathed through my mouth.

I only heard snippets, but the Obermeyers were clearly in a fight and the Mrs. did not want to wait in the car.

"...we couldn't stop at the store, Chas, and had to drive all the way home," a female voice hollered. The soft clicking of her heels grew louder.

"How can I get investors if I'm not using my own wine cellar?" Chas called back, his voice closer.

I gasped. Ransom covered my mouth with his hand. I couldn't breathe. I inhaled slowly, adding leather to the list of scents clinging to Nick Ransom. His entire body pressed against mine. You couldn't fit a stick of gum between us. I clutched his shirt in my fists for balance. I didn't want to press into Ransom, but I also didn't want to lean on the wall of wine and have it topple over and crush Chas. I wiggled forward away from the beam.

Our eyes locked. He gently slid his hand from my mouth, skimming down to my neck. He could feel my pulse. Hell, I could feel my pulse. It rattled my teeth with the force of rocket booster.

"I'll just grab the Insignia," Chas said. He was at the door.

My eyes jumped to the right where a dark wine bottle stood upright. It had a burgundy and gold label. Joseph Phelps, 1997. "Insignia" typed in gold in a tight black box. My eyes widened as big as dinner plates.

"No, Chas. The Fumé Blanc, the one from Dry Creek. She's serving scallops," his wife said from the doorway.

I held my breath while Chas selected a bottle from the other side of the cellar. I released the fistfuls of Ransom's shirt and spread my hands on his chest. I was becoming more nervous about Ransom's fingers on my skin than Chas rummaging around behind us.

I let out a jagged sigh as the clicking of footsteps faded on the hardwood floors. A door shut in another part of the house and we were left in silence.

Ransom and I remained locked together.

"You changed your hair," he finally said. "I like it, it's softer, more..."

"Flat? It was the eighties. Big was in." He was staring down at me. His eyes were so very blue. And dark. And steely.

Uh-oh. I recognized that look. It had been twenty years, but my nerves were humming all the same. We had this encounter earlier in the library at the Big House, the one that started with this look and ended with his hand up my dress.

I gulped. "Listen," I whispered. "What, um, are we doing?"

"Reliving my favorite memory."

I squirmed to make room and ended up rubbing against him. He froze.

"Feels like there's more to it," I said.

"There's always more to it," he whispered. He leaned forward and kissed me. It was strong, hard, and full of electricity. I reacted as if jolted by a taser and the fire spread quickly. His hand was under my blouse seconds later, around my back, quickly slipping beneath my waistband.

Man, he felt good. If there had been more room, I would've jumped up and wrapped my legs around his waist. Instead I whacked my head on a beam of redwood and nearly bit his lip.

He slowly pulled back. He ran his hand through his hair, then cracked his elbow on a wine slot.

I ducked out of the tight space. I smoothed my blouse and turned to face him.

"I'm sorry, Red, I can't do this," he said. He straightened his shirt. The second button down was missing. I think I'd ripped it off. "I'm supposed to be at my own dinner party right now."

I didn't know if he was sorry he kissed me or sorry we couldn't continue. "Why are you here? Were you following me or do you have something on Chas?"

"You," he said. "I'm here for you. Cherry said you were on your way over to the hospital, so I waited, then followed you here. Why would I follow Chas?"

I walked back to our tiny hideout and handed him one of the Insignia bottles. "That's the wine from Leo's study. The night he was murdered."

Ransom stared at the label. "Interesting, but it doesn't prove anything. Other than the cork's probably dried out from the bottle standing upright. There were probably a thousand bottles of this wine sold."

"Yes, but a remarkable coincidence. Did you find any fingerprints on Leo's bottle?" It felt surreal to be having this conversation after two minutes of debauchery behind the wine rack. Especially since my lip gloss was now evenly distributed between my lips and his.

He shook his head. "No, none. The bottle was wiped clean."

Ransom followed the killer's lead and wiped the bottle with his shirt after he set it back on the shelf. He also wiped the cellar doors after we closed them, and the door handles when we left through the side door.

I replaced the rock (Ransom wiped that, too), retrieved my clipboard from the hydrangea, and we walked to our cars. His was parked right behind mine. Like a shark about to eat a guppy.

"I really have to go," he said as he opened my car door. "I've already kept Reena waiting too long."

Right, Reena. Now I didn't feel so bad about his glossy lips. I started my car and shifted into drive.

"Stay out of trouble, Red. And other people's houses."

"You do the same," I said and sped down the street. It would've been way more dramatic if I didn't have to circle around the cul de sac and pass him again.

TWENTY-FOUR

I spent a quiet night at home with take-out from Fiesta Cantina. I ate taquitos and watched the sun go down from the deck. I tried to sort out Matty's kiss, Ransom's kiss, my slashed tires, the battle of the Delafield House, and the case of the coincidental wine bottle. But my brain was gum and I decided to read Sue Grafton instead. Kinsey Millhone always catches her killer one way or another. That gave me hope and by morning I was ready to face something even bigger than the Hirschorn investigation: The Ballantynes were coming home to the Big House.

As I rode my bike to work, I heard the steely roar of the Ballantyne jet overhead, approaching the landing strip. With the airport less than a mile away, and only ten flights a day, it's pretty easy to figure out someone's arrival. The day was sunny and bright with high wispy clouds sailing across the sky, but a storm was rolling in for tomorrow. As long as it didn't hit before nine tonight, I didn't care if it rained for a week.

I stashed my hipster in my office and scooted out the front steps where Tod was already waiting.

"What are you doing here?" I asked.

"I work here. You often abuse my services, overask for favors, interrupt my workday..."

"Shouldn't you be picking up the Ballantynes at the airport?"

"I dropped off the car early this morning. They're bringing guests, remember? The nice couple from Australia. I think the Ballantynes are following them to the Outback tomorrow to look for dingoes."

"Maybe a dingo ate chor baby," I said with a heavy Australian accent.

Tod ignored me.

A minute later Mr. Ballantyne drove up in a white Rolls Corniche convertible circa 1985. It looked like a parade float. Mrs. Ballantyne rode shotgun and a smiling couple waved from the backseat, all wearing fancy hats and big sunglasses.

"Elli, my dear," Mrs. Ballantyne said as she stepped out. She kissed both my cheeks and squeezed me tight. She was a beautiful woman at seventy-two, a full two years older than her husband. She had rosy cheeks, piercing blue eyes, and short white hair. She skipped makeup in favor of sunscreen and had more energy than a five-year-old on Christmas morning. She stuck her tiny arm through mine. "Do tell everything you've been up to. Getting into trouble, I assume. I can't wait to hear all the juicy details!"

Tod unloaded the luggage from a trunk the size of a steamship while Mr. Ballantyne unloaded his guests from the rear.

"Hello, Elliott! So good of you to meet us," Mr. Ballantyne bellowed. He also kissed both my cheeks and squeezed me tight.

Mr. Ballantyne was a tall man at six foot even and resembled a scarecrow with sticks for arms and legs and knobby knees and elbows. His booming voice flowed out of him naturally, as if all the world's a stage and the audience sat in the last row of the theatre. "This is Mrs. Polly Pullman and her husband, Mr. Timothy Pullman."

I shook their hands in turn. If I didn't know they were married, I'd swear they were siblings. Both had sandy blond hair, green eyes, and freckles brushed across their cheeks. I pegged them as in their fifties, maybe sixty at most.

"I'm sure you've had a very long day," I said to Mrs. Ballantyne. "Shall we get you upstairs and settled? The party begins at five this afternoon. Carla's in the kitchen all day, I'm sure she can send lunch up when you're ready."

"You are such a thoughtful delight, Elli," she said. She turned to her husband. "Edward, do you mind if we rest before lunch? Maybe we can dine in the reflection garden?"

He wrapped his arm around her. "Splendid idea, Vivi."

"Agreed," said Mrs. Pullman.

Mr. Ballantyne looked over his shoulder at me. "And on the other matter, Elli? I trust no news is good news?"

"Absolutely," I said. "I expect nothing but a delightful afternoon."

Tod carried their bags into the house and up the center staircase to their private residence on the third floor. It was larger than most homes with an enormous master's chamber, a trio guest suites with private baths, his and hers sitting rooms, a game room, a media room, and a balcony that wrapped around the entire backside of the house.

I spent the rest of the day on the back lawn, assisting with table linens, pounding in stakes for the games, and directing traffic (no, the bar doesn't go on the first tennis court; yes, I would like the twinkle lights over the pergola and not thrown haphazardly on the azalea bushes).

After a quick shower at my cottage, I dressed in my best Gatsby attire: a long petal pink chemise with a deep v-neck collar and a striped silk scarf tie just above a pleated skirt. I set my hair in thick waves and stuck a large flower pin in my hair.

At four-thirty, I arrived back at the Big House, ready to inspect the grounds and gulp down a quick cocktail before the guests arrived. Matty might stand me up, Ransom might show up, and there's probably a killer on the grounds. Maybe two cocktails were in order.

"Well, aren't you beautiful," Matty said to me when I walked into the foyer. "Fitzgerald could've been writing about you."

I curtsied. "You look quite dapper yourself, Master Gannon." He was right off the pages of a Ralph Lauren costume ad in plaid knickers, argyle vest, and a floppy newsboy cap. "Shall we entertain ourselves with a libation?"

He agreed, and we walked arm and arm to the back where we could romp around the lawn like kids summering in East Egg at the Buchanan mansion. After watching a heated tennis match and a spirited croquet game, we decided to find a sport of our own. I chose horseshoes over lawn darts. I was more comfortable hurling iron across the yard rather than flinging daggers through the air.

The warm evening air smelled like sweet magnolias and fresh cut grass. The crowd was especially electric. If receiving an invitation to the Big House was like getting a Golden Ticket, then attending when the Ballantynes were in residence was like taking a ride in the Wonkavator. Mr. and Mrs. Ballantyne moved through the party with an experienced hand, gracing each couple and group with lively conversation and glittery tidbits about their latest journey.

"Looks like they're taking photos with the school kids," Matty said after the second inning of horseshoes. "Don't you want to go over there? You deserve it for organizing this whole thing."

I watched the Ballantynes with the crowd of players and coaches. Flash bulbs sparkled as the photographers snapped the couple surrounded with the kids in uniform. "No, I could use a break from the attention. I'll meet with the players later, deliver the equipment, something like that."

He lobbed a horseshoe straight at the stake. He hadn't missed one yet. "You could help coach the team next year. I'm sure they'd love to have you."

"Ha. Turns out I throw like a girl." I pitched a horseshoe at the post and it hit with a satisfying clang. "Except in horseshoes, of course."

"Of course."

We walked over and picked our horseshoes from the sand. I'm sure true diehards might balk at the use of sand instead of dirt around the stakes, but I could only carry so much hand-sanitizer.

"Good thing we're playing house rules or we could be here all night," I said as we both scored points in the next inning.

"I wouldn't mind that at all. But one more for me, and I win," Matty said. He lifted his last horseshoe up and effortlessly slung it down the lane. It clomped into the sand, sliding right around the ring.

He leaned in close with his hand low on my back. I felt his heat through my shirt. "Too bad we didn't have something riding on this game. I say next time we make our own rules."

My knees weakened and I nearly slipped in the grass. Hey, I like changing the rules just as much as the next slightly obsessive, barely compulsive hot-blooded girl.

The dinner bell rang on the other side of the backyard. We slowly made our way to the dinner line. He held my hand in his. I couldn't remember the last time a man took my hand as we walked. Or when I wanted one to.

Matty and I followed the end of the line toward the buffet. Tod and Carla manned the front table, Chef Carmichael ran the last table, and liveried servers assisted guests with their dinner plates. I was all but starved by the time we reached them. The passed hors d'oeuvres consisted of jumbo shrimp, lump crab cakes, Cajun scallops, and one lone non-seafood item: fried green tomatoes.

"A buffet, Carla?" I said.

"Yes, I know you hate them, but table service on the back lawn would be a nightmare and you know it. My fried chicken would wilt."

"I know, I know. But still. All this food out in the open, people sneezing on it, and then I'm supposed to just eat it?"

"Yes, just like Weird Al says," Tod said.

"You're invoking Weird Al?"

"It seemed appropriate."

"You're a special person, Tod," I said.

Carla handed me a covered plate from behind the table. "So are you, Elli, so are you. Now go on and enjoy, I doctored this up just for you."

Buttermilk fried chicken, coleslaw, macaroni and cheese, and mashed sweet potatoes. "Carla! Thank you so much." It looked fantastic. And so much better than Matty's which was piled with catfish, dirty rice, and collard greens.

I followed Matty to the last table with open seats. It sat beneath a blooming magnolia in the center of the lawn. Deidre Burch and her husband, Anton, were already there.

"I have an exciting new project for the board," I said to Deidre after we sat. "Leo created the most wonderful proposal for the Shelter Initiative, a new homeless program for the county. We'll have a dedicated center with a kitchen, semi-private sleeping rooms, and counselors. Plus, full funding from the Ballantyne. I just need someone to chair the committee."

"It sounds wonderful," Deidre said in her lovely southern drawl. "And an easy committee to chair. Always a good thing. I'm sure the board will approve it as soon as it's proposed."

I smiled and jumped with inner glee. "It will go on the agenda for the very next meeting. You'll be perfect."

"I appreciate the thought, but I'm proposing a new literacy committee. I can't possibly chair another committee. Don't you worry, sugar. It'll be a snap to find someone else on the board."

I nodded and kept my smile in place. Some snap. I was almost out of board members to ask. I took my first bite of sweet potatoes and nearly choked on them when Reena and Ransom approached our table.

"May we join you?" Ransom asked.

I felt Matty stiffen beside me. Reena didn't look too pleased either, but she sat down anyway.

"So Reena, how is your Mumbai project doing?" Deidre asked after they settled in.

"It's a daily struggle, Deidre. Half of the people don't want the help while the other half are merely indifferent," Reena said. "We have a new teacher arriving in Mumbai next week. He's very charming and quite entertaining. We are hoping he will be able to encourage the students to return each day."

I chewed and swallowed my chicken without actually tasting it. I couldn't have been more uncomfortable with Matty's arm around my chair, Ransom sitting across the table, and Reena shooting death-ray eyes at me.

"Elli, I've been meaning to ask you all night," Deidre said. "How's your car? What a fright for you, and so violent, right here on the island."

Ransom's head snapped up. "What happened to your car?"

"All four tires slashed," Matty answered. "I'm surprised you haven't heard, seeing how you're a detective. I bet the entire island knows by now."

Ransom's gaze flicked to Matty and then to me. "She didn't mention it when we were together last night."

"Last night?" Matty and Reena said at the same time.

I stuttered, which only made it worse. Not a single real word came out.

Reena laughed. Seductively. Her hand on Nick's arm, her eyes on me. "Nick was with *me* last night. Until *very* late."

"Our engagement was earlier," I said to Reena. "He saw me first."

"Excuse me?" she replied.

Did I just say "he saw me first?"

Ransom leaned over to Reena, but she was pissed. She threw down her napkin. "Where exactly did you two meet?"

I looked at Ransom, then back at Reena. And never once up at Matty. I put my hand on his thigh instead. Rock hard and unforgiving.

"We met to discuss wine," Ransom said smoothly. "Elliott here suggested a vintage I hadn't paid much attention to. It was very brief."

Reena's glare never left me. She picked up her fork, her grasp so tight, I almost ducked. It was one thing to throw pastries, but another to throw the silver. Those tines were sharp. But then she set it back down. "I've forgotten the chutney. If you'll excuse me."

Ransom stood. "Let me," he said to her.

She smiled warmly at him. "Thank you, Nick, but I'll only be a minute. I need the walk."

I watched her walk toward the buffet in her ivory chemise with silk buttons and an ostrich feather in her hair.

"What happened to your tires, Elliott?" Ransom asked.

"A particular student at Seabrook Prep didn't appreciate my investigative techniques and gave me a parting gift," I said.

"So this happened under your nose, Gannon?"

Matty leaned back in his chair. He looked calm on the outside, but his leg muscles were still clenched beneath my palm. "I'm Headmaster, not security. It had more to do with the murder investigation you have yet to solve than it does with one of my students."

"Were you questioning Tra—" Ransom said.

I threw up my hand to stop him. Deidre and Anton were watching the conversation like spectators at a ping pong match.

"I'm questioning whomever I deem necessary, Ransom. As Matty said, you haven't yet solved your case."

"The case is solved, Lisbon," Ransom said. "You're just stubborn."

Pot, meet Kettle, I almost said, but stuck my chin out instead and pointedly looked away. I was not going to engage Ransom in front of Matty or the Burches. I saw Reena fawning over Mrs. Ballantyne near the buffet. I mentally rolled my eyes, then caught sight of Jane striding across the grass with Chas closer than her shadow, practically chasing her. I couldn't hear what they were saying, but I didn't have to. Chas looked ready to rip Jane's head off by her hair.

"It looks like we both want the same thing," Matty said. "Elliott to stay away from you."

I jerked my head back. "What did you say?"

"I never said I wanted her away from me," Ransom said. "Just my investigation. I certainly didn't mind it yesterday, did I, Red?"

Oh Lord. In front of Matty and Deidre and everyone else. How did I get wrapped into a love triangle (rectangle?) and a murder investigation. "Excuse me, I have to settle something. You two aren't the worst of my problems right now."

I left the table as Reena sat back down. Fine, I thought. Let her feel the heat for a while. I climbed the steps to the patio and watched in alarm as Jane and Chas tangled near the pool.

"Don't you dare threaten me, Obermeyer," Jane hissed. "I have the law on my side."

"Bullshit. You blackmailed Leo into giving up that land and then you killed him. You're going down and I'm going to watch. Hell, I'm going to help."

"Go on home and drink away your sorrows. Your little Buffalo Bill's project will never see the light of day, not as long as I'm heading up the Historic Society. And the Ballantyne board, come to think of it. What have you got? I'm not sure a mountain of debt will actually help you, you know?"

"You bitch," he yelled. "You'll not only rot in prison for killing Leo, but I'll wipe your name through the mud so deep, no one will find it a hundred years from now."

"Stop it, you two," I said. I marched between them and pushed Chas back. "Enough. We're at a *party*, people. The Ballantynes are less than a hundred feet away."

"Maybe I should have a long chat with Edward," Chas said. "Let him know what his little pet has been up to in his absence."

"You'll do no such thing, Chas," I said. "Just back off."

He pointed his finger at Jane's face. "I'm suing you for everything you're worth."

"Get in line, asshole," Jane said with a laugh as Chas stormed off.

"Are you crazy, Jane? Mr. Ballantyne will croak if he hears about this."

"He'll croak when he hears what a crack investigator you turned out to be. Elliott, you are an idiot. You've caused more problems than you've solved."

"I got you out of jail for your auction! Do you know how hard that was?"

"Please. My attorney did that. But if you don't start figuring this shit out, I could lose my seat on the board."

"Jesus, Jane, aren't you paying attention? You could lose your *life*."

"Don't be so melodramatic."

"South Carolina is a death penalty state. Leo's murder was premeditated. They will kill you. You were there. A witness saw you driving away from Leo's house right after the murder!"

"I was not there. This is your problem. You don't listen. Now, if you'll excuse me, I have to call my attorney. Chas is like a dog with an old soup bone with this ridiculous Buffalo Bill's project. I may have to snatch it away before he really digs in."

"No way, Jane. Not a chance. No one is suing anyone. That won't solve anything."

"No, Elliott. It will solve everything," she said and calmly walked away.

Great, I thought. Great, great, great.

I turned around and slammed right into Ransom.

I punched him in the chest. I think it hurt me more than him. "What is wrong with you? How could you tell the entire table about our...*thing* yesterday?"

"Clearly I didn't mean to. And you didn't help by calling it an engagement."

"Discreet, Ransom. I'm supposed to be discreet. Quiet, private, on the down low. You can't blab every move I make to a full table at a dinner party!"

"Why didn't you tell me someone's threatening you?"

"It's not your concern." I took a step back. "Why are you here, by the pool?"

"I saw you follow Jane. I wanted to see what she was up to."

"You think she'll just blurt out that she killed Leo?"

"She'll admit it sooner or later."

"You're wrong, Ransom. So so wrong. Jane didn't do this and you're not listening to me."

"Why can't you trust me, that I know what I'm doing?"

"Trust you? Never. You had your chance."

"This isn't about us. It's about you withholding evidence and obstructing my investigation."

"I'm not obstructing."

"The hell you're not. You're protecting the Foundation."

I threw my hands up in exasperation. "Of course I am, but I'm not protecting a killer. You are set on Jane but there other suspects. Travis, Chas, Joseph, Cherry. You're just mad you didn't find out about the red car yourself so you could tuck it away before anyone else heard about it."

Ransom took a step toward me. "Watch it, Lisbon. I admit you're damn sexy when you're all worked up, but be careful with your accusations."

My temperature started to rise. Either because he called me sexy or because he was frustrating the shit out of me. "Someone framed Jane, I know it."

"If it walks like a duck, and quacks like a duck..."

"If I'm the killer and I wanted to frame Jane, I would use the most obvious Jane weapon. Everyone knew she hated Leo and that damn trophy."

"Or maybe, Elliott, she killed him. I have solid evidence."

"Oh, like the ripped form? Half the island heard her threaten to kill Leo's project. That's not evidence."

"You're forgetting the best part. Jane was there that night, remember? The neighbor saw her car."

"Her car, Ransom, not her. Do you know how many black Sebring convertibles are on this island?"

"With a driver wearing a bright scarf?"

"It's an island!"

I swear he rolled his eyes at me.

And Heaven help me, I pushed him into the pool.

TWENTY-FIVE

It was an accident. Sort of. I only meant to push past him, elbow him out of my way as I righteously stalked across the deck. But I used too much force. And maybe both hands. Man, if you could've seen the look on his face, you could've sold it.

I rushed back to our table, but it was empty. No Deidre, no Matty, no leftover buffet plates. Not even a lone dinner roll. I checked my watch and gasped. I'd been gone longer than I thought. Most of the guests were now watching a rousing mixed doubles match down on the grass court.

I spotted Tod at the bar.

"Have you seen Matty? I think I better sneak out of here before Nick Ransom climbs out of the pool."

He raised his eyebrow. "A little overdressed for a dip."

"It was unscheduled. Matty?"

"He left while you and Detective Handsome were duking it out. Or maybe it was you and Jane. Either way, he's gone."

Shit. I screwed up again. "Can you and Carla wrap things up? I'll owe you."

"You already owe me."

"I know, I know. National debt proportions and all that. Just help a girl out, okay?"

He nodded toward the patio. "I see a tall man by the pool. You better scoot. You don't want to get caught in the car with your top down, so to speak. He might lift you right out."

I crept around the side of the house as if I was a cat burglar rather than the director. I slid into my car and hustled home, barely slowing down until I parked in my garage. I went into the house and leaned against the door with a sigh. So this night didn't go so hot. Matty's pissed, Ransom's pissed, and I was starving.

I grabbed the phone and pushed the five key, the one for emergencies.

"John's Pizza," a low baritone voice boomed into the phone.

"It's Elliott Lisbon on Spy Hop Lane. I need a Hawaiian bbq pizza stat."

"Sorry, Elli, I got a driver out sick. It's gonna be at least an hour and a half."

My heart sank and tears sprang into my eyes.

"Never mind. I'll be dead by then."

I hung up and sullenly whipped open the refrigerator door. I stared inside. A half-gallon of skim stared back. I opened one of the cooling drawers. Two packages of string cheese and a dozen fat free pudding cups. Well, crap. Doesn't anyone go grocery shopping around here? I checked the freezer. Three boxes of mint Girl Scout cookies and two diet dinners so frozen over, they'd become one with the ice machine.

I snatched the skim milk and poured a bowl of cereal. I ate it right over the sink. Ten minutes later, I dragged my tired butt upstairs and into bed. I had the day free tomorrow and I was going to sleep until noon.

Then come hell or high water, I was solving this murder case and dumping the evidence right over Ransom's head. We'll see who's right, I thought as I drifted off to sleep.

I woke up feeling groggy and hung over, even though I only drank a single Mint Julep. The skylight over my head was grungy like my mood. I burrowed deeper under the covers.

Matty left the party without speaking to me. Probably take more than a picnic lunch with a fruit cup to make it up to him. I may have really blown it and we hadn't even had one single real date. And I wasn't winning favors with the police, either. I didn't even want to know how Ransom explained his impromptu plunge into the pool.

Better not worry about all that now, I thought. If I could just solve the case, prove I'm not a complete bag of air, everything will be peachy.

I finally talked myself out of bed at ten o'clock. Within the hour, I was dressed in cropped cargoes, a sturdy blue tee, and ballet trekkers. Serious crime-solving, get-this-shit-done, run-all-over-town-if-I-have-to gear. I spread out my notebook on the living room trunk table with the last of my cereal and begun theorizing.

I needed to narrow down my suspect list. First: Jane. Did she or did she not kill Leo? I think not. And not only because I wanted Ransom to be wrong. No, Jane didn't kill Leo because she said she didn't kill Leo, and I believed her. She never lied, not once. She didn't make up an alibi, she simply refused to give one. Whatever Owen Dobbs saw that night, Jane did not murder Leo. She was nasty, mean, unpleasant, scalding, blunt, and more difficult than a wet cat in a bathtub, but she didn't lie.

Which left Chas, Travis, Bebe, Joseph, and Cherry. And wine futures, secret affairs, real estate scams, blackmail, and money—both of the sock-it-away and strike-it-rich variety. I felt as if I had dozens of puzzle pieces, but I didn't know if they all belonged to the same puzzle and I didn't have a picture on the box to compare them to. I needed either more pieces, or less.

I wrote the names of my suspects in the back of the notebook. I'd already spoken to them multiple times. I'd spoken to everyone. I flipped through the pages. Well, not everyone. Ransom and I only spoke to one actress, not both. If Jenna's interview was interrupted, why not Brooke's? According to my notes, she was due back from Athens yesterday. A drive out to Savannah would at least buy me time until I thought up something better.

The sky remained blanketed in gloomy gray clouds, so I left the top up. I didn't want to get caught in a sudden storm and ride around all day with my pants in a puddle. Get-this-shit-done pants are less effective when wet.

I cruised over the Palmetto Bridge and into Summerton through light traffic. Vacationers and residents must be tucked in for the day, pushed indoors by the threat of rain and air thick with humidity. Enough that I kicked up the a/c as I hurtled toward Savannah with the case on my mind.

Brooke wasn't the only one I had yet to talk to. I didn't call on Gina Beckendinga, Bebe's roommate at the Scrapper's convention. Just because Ransom said Bebe's alibi checked out, didn't make it true. Ransom believed Travis the first time around, and the same for Mrs. Jones, the neighborhood watch captain and spotter of Cherry's car in the drive.

Some hotshot investigator he is, I thought. But he definitely knows something I don't. Something has him clinging to Jane.

And then there's Buffalo Bill's. Brandon, the nervous salesclerk, probably wasn't the only one to hear Joseph and Leo arguing. Any one of the staff could've heard threats or promises or any one of a dozen revealing tidbits. I just needed another puzzle piece and a hint or a glimpse to start snapping them together.

I sailed over the Talmadge Bridge into Savannah shortly before eleven. I parked on Jones Street in front of Jenna's brownstone. I quickly jotted a list of new interviewees in my notebook, then dog-eared the page with Gina's information on it. She lived in Savannah. I could stop by while I was in the neighborhood, then hit Buffalo Bill's on the way back. With Joseph and Cherry at the hospital, I bet the staff would tattle like kids in a schoolyard.

I climbed the metal stairs and knocked on Jenna's door. I waited in the small foyer, then knocked again.

Jenna answered the door in wrinkled sweatpants and a stained shirt. Her braids were unkempt, frizzy strands poking out like she'd slept for a week and forgotten to wash them. Or her clothes. Or her face.

She stared through swollen and runny eyes at me. "Oh, you're the lady from last week, with the police," she said when she saw me. A small sob shook her shoulders. "Have you come about Brooke?"

"What about Brooke?" I asked with my hand on my heart.

"She's dead," she hiccupped. Fresh tears ran down her face. "Killed in a hit and run four days ago."

"Oh no, Jenna, I'm so sorry. What happened?"

She opened the door wider and dragged back into the apartment. It smelled like sour milk and basement mold. Every shade was drawn with only narrow strips of light peeking in from the sides. Jenna balled herself up on the couch beneath an afghan and blew her nose. "She was my best friend. Since the fifth grade. I can't believe she's gone."

I sat by her feet and patted her legs. "Tell me."

"She was staying at her boyfriend's house, he lives on the UGA campus. She went to dinner with a couple of friends, then drove back to his house, but she never made it." Jenna hiccupped again. "A car came out of nowhere. They said he was probably drunk, and it was late, so Brooke may have been asleep at the wheel anyway, maybe drifted over a lane. I guess, it was, you know, instant."

"Did they catch the driver?"

"No. No one really saw much, it happened so fast." Jenna closed her eyes and pulled the afghan higher.

Four days ago was Sunday. The same day Joseph was attacked. Quite a coincidence, I thought. Athens was no more than two or three hours from the island. But why kill Brooke?

"Would you mind if I looked around Brooke's room? Just for a minute."

She shrugged her shoulders. "Sure. Her mom won't be here until next week. We're gonna box her stuff up, you know? It's the door behind me, but I can't go in there. I don't think I can take the sight of her things right now."

"No, no, you just rest. I'll be right back."

I picked my way through the apartment and slowly opened Brooke's door. I stood frozen at the sight. The room was trashed.

Clothes ripped and dumped on the floor; the mattress slashed until the old springs popped out; broken DVDs, metal reels, VCR tapes snapped into pieces.

I stepped back. "So Jenna, you haven't seen this mess?"

Jenna tilted her head back over the side of the couch and looked at me upside down. She tried to smile. "Brooke's a bit sloppy, I know. She'd always say she was going to clean up on Saturday, but then never did."

"Jenna, this is more than sloppy."

She peeled herself off the sofa and slumped over to the doorway. Her breath sucked in so hard, I thought she was choking. "Oh my God!" She slapped her hand over her mouth and started to enter the room.

"Wait. Don't touch anything. Let me look around, okay? Go sit on the sofa and wait for me."

Jenna went back to her blanket with her eyes popping out of her head.

I gingerly tiptoed around the mess, not touching a single thing with my hands. I knelt near the clothes, then the mattress. My mind raced. Definitely not a coincidence. But what was the killer looking for? What could Brooke possibly have? And why only search this room, why not the entire apartment?

My heart stopped. Because he finally found what he was looking for.

The room was only nine feet by nine with a frameless double bed against the left wall, a closet on the right, and a desk under the window. I didn't have to worry about opening the desk drawers because they were broken on the floor, the contents now mixed into the mishmash of Brooke's meager belongings. I looked through the closet, but there were only clothes. No empty shoeboxes or garment bags. Just tattered remnants of fabric dangling from cheap plastic hangers, rags that were once typical college girl clothes: jeans, sweats, tees. I turned back to the desk. No computer, but no ports either. No leftover power plug or internet cable indicating one belonged there. What else did she have?

I studied the destroyed movie tapes and discs. Only they weren't movies, they were auditions. Each case marked with the date and time. They started with an audition for a furniture commercial six years ago and ended with a small role in a TV pilot last month.

Leo's commercial!

My hands shook as I gently kicked through the pile of DVDs. It was missing.

"Jenna, did Leo Hirschorn give you a copy of your audition from Buffalo Bill's?"

"Yeah," she called back. "It's on DVD. We always get a copy when they film it."

I joined her in the living room. "Do you happen to have Brooke's tape?"

"No, she kept her own. But I have my copy and she's on it. I had a techie friend from SCAD dupe a copy for Brooke with just her audition on it, but mine's the original with both."

I could barely think straight I was so excited. "Can I borrow it?"

"Sure, I guess. You think Buffalo Bill's wants it back?" She went into her room and came back a few seconds later with a slim clear jewel case in her hand.

"I'm not sure. But this was never in Brooke's room, right? Not part of the mess in there?" I tucked the DVD into my hipster.

"No. Like I said, I never opened her door after her mom called to tell me that Brooke, that Brooke…" She sniffed and took a deep breath. "When she called to tell me."

I led her back to the couch and we sat down. "Listen to me. I need you to call the police and report the break-in. Tell them everything you know about Brooke's accident, too. It's important."

"Break-in?" She hopped to her feet in a panic. "Oh my God, you mean it's related? Someone, I mean the killer, I mean, oh my God." She ran around the sofa. "What do I do?"

"Calm down," I said, but she didn't hear me. "Jenna! Calm down!" I shouted and pulled her back to the sofa. "I'm not sure someone broke in, but don't talk to anyone but the police, do you hear me? Do you have a friend you trust who can come over right now?"

She nodded. "My mom's coming over. She's worried I'm not eating." She picked up her cell phone and dialed her mom. "Mom," she said and started to cry again. "Okay, yeah, okay. Thanks, mom." She turned to me. "She's just turning onto Jones now."

I had to get out of there quick. I didn't need a protective mother asking too many questions. The DVD wasn't part of the wreckage, but sooner or later the police would want it back. "As soon as she gets here, you call the police. Lock the door behind her and wait for them. Do not go back in there, okay? The police will handle everything."

I walked to the door. "You'll be okay. What does your mom drive?"

"A tan Cadillac," she said. "And thanks. Brooke's mom would've totally freaked out when we opened her door." I hugged her and left. I heard the deadbolt engage behind the door and hustled down to my car. I threw it into drive and whipped a U-turn in the street.

I waited until I saw her mom pull up out front, then I drove over the Talmadge Bridge like a bat out of hell.

TWENTY-SIX

I drove through Hardee's for a western bacon cheeseburger and a Pepsi to eat in the car as I zipped back to the island. I dripped bbq sauce into my lap, but I didn't care. I dialed information and the operator connected me to the M.E.'s office.

"Fleet," Harry groused into the phone.

"Harry, it's Elliott Lisbon. I think I found another murder, connected to Leo Hirschorn's. An actress out of Savannah. But I need your help."

"What the hell does an actress have to do with the Hirschorn case? Was she hit over the head with a trophy, too?"

"Leo interviewed her before he died. Now she's dead. Run off the road four days ago. They're connected, I just know it."

"I'm busy, Lisbon. Got enough troubles without having to track down more, especially a car accident out of Savannah. Have you seen my office? I got more paperwork in here than the damn IRS."

"Athens, Harry, not Savannah. She was up at the University. Please, please, can you at least make one small tiny phone call and find out what really happened? Come on, Harry, her bedroom was ransacked just like Leo's house, and then some mysterious un-named driver runs her off the road and kills her? It sounds suspicious, right?"

He didn't answer me, but he didn't hang up, either.

"I'll owe you."

"You already owe me, Lisbon."

I tapped my fingers on the steering wheel as I sped over the bridge onto the island. "Come on, Harry, it's one call. It's the missing piece. I'm telling you her room was ripped to shreds, not just tossed. It was destroyed."

I heard papers shuffle on his desk. He grumbled something that sounded like "bust my chops" and "goddamn bellyache." Then he sighed. "Give me the name. I'll call if I run out of things to do. But no promises and don't bug me."

"Thanks, Harry. The name's Brooke Norman, killed this past Sunday in Athens. That's all I know." I gave him my cell number and begged him to call back as soon as he heard.

I called Ransom. It rolled straight to voicemail.

"Nick, it's Elliott. I think I've found something on Leo's death. Call me as soon as you get this. It's important." I clicked off and called the Island Police station.

Ransom was out and Parker had the day off. The desk sergeant wouldn't give me her home number, so I left a similar message on her voicemail in case she called in. This whole thing with Brooke might be nothing, but after the red VW disaster, I wasn't taking any chances.

I pulled into my driveway, dashed inside, threw my handbag on the counter, and put the DVD in the player. I fiddled with the remote until I could find the right channel for it to play.

I watched Jenna's interview first. She was right, nothing much happened and it lasted all of twelve minutes. Then a bright young girl's face popped up on the picture. The camera loved her. She had soft brown hair that fell just past her shoulders. She wore it parted on the side with a leather clip in her hair. Her shirt was pink with brown suede fringe and she held a matching cowboy hat in her hand.

I couldn't see Leo, but I heard him. It was haunting to hear his voice, strong and booming. No hint that in a few weeks' time he'd be dead. Or a week after that, this lovely girl sitting in front of him would be dead, too.

Leo started the audition by telling Brooke about his plans for a mock Price is Right game show commercial. They chatted back and forth for about twenty minutes, comparing their favorite episodes and prizes, different ideas on how to incorporate the western theme into the show.

Then Leo asked about her experience. "Why don't you tell me all about yourself there, darlin'. What kind of experience you have with makin' commercials?"

"Why, all kinds," she said in a lilting southern drawl. "I starred in a bunch of commercials last year. One was for a new wireless service, I played a waitress in a coffee shop who used her phone to find a better job. It ran for almost six months. I've also been in movies. I was an extra for *Sweet Home Alabama*. They filmed up near Rome, Georgia, just north of Atlanta. I was just a little girl then, barely a teenager. But my mama loves Reese Witherspoon and drove me all the way from Mobile to see her. That's when I first fell in love with acting."

"Have you done much modeling or improv work? As a product model on the game show, you won't need to say much, just an occasional squeal as you show off prizes."

"Oh sure. I had one job for an infomercial, for a company called Humanitarian something. I played a teacher to help poor kids in Africa, showed programs and brochures with kids living in crooked shacks on mounds of trash. I had to stay in character for the whole interview from the time I got out of my car until I left. Then there was another job where I wore a nun costume, it was hotter than a—"

"Wait, go back a second," Leo interrupted. "What was that about being a teacher in Africa?"

I held my breath as the hairs on my arm prickled with goose bumps, afraid to hear her answer.

"It was for a charity school in Africa, but we filmed it in Atlanta. In a fancy boardroom full of people, talking about how these poor kids had tiny classrooms and no supplies. I didn't have many lines. But I showed them all the pamphlets, passed around school-

books, stuff like that. The coordinator lady thought I was a natural."
Brooke laughed. "Of course, she had no idea I was a professional."

"How's that?"

"Well, one day my boyfriend called up. His roommate's girlfriend got appendicitis only days before the shoot. The coordinator
was pitchin' a fit because she needed a replacement, but it couldn't
be anyone professional, had to be a student with no acting ambitions." Brooke leaned forward. "You know on infomercials, they
don't want the audience to recognize an actor, ruins the whole sales
pitch. Here you think some nice lady bought a whole set of knives,
and she's really just a plant. So anyway, my boyfriend and I pretend
I'm just his small town girlfriend still living in Mobile."

"How very clever of you, little darlin'! Can you tell me anything else about this meeting?"

She tilted her head and tapped her index finger against her
cheek. Then she smiled like a teacher's pet with the right answer.
"Well, did you ever see that movie Slumdog Millionaire? The one
where they play the Who Wants to be a Millionaire game in Africa?
The pictures in the brochures looked just like that place. There was
one of a little boy holding an old can of beans. So sad."

"Do you remember the coordinator lady's name by chance?"

"Reba, I think. She was very beautiful, hair all the way to her
waist."

"Could it have been Reena? Reena Patel?"

She shook her head. "I don't remember. Oh God, do you
know her?" Brooke's eyes went wide and her face dropped. "You're
not going to tell her I'm a real actor are you? She might make me
give the money back and I already spent it."

"No, no darlin', don't you worry about a thing. This won't
cost you anything," Leo assured her.

Only your life, I thought.

I hit pause and sank into the couch. This DVD wasn't just a
missing puzzle piece, it was the picture on the damn box.

Not a teacher in Africa, but one in India. Mumbai, to be exact. I'd bet dollars to donuts the boardroom Brooke mentioned was

at the Lafferty Foundation. And I'd also bet Leo thought the same thing. As a board member, he would've interviewed Reena about Mumbai Humanitarian before the first meeting—before the May Bash, before he was murdered.

But what did it mean? Was Reena boosting her credentials? The Lafferty had a very rigorous approval process and would've insisted on meeting Reena's teachers. Probably cheaper to hire an actress for the day than to fly a real one to the states from India. Especially a nice southern girl who would say exactly what Reena wanted her to. No need to worry about a real teacher accidentally blabbing about using grant funds for teachers instead of students. Fancy dinners, flying first class, luxury accommodations. If Reena was hiding teachers, she could be hiding anything. I knew I wasn't crazy for hating her.

If the folks at the Lafferty discovered the Mumbai meeting was nothing more than theatre, they would cancel the grant faster than they could draft the paperwork. Then sue the crap out of her. Damages, fraud, and every penny they originally gave her. Plus, Reena would be blacklisted. No other foundation, including the Ballantyne, would even speak to her, much less consider a grant application. As a board member, Leo knew the impact of this kind of information. Did he tell her about the video? Blackmail her? He was certainly desperate for money to save Buffalo Bill's.

I stared at Brooke's smiling face on my TV. Shit, Leo, what did you do?

TWENTY-SEVEN

I ejected the DVD and popped it back into its case. I grabbed my notebook, handbag, and keys, and left through the garage. Then I stopped.

I didn't want to keep the DVD with me. What if I lost it or something happened to it? I dashed back inside. But where to hide it? I stuck it in the freezer behind the block of frozen dinners. I was halfway out the door when another thought hit me. Does temperature affect discs? I quickly plucked it from the freezer. I needed a new spot. Cereal box? Underwear drawer? Linen closet? I ended up stashing it in my printer, beneath the stack of paper in the paper tray.

I ran over to Ransom's house and knocked on his door. No answer. I peeked in the window. The place looked dark and deserted. I ran back to the Mini and sped out of Oyster Cove with no real destination in mind. I left another voicemail on Ransom's cell. Seriously, the man hounds me for days and then won't return my calls even though I used the words "urgent," "important," and "for shit's sake, call me already."

I jumped onto Cabana Boulevard heading south, piecing together my theory. Reena Patel killed Leo Hirschorn in a blackmail scheme gone awry. In a freak act of serendipity, Leo discovers Reena used fake teachers to get the Lafferty grant. He demands money in exchange for silence, maybe even offers to secure the Ballantyne grant. She denies his outrageous claims, but Leo explains the audition with Brooke Norman and Reena wants proof. She sees the video with Brooke, recognizes her as the student she hired, and freaks.

But the video isn't exactly ironclad. Brooke never mentions Reena's name or even Mumbai, repeatedly saying the children of Africa. The only solid clue is a description of a picture on a brochure of a boy playing with a can of beans. And I couldn't even be sure she meant the same one. I decided to visit Reena's office and see the painting again, maybe pick up some new reading material, and for the first time in my life, hope the lady in question was off gallivanting with Nick Ransom.

About the time I pulled into the parking lot for Mumbai Humanitarian, the skies let loose with a deluge of rain. Thick heavy drops spattered my windshield and within ten seconds, rain fell with the intensity of Victoria Falls, buckets of water cascading straight down in solid sheets.

I parked as close to the door as I could get. I grabbed my umbrella from behind my seat. I hopped out and ran to the entrance, flying through the glass door and skidding across the marble floor. I shook myself off, tucked the umbrella in a corner by the door, and climbed the stairs. I plastered on a big fake smile, the one I reserve for Ballantyne functions when the night has dragged on too long and the guests are reluctant to leave.

Shania, the receptionist, quickly shut her book when I entered.

"Hi Shania, I'm Elliott Lisbon with Ballantyne Foundation."

She looked at me blankly and tapped her pencil.

"I'm working on Reena's grant application?"

Still no recognition. Okay, then. "Is Reena in?"

"No, ma'am. She's out until tomorrow. You want an appointment?"

My fake smile turned genuine and I was giddy with relief. "No, no. I can catch up with her later. Maybe you can help me. Do you have any brochures about the program, something I can read over and stick in the file?"

She nodded and walked into Reena's office. While she was gone, I spun around and examined the picture on the wall. I stubbed my toe on the coffee table and almost fell over. The picture was just as I remembered it: piles of garbage, lopsided shanties, and a little boy in a dirt road holding a can of green beans. I quickly snapped a picture with my cell phone. Shania returned a millisecond later.

"This is quite compelling," I said and pointed to the picture on the wall.

"Oh yeah. Disgusting, right? Who wants to live like that?"

Nobody, I thought. That's the point.

She handed me a thin color pamphlet with the same picture of the little boy on front. It was narrow, with only two slim pages on the inside and information on back. No pictures of Brooke, but there were other teachers. It wouldn't have really mattered, most brochures are staged anyway. I tapped it on my hand and racked my brain for more questions. I glanced at the teacher on the inside.

"Do you have a list of teachers you currently employ?" If I could prove she hired Brooke, some kind of record to tie them together, I'd have her for sure.

Shania nodded, but looked uncertain, almost nervous. "Yes, but I'd have to check with Ms. Patel on that. She keeps all the records private. Why would you need something like that?"

I backtracked, trying not to arouse her suspicions. "Oh, just part of the evaluation. See how many teachers on staff, that kind of thing," I said casually and smiled.

She picked up her book, but continued to stare at me.

"Well, thank you for this." I waved the brochure and left. I clattered down the stairs. The rain had lightened for the moment, but my umbrella was missing from where I'd left it in the lobby. Crap. The rain wasn't *that* light. And who steals an umbrella?

I ducked my head, sprinted to my car, and dove into the front seat. I cranked the engine and drove out to Cabana Boulevard. After three miles of aimless driving, I pulled into a deserted parking lot next to Captain Blackbeard's Mini Golfland.

I studied the Mumbai Humanitarian pamphlet closely, looking for any clue possible. Nothing seemed unusual or suspicious. At least it had stayed dry in my handbag.

What else did I know about Reena? Not much. I'd barely even looked at her file. Which I'd left back in my office. I grabbed my phone and dialed the Big House.

"Tod, who told you Reena had family money?" I asked when he answered the phone. But then I realized he hadn't answered, it was his voicemail. Where the shit is everybody today, I thought, as I waited for Tod to finish his oration on leaving a message.

I heard the beep and repeated my question about her family money, then added strict instructions. "Call and verify this information, Tod. Don't just take their word for it, get somebody else's word for it, too. This is important," I stressed.

Then I called Jeremy Turco, the youngest member of the Ballantyne board. During the board meeting, he made an obscure comment about seeing Leo dance with a lady in a red dress. I was betting it was a Hot Damn! dress.

"Hi Jeremy, it's Elliott. Do you remember at the board meeting last week you said you saw Leo dancing with a woman?"

"Sure. That meeting was legendary. Jane dragged out by the police right in the middle. It was awesome."

"Yes, but about Leo. Was the woman Reena Patel?"

"The Mumbai lady? I don't know. I never met her, I don't know what she looks like."

"Did you read the packet? Her picture's inside."

He laughed sheepishly. "Well, I haven't had time, really. With the new season at the beach opening up and all."

"That's okay. Did she have really long hair and tan brown skin like she was from India?"

"Could be," Jeremy said. "She was totally hot, and yeah, she was definitely exotic."

"Could you hear anything they talked about?"

"Not really. I was checking her out pretty heavy when my date smacked my arm. She was standing right next to me."

"Could you think about it? Maybe call your date and see if she heard anything? It would really help my evaluation, Jeremy."

He said he would and we hung up.

What else did I know about the actual murder? Obviously a big fat frame-up like I thought. Reena drugs Leo with Chas's Insignia wine (which had no fingerprints), clocks Leo over the head with the Humanitarian of the Year trophy which Jane hated (which also had no fingerprints), and trashed the place looking for the video of Brooke's audition (a copy of which was now stashed in my cottage). What else happened that night?

Neighbor Owen Dobbs saw Jane speeding away from Leo's.

I dialed information on my cell and made a series of calls over the next fifteen minutes. I hit pay dirt on the seventh call.

"Sunshine Car Rental, Bianca speaking. May I interest you in a minivan today?"

"Hi Bianca, this is Reena Patel, I rented a black Sebring last Friday. Did I get charged for a full tank?"

I heard the clacking of a keyboard.

"I know I filled it up the day I turned it in," I said. "But I didn't check the gauge."

More clacking. "Sorry, I don't have a record of the rental," she said. "Are you sure it was Sunshine?"

"Well, I think so. But it was probably under my associate's name, she's the one who drove that day, I was just a passenger. Try Shania Carter."

I tapped the steering wheel and watched the rain pour down over the bow of a pirate ship on the fifth hole of the mini golfland. It's nearly impossible to do anything anymore without using your real name, and cash is obsolete. A hundred years ago, you could walk around with a chunk of gold. It would get you a hotel room, dinner in a saloon, a new horse & buggy rig. But in today's security climate, you need a valid ID and credit card. Unless you lift your receptionist's valid ID and credit card.

"Sure, here it is," she said. "No gas charge, ma'am. Says it was full when it came back."

"Oh great. And that was for the black Sebring convertible, right?"

"Yes, ma'am. Can I do anything else for you?"

"Could you fax the receipt to my home office, please?" I rattled off the fax number at the Big House and said goodbye.

Hot damn and holy shit. I did a rousing celebratory dance in the front seat. So Reena rented a car identical to Jane's. When Owen Dobbs saw her turn around and go back, she hadn't forgotten anything, she was trying to be seen. I've got her now! And I've got the receipt, baby.

Then my smile faded and I fell back against the seat. I'd been running on adrenaline for an hour and was starting to crash.

I didn't really have her. So she rented a black convertible. I heard my own taunting words hurtle back at me: It's an island! Everyone drives a convertible. Doesn't mean Reena drove hers to Leo's or that Owen Dobbs was mistaken.

I needed better evidence. I needed more than a rental car receipt and a brochure. I needed to go back to Reena's office and find that teacher's list.

TWENTY-EIGHT

The sky had darkened from gloomy to murky and the rain now fell in waves. Tidal waves. We were getting a month's worth of rain in one day. It's the trade-off for eight days of sun and blue sky: three hours of torrential downpours wedged between ten hours of sludgy gray clouds and light drizzle. Nothing unusual about that, but the timing sucked. I checked my watch. Almost five o'clock. Had to be close to quitting for Shania. With Reena gone and the hammering rainstorm, she should be locking up any minute.

I parked around the backside of Reena's office building. I tucked my handbag under my seat, slid my phone into my pocket, hooked a penlight to my key ring, and made a dash for the glass door around front. I slipped into the alcove beneath the staircase, barely hidden by a potted palm. As long as Shania didn't look around when she left, I'd be okay.

Five minutes ticked by, then ten. I was soaked. My shirt clung to my skin, my hair was pasted flat to my head, and my feet squished in my trekkers. I squeezed the water from my hair and my tee, adding to the growing puddle on the floor. The air conditioning in the lobby was set to meat locker. I reassured myself that a nasty cold was a small price to pay to nail Reena Patel. Office workers slowly streamed out of the building. Most took the stairs and no one spotted me.

After twenty minutes, I heard the elevator ping. Three people exited: a man and two women. No idle chitchat for this crowd, just hollow footsteps on the marble floor before they dashed out to their cars.

I listened as the elevator rose, paused, then returned to the lobby. This time I heard one man and one woman. "Well, wouldn't you know it, I'm parked on the other side of the lot," the woman said.

"Here, use my umbrella," a man's voice offered. "I've been running back and forth for the last hour, I'm practically soaked anyway."

I peeked out and watched him hand my brown and white polka-dot umbrella to a young woman. I almost leapt across the foyer. I loved that umbrella!

"Why, thank you," she said. "But here, we can share."

"Well, if you don't mind," he said and they hustled out the door, huddled together beneath the umbrella dome.

What a thief and a scoundrel! I mentally snatched my umbrella from his hands and smacked him over the head until he apologized. I smiled at my victory, then scolded myself. Focus, woman, focus.

Oh crap. A second later I jumped into the elevator car and hit the "2" button.

So here's the thing. I literally had no way of breaking into Reena's office. I don't know how to pick locks, with sharp metal tools or credit cards or anything. And I'm pretty sure she wouldn't have a fake rock with a hide-a-key in the hall. My options were limited to the outside balcony. I pictured myself: shimmy up the outside wall, hoist my legs over the slick wet balcony railing, then stand in a downpour rattling the sure-to-be-locked balcony doors.

New plan. I needed to somehow talk my way into Reena's private office without raising any alarms with Shania. I'm the Ballantyne Foundation Director. I'm entitled to look at their client list. And I can certainly outwit Shania, the puzzle playing ditz at the door. I hustled down the hall hoping she hadn't left yet.

I entered the office with a sappy smile on my face, but the room was empty. "Shania?" I hollered. I peeked into Reena's office, but she wasn't there either. Ladies room? Or maybe she forgot to lock the door when she went home. Either way, I didn't care.

I quickly threw the bolt on the main door. If she was in the little girl's room, her knocking would give me enough time to scoot out of the office and innocently open the door. Of course, she may have taken her keys.

Can't worry about that now. I went straight for Reena's desk in the other room. The black sawhorse desk held only three drawers, two matching deep ones on either side of a long slim one in the center. All three were locked.

She had to keep a spare key around here somewhere. Everyone does. And it's not like these suckers were bank vault quality, probably only needed a bobby pin to pop the lock. Only I didn't have a bobby pin. I tried every key on my ring, but none fit. I checked on her desk, under a black leather blotter, behind a sleek silver lamp. Nothing.

I looked around the room. The bookshelves, directly across from her desk. She must have had over two hundred volumes crammed into the cases. I skimmed the book tops, but none looked to be bulging due to a key jammed between the pages. I ran my hand along the shelves, then behind the cases. No key, but plenty of dust. I wiped my dirty hands on my wet pants and made mud.

I crawled beneath the sawhorse. It was really dark under there. Heavy drapes edged the balcony doors and the barely visible gloomy sky made it slightly better than working in a cave. I tried to dig the penlight out of my pocket and smacked my head on the center beam of her desk. Tiny stars sparkled in front of my eyes and I had to slap a hand over my mouth to keep from crying out. I rubbed my head. It felt wet and sticky and I got lightheaded. Wet from the rain, I told myself, not blood. I heard a small rustle when my hand scraped the underside of the desk. I readjusted and felt a tiny key held to the rough wood with scotch tape.

I glanced at the doorway. No sounds, no shadows.

I peeled the tape back and climbed into the leather desk chair. I slipped the key into the large drawer on the left. I clicked on my tiny penlight, but the drawer was mostly empty. Must be her purse drawer. There was a makeup bag, hand mirror, two scarves, and a pair of sunglasses. I closed and relocked it, then tried the large drawer on the right.

It was filled with files. Each had a neatly typed label on the top tab. Teachers, Educational Materials, Vaccination Supplies, Donation Requests, Travel and Accommodations. I quickly leafed through the pages. They looked very organized and professional. Until I read the file marked Sanitation.

The top sheets detailed plans for toilets, irrigation, sump pumps, and other equipment. Another sheet explained (in depth) the concern over diarrhea and disease caused by the fecal matter running into the water. Wedged in the middle of the file, tucked between the poop report and a budget analysis for a sanitary system adjacent to the classroom, was a list of teachers names. I scanned the list.

Bingo.

My finger stopped at Brooke Norman, age thirty, Master's Degree in Education from the University of Alabama, two years internship at Seabrook Preparatory School, currently on a teaching mission in Mumbai.

Brooke was no more thirty than I was. She was barely twenty-two. I wondered how many names were legitimate. I studied the sheet behind the teacher's list. It was taken from a financial ledger with a dollar figure next to each item on a very long list of items.

Even with my mediocre math skills I figured out Reena was cooking the books. Two sheets later I found the articles of incorporation for a company called RP Enterprises with Reena Patel as sole proprietor. So not just phony teachers, but the whole shebang was a fraud.

Why you bitch, Reena Patel. Threaten me with cancelling your grant application. Who's in trouble now?

I needed those papers, but I didn't see a copy machine out front. Shit. Take them or leave them? Take them or leave them? How much longer would I be left alone to snoop?

My phone rang and I jumped straight up out of the chair. My heart was pounding so hard, I thought it would pop. I dug the phone out of my pocket to hit the ignore button, then saw Harry Fleet's name.

"What did you find?" I whispered excitedly. Had to be good if he called me so soon.

"What the hell did *you* find? I want to know how this is related," he barked into the phone.

I started pacing. "First tell me about Brooke Norman."

"Same chemicals in her blood as Hirschorn. Same everything: GHB, oxycodone, and diazepam."

"Man oh man. That's a specific cocktail of drugs. No way it's random, right?" I peeked out the window into the parking lot. I saw my Mini through the rain sitting alone in the back lot.

"Now you tell me, Lisbon. How is this death related to Leo Hirschorn?"

"I'm not sure, Harry, but I have an idea—"

The phone was knocked from my hand and my face slammed into the wood frame on the balcony door.

TWENTY-NINE

It was dark. It smelled rank and tangy. Gasoline. Bobby the mechanic? Was I still at the dealership fixing my slashed tires? My thoughts swirled and bounced, disconnected and jagged. I couldn't string two together. My eyes adjusted to the lowlight. My face hurt. I tasted blood on my lips, in my mouth.

Then I remembered my face slamming into the door. Reena's office! I struggled to get up, but something heavy pinned me down. I tried to push up with my hands and push off with my feet, but I had no strength. I used my elbows and squirmed forward. I freed my back and twisted my head around. A bookcase was on top of me. It was ridiculously heavy, like concrete block instead of wood.

"I see your investigative skills have improved since you were last here," Reena said.

I whipped my head around and nearly passed out again. Nausea crept up my throat while my head spun round and round. My vision slowly cleared. Reena stood behind her desk across the room. With a box of matches in one hand and a gun in the other.

I tried to scramble forward. I flailed my arms and bumped into a red gas can with a yellow spout. From the hollow sound, I figured it was empty.

"Let's not play games, *Red*," Reena said and lifted the gun toward my face. "As much as I enjoy watching you squirm, I like you right where you are. Not so funny now, is it? You fight with cake, I fight with fire."

"So, how much money did Leo demand?"

"That greedy little fuck wanted half the Lafferty money. Half!" she said. "He said he wouldn't take a dime of the Ballantyne grant."

"How noble."

She snorted in the most unladylike manner. "Ain't that the truth. But how could I trust a blackmailer? He'd want more and more, stick his grubby hand out every time I received new grant money."

"No honor among thieves." I slowly tested my strength against the bookcase and felt it give a little. It wasn't as heavy as I thought, I was just weaker. Both from the blow to the face and a lifelong avoidance of exercise.

"Hey," she snapped. "I worked hard to get where I am. This entire operation is mine. What the fuck do you own?"

The gasoline fumes made me lightheaded. I shook my head to clear away the fog. "And Mumbai? What about your people?"

She barked out a laugh. "My people are from Cleveland, genius." She set down her gun and held up the file I'd found in her desk. She stuffed it into a wastebasket sitting in the middle of her desk. "My last mistake. After that dumb bitch Brooke. She lied straight to my face, said she'd never acted once in her life. Not even a school play." She pulled a match from the box.

"What are you doing?" I yelled. "This place is full of gas fumes."

"No, just you, and I can't wait to roast you like a pig," she raged. "You think you can just trot all over town, spread lies about me? Try to wedge between me and Nick? Steal my life and call me a thief?" She struck the match.

I covered my head and squeezed my eyes against the explosion, but none came. The folder flashed into flames. The fire consumed the wood basket in seconds. I started to doubt her assertion that I was the only source of gasoline in the room. I began breathing through my mouth to avoid the smell, but then I tasted the gasoline and my thoughts bounced around my head like a pinball.

"You'll burn, and I'll waltz out of here the victim," Reena said as she picked up the gun. "Crazy Elliott Lisbon tripped over the bookcase while burning down my office. Can't do anything right, can she?" She walked around the desk, then toward me.

Smoke and flames rose from the wastebasket. Searing hot fire quickly spread to the desk, racing across the flat top, down the legs, then jumped to the chairs. "And why would I burn down your office?" I wiggled under the bookcase. I had to get out of there before the fire scorched a trail across the carpet.

"Don't move!" she screamed. "I'll blow your fucking head off!"

She stepped closer. Her back was against the balcony drapes, only ten feet away from me now. The fire jumped to the wallpaper behind the desk. "Jealousy, of course," she continued as if we were chatting over tea and crumpets. "Everyone can see how crazy jealous you are of me. Refused to approve my grant application, threw yourself at my fiancé. You attacked me in my own home. You attacked Nick just last night, tried to drown him in the pool." The gun bounced while Reena ranted. At the bookshelf. At the carpet. At my head.

My left arm lay outstretched in front of me, slightly to my left, while I kept my right directly under me, palm flat on the carpet.

Reena inched closer, now only five feet away, her voice scratchy and shrill. "And then I found you in my office, trying to burn it down. I had to shoot you in self-defense."

I needed her closer, and more unstable. "You've lost your mind if you think anyone, including my sweet darling Nick, will believe you."

She stomped forward, her gun arm swinging. The thick smoke grew heavier. The air hotter. Crackling, burning, choking.

One more step. Then the gun bounced from my head to the floor.

I braced with my right hand and reach out with my left. I latched on to her ankle and yanked as hard as I could.

Reena let out a short scream, more surprise than anything. She hit the ground in a crash.

I scrambled up, kicking at the bookcase as I tried to stand. It flipped over and blocked the doorway. I stepped toward it, but Reena grabbed my foot.

I screamed at her to let go. Mistake. My throat filled with smoke. Burning soot choked me. Reena twisted my ankle, but I clamped onto her arm, scratching and clawing. I couldn't stop coughing and tears streamed down my cheeks.

Reena yelled into the black air. Mad, insane words. She pulled at my leg and punched my thigh. Flames shot up the wall and engulfed the room. Time was measured in seconds.

With my fists clenched onto her shoulders, I slammed my knee into her face and she tumbled backward, directly into the flaming balcony drapes. Her scream lasted only a second before fading into the flames.

Like a streak of lightning, a line of fire spread from the curtains to the carpet to the case to the books—all in a flash of a single second.

I ran for my life. I crashed into Ransom as he burst through the outer door.

He hauled me to the ground, then he fell on top of me to smother the flames. His hands were all over my body, searching for sparks and flames.

I couldn't feel any pain. I choked and coughed, but couldn't croak out any words.

He picked me up and carried me down the stairs, out into the lot. We collapsed on the lawn in front of the building next door. He held me close while rain poured down on the both us. I lifted my face to wash away the gritty soot and slimy gasoline.

Three fire engines and four squad cars crowded the office lot. The rear doors of an ambulance flew open, and a paramedic climbed out with a gurney. I saw Pete, Matty's brother, in full fireman gear, run over to our huddle on the grass.

Ransom lifted me to my feet.

"Oh God, Elli, you're okay," Pete said as he crushed me in a bear hug. He pulled me toward the ambulance where a crowd of people hovered.

Matty pushed through and my breath caught when I saw him. He looked awful. His face was chalk white, and he broke into a run. He held my face between his hands, and without a single word, he kissed me.

THIRTY

I tilted my head to the clear Carolina blue overhead, letting my freckles pop in the hot sun. I closed my eyes.

"Are you sure you're feeling okay? Maybe you should still be at home," Carla said. She and Tod had joined me for lunch by the pool at the Big House.

I'd spent the previous three days holed up in my cottage, though not always alone. Carla provided constant nursing and meal service. Her chocolate cupcakes with buttercream frosting sped my recovery. Cherry dropped off a get-well blender, in red, of course. Tod persuaded Tate Keating to do a weeklong feature piece on the Ballantynes' philanthropy. And Jane finally showed a sliver of appreciation by taking over Leo's Shelter Initiative with nary a complaint.

Matty kept me company when I wanted it and left me alone when I needed it, which made him sexier by the day. I love a man who knows when to leave me alone. He asked me out on a real date, in a two weeks' time, once I was truly healed. I accepted. I decided not to overanalyze where it would lead and what could go wrong, and just enjoy the ride.

Today was my first day out, and other than my statement to the police, I'd yet to talk about the burning of Mumbai Humanitarian. Although by now, I'm sure these two knew more than I did.

"Yes, Carla, I'm fine," I said. I wore a light cotton sundress long enough to cover the thin white bandages on the backs of both my legs, which were propped up on a cushy ottoman. "The burn is healing nicely, barely more than a bad sunburn now."

"You should still be careful," Ransom said.

I opened my eyes, using my hand to shield them from the sun and watched Ransom walked toward us, wearing faded jeans, a tight white tee and flip flops, and carried a bright red gift bag in his hand. He pulled out a chair and joined us at the table.

I nodded, then tilted back to the sun trying to tan over the colorful bruise on my left cheek. "I'm careful."

"So why didn't you light up like briquettes on a bbq with all the gasoline soaking your clothes?" Tod asked.

"Turns out I was wet from the rain, not gas," I said. "Reena had poured it all over the room, but avoided dripping a single drop on me."

"She wanted it to look as if Elliott tripped while dousing the room," Ransom said. "She may have thought it would look suspicious if Elliott was drenched in gasoline. How could she soak herself if she fell down?"

"Why not just pour the gas on the carpet surrounding Elliott," Tod said. "Make it look like the gas can drained when it fell. That would've been the way to go."

"Maybe next time," I said.

"Just saying."

"Reena was in a hurry. Her whole plan was thrown together in minutes," Ransom said. "We'd been out together when she got a call from her receptionist. Reena told me there was some kind of conference call with Mumbai and she had to rush back to the office. I dropped her off in the pouring rain and left."

I put on my sunglasses and leaned back farther in the chair. I'd heard all this before. It bothered me to hear it again. Reena's screams still haunted me late at night, when I was alone under my skylight. Though I did find comfort in soft voices around me now, mingling with the bird calls and lapping pool filter.

"Where was the receptionist, when Elliott was in the office?" Carla asked Ransom.

I heard her pour another glass of lemonade iced tea and the ice cubes rattled in the glass.

"The suite next door, flirting with a dentist," Ransom said.

"Why did you go back?"

Ransom cleared his throat. "We suspected Mumbai Humanitarian of fraud, been under an interagency investigation for months. Which is why I was dating her. But she was extremely careful. We had a wiretap on her office phone and a unit monitoring her calls. After I dropped Reena at the office, I checked my voicemail. Besides Elliott's urgent messages, I had one from the unit captain. Reena's receptionist had called Reena to tell her Elliott was asking about the brochures, a teachers list, and secretly snapped a picture of the boy on the wall. When I couldn't get Elliott on the phone, I raced back to Reena's office."

"Elliott, you should never have gone in there like that," Carla said. "Do you know how dangerous that was? How foolish?"

I raised my hand. "We agreed. No finger-pointing, no lectures. I solved Leo's murder and saved Jane from the electric chair. I am the hero of this sad tale."

"So it all boiled down to a silly appliance commercial?" Carla asked.

"Mostly," I said. "It certainly spun Leo's wheels. He was desperate to save Buffalo Bill's and discovering Reena's fraud was like finding a treasure map on the sidewalk. He picked it up and followed the trail."

"He took Brooke's picture to the Lafferty Foundation. A secretary—"

"Gayle Everheart's personal assistant," I interrupted.

"—identified Brooke as one of the teachers from Mumbai Humanitarian," Ransom continued. "Leo dug further, ended up with an entire file of incriminating evidence against Reena, then demanded five million dollars—"

"Half of the Lafferty grant," I interrupted again.

"—to keep quiet. With the first board meeting looming on Monday, they struck a deal. They met at his house after your party at the Big House. Leo asked for the money and Reena killed him instead."

"Well, he certainly wasn't the smartest member of the board," Tod said.

"Tod! You can't say that," I said and sat up.

"Why not? How did he think such a ridiculous scheme could ever work?"

Carla nodded. "It's the truth, chicken. That cowboy hat squeezed his brain too tight thinking he could threaten a crazy woman with exposure and get paid five million dollars for it."

I ate the last tea cookie on the plate and sipped my lemonade. I looked sideways at Ransom. "Did you stop by to get some sun or did you have something else on your mind?"

"Care to take a walk?"

"Sure," I said. I slipped on my shoes and turned to Carla. "You'll excuse me? We won't be a minute."

"You take your time," she said. "We'll be out here all day."

Ransom and I walked down the lawn to a narrow path on the other side of the reflection garden.

Ransom broke the silence first. "Are you sure you're okay?"

"Yes, Nick, I'm fine. Honest." We walked side by side, his left hand brushing my right. A light breeze carried the scent of his cologne and I breathed deeply. It went nicely with the blooming jasmine bordering the brick path.

One hundred feet later, the path opened to an expansive lawn bordering a beautiful lake with bonfire pits arranged by the water's edge. Six large brick circles with fresh cord wood piled in the center. We sat in matching Adirondack chairs facing the water.

"I fucked up," Ransom said. "I never should've put you in danger. Reena was very careful and our investigation was dragging. We needed more evidence, but if I thought she was a threat, I would've told you. I should've told you anyway."

"I understand," I said. He still could've told me. But I was just so happy to be alive and wasn't actually all that mad. Yet. I figured the anger would come later. Then I'd let him have it.

"This is for you," he said and handed me the gift bag.

I untied the large bow from the handles. I reached in and lifted out a vintage Brunswick bowling pin with a red crown ring around the neck and a large B stamped on the front.

"How did you know?" I whispered.

"It was in the window at that shop in Savannah. I thought it matched your game collection."

"It does, it's perfect. I can't believe you remembered it."

"I remember a lot of things." He caressed the back of my hand. "I remember the wine cellar. The first night I saw you again in the library. The first time I kissed you twenty years ago."

I blushed and set the bowling pin on the edge of the brick fire pit. "We can't go back, you and me. I've got a date with a nice guy, you know. A new life."

"Don't count me out yet." He leaned over and tucked my hair behind my ear. He softly kissed my cheek. "I'm sorry for everything. I won't make those mistakes again."

"You better not or the next time you get in the middle of one of my investigations, I'll kick your ass."

"Next time? What next time?"

I laughed. "This island is full of surprises, Nick. I'm now twenty-seven hours closer to getting my PI license." Would've been more, but I couldn't very well include my trip to Milo Hickey's poker game or Chas Obermeyer's wine cellar. But I was getting there.

I propped my feet on the bonfire pit next to the Brunswick and tilted my head toward the sun.

And next time, I thought, I'm calling the shots.

Kendel Lynn

Kendel Lynn is a Southern California native who now parks her flip-flops in Dallas, Texas. She read her first Alfred Hitchcock and the Three Investigators at age seven and has loved mysteries ever since. Her debut novel, *Board Stiff*, won several literary competitions, including the Zola Award for Mystery. Along with writing, she spends her days editing, designing, and figuring out ways to avoid the gym but still eat cupcakes for dinner. Catch up with her at kendellynn.com.

Be sure to check out Elliott's prequel novella:
SWITCH BACK
featured in
OTHER PEOPLE'S BAGGAGE

IF YOU LIKED THIS HENERY PRESS MYSTERY,
YOU MIGHT ALSO LIKE THESE...

FRONT PAGE FATALITY

by LynDee Walker

Crime reporter Nichelle Clarke's days can flip from macabre to comical with a beep of her police scanner. Then an ordinary accident story turns extraordinary when evidence goes missing, a prosecutor vanishes, and a sexy Mafia boss shows up with the headline tip of a lifetime.

As Nichelle gets closer to the truth, her story gets more dangerous. Armed with a notebook, a hunch, and her favorite stilettos, Nichelle races to splash these shady dealings across the front page before this deadline becomes her last.

DOUBLEWHAMMY
by Gretchen Archer

Davis Way thinks she's hit the jackpot when she lands a job as the fifth wheel on an elite security team at the fabulous Bellissimo Resort and Casino in Biloxi, Mississippi. But once there, she runs straight into her ex-ex husband, a rigged slot machine, her evil twin, and a trail of dead bodies. Davis learns the truth and it does not set her free—in fact, it lands her in the pokey.

Buried under a mistaken identity, unable to seek help from her family, her hot streak runs cold until her landlord Bradley Cole steps in. Make that her landlord, lawyer, and love interest. With his help, Davis must win this high stakes game before her luck runs out.

Available Now
For more details, visit www.henerypress.com

Diners, Dives & DEAD ENDS
by Terri L. Austin

As a struggling waitress and part-time college student, Rose Strickland's life is stalled in the slow lane. But when her close friend, Axton, disappears, Rose suddenly finds herself serving up more than hot coffee and flapjacks. Now she's hashing it out with sexy bad guys and scrambling to find clues in a race to save Axton before his time runs out.

With her anime-loving bestie, her septuagenarian boss, and a pair of IT wise men along for the ride, Rose discovers political corruption, illegal gambling, and shady corporations. She's gone from zero to sixty and quickly learns when you're speed-ing down the fast lane, it's easy to crash and burn.

Available Now
For more details, visit www.henerypress.com

$\mathcal{L}$owcountry BOIL
by Susan M. Boyer

Private Investigator Liz Talbot is a modern Southern belle: she
blesses hearts and takes names. She carries her Sig 9 in her Kate
Spade handbag, and her golden retriever, Rhett, rides shotgun in
her hybrid Escape. When her grandmother is murdered, Liz high-
tails it back to her South Carolina island home to find the killer.

She's fit to be tied when her police-chief brother shuts her out of
the investigation, so she opens her own. Then her long-dead best
friend pops in and things really get complicated. When more folks
start turning up dead in this small seaside town, Liz must use more
than just her wits and charm to keep her family safe, chase down
clues from the hereafter, and catch a psychopath before he catches
her.

Available Now
For more details, visit www.henerypress.com

PORTRAIT of a DEAD GUY

by LARISSA REINHART

In Halo, Georgia, folks know Cherry Tucker as big in mouth, small in stature, and able to sketch a portrait faster than buck-shot rips from a ten gauge -- but commissions are scarce. So when the well-heeled Branson family wants to memorialize their murdered son in a coffin portrait, Cherry scrambles to win their patronage from her small town rival.

As the clock ticks toward the deadline, Cherry faces more trouble than just a controversial subject. Between ex-boyfriends, her flaky family, an illegal gambling ring, and outwitting a killer on a spree, Cherry finds herself painted into a corner she'll be lucky to survive.

Available Now
For more details, visit www.henerypress.com

THE AMBITIOUS CARD
BY JOHN GASPARD

The life of a magician isn't all kiddie shows and card tricks. Sometimes it's murder. Especially when magician Eli Marks very publicly debunks a famed psychic, and said psychic ends up dead. The evidence, including a bloody King of Diamonds playing card (one from Eli's own Ambitious Card routine), directs the police right to Eli.

As more psychics are slain, and more King cards rise to the top, Eli can't escape suspicion. Things get really complicated when romance blooms with a beautiful psychic, and Eli discovers she's the next target for murder, and he's scheduled to die with her. Now Eli must use every trick he knows to keep them both alive and reveal the true killer.

Available August 2013
For more details, visit www.henerypress.com